I felt fine at first—not afraid, because I didn't know what to be afraid of. The memory loss could be a temporary thing. Then I noticed my eyes automatically searching for cover, places to hide. Scanning people's faces, judging their expressions as friendly or menacing. Watching the way they moved, seeing if they were preparing to attack. Nobody was.

Paranoia, I thought. I struggled to appear calm on the outside. Inside I was feverish, eyes darting at everything, grasping for calm thoughts.

Eventually I couldn't take it anymore.

FALSE MEMORY

DAN KROKOS

Hyperion

New York

Text copyright © 2012 by Dan Krokos

All rights reserved. Published by Disney • Hyperion, an imprint of Disney Book Group. No part of this book may be reproduced or transmitted in any form or by any means, electronic or mechanical, including photocopying, recording, or by any information storage and retrieval system, without written permission from the publisher. For information address Disney • Hyperion, 114 Fifth Avenue, New York, New York 10011-5690.

First paperback edition, 2013

10 9 8 7 6 5 4 3 2 1

V475-2873-0-13121

Printed in the United States of America

ISBN 978-1-4231-4984-2

Library of Congress Control Number for Hardcover Edition: 2011053532

Visit www.un-requiredreading.com

SUSTAINABLE FORESTRY INITIATIVE

Certified Chain of Custody
Promoting Sustainable Forestry

www.sfiprogram.org
SFI-01054

The SFI label applies to the text stock

to Adam Lastoria
bad boys for life

In the food court I find a mall cop leaning against a pillar. His eyes sweep over the tables, fingers rolling a whistle in front of his sternum. His left hand taps a beat on his thigh. C. Lyle, according to his name tag.

I walk up to him. It takes five seconds for him to look at me. "Hello," I say. "I lost my memory. I was wondering if you could help."

"You lost your memory?" he says.

I don't know why he asks. It's clear he heard me perfectly.

"Yeah. I don't know where I'm supposed to be," I say.

He stands upright, arching his back to push off the pillar. Fuzzy blond wisps cover his chin, and acne pocks his forehead—not all of him made it through puberty.

"What's your name?" he says.

"Miranda North."

"And how old are you?"

"Seventeen."

One corner of his mouth goes up, and I know it's fake because no one smiles that way naturally. I remember that.

"Doesn't seem like you've forgotten all that much. You remember who you are."

Half true. I remember my name and age. I remember what a mall cop is. I don't remember anything about my life. Here's hoping that's normal for amnesiacs.

The crowd pulses behind me, makes me step closer to C. Lyle. I try to block them out; being in the open like this makes my skin itch, and I don't know why.

"I don't remember anything else," I say.

It's true. This morning I woke up on a bench, staring at the Terminal Tower. I know that's in Cleveland, and my first thought was what bad luck to wake up in Cleveland with no memory. Not San Diego, or Dallas, or a place where the sun shines more than three days a year. The logical reason I'm here is because Cleveland is my home.

I know my name is Miranda North, and I know I'm in the second half of seventeen. I have four hundred dollars cash in my pocket.

"Why would I lie?" I say.

"Because you're a kid, and kids like to mess with security guards."

Can't imagine why. If he wants me to stand here until he's forced to deal with me, I can play that game.

After wandering the city for a bit, I found a mirror in a public restroom and didn't recognize the girl staring back at me. I mean, yes, I knew it was me. Obviously. But if you had asked me what color my hair was before then, I wouldn't have been able to tell you. It's reddish-brown, straight, a little past my shoulders. I'm muscular, like I work out all the time. The contours of my stomach are visible without flexing. I'm not bulky, but there's nothing soft about me. Maybe I'm a gymnast. My eyes are the same color as my hair, which seems odd.

I drifted into the mall after that. I felt fine at first—not afraid, because I didn't know what to be afraid of. The memory loss could be a temporary thing. Then I noticed my eyes automatically searching for cover, places to hide. Scanning people's faces, judging their expressions as friendly or menacing. Watching the way they moved, seeing if they were preparing to attack. Nobody was.

Paranoia, I thought. I struggled to appear calm on the outside. Inside I was feverish, eyes darting at everything, grasping for calm thoughts.

Eventually I couldn't take it anymore. I had to ask someone for help. I rode the escalator to the food court on the second level. Found a table in the corner to rest and think. Then I saw C. Lyle leaning against his pillar.

"Just . . . let me use a phone or something." Maybe if I'm holding a phone, my fingers will remember a number my brain can't.

C. Lyle really studies me for the first time. It's like his eyebrows are trying to kiss between his eyes. "Are you messing with me?"

I'm trying to be calm and reasonable, but this emptiness inside my chest widens, this fear I might never remember who I am.

With that awful thought, my eyes ache, as if I stared into the sun for a few seconds. The cramp spreads through my brain into a full-blown headache, which I could do without right now. I blink a few times. Over my shoulder, the line curls away from Charley's.

"No," I say. "I'm not. I was hoping my memory would come back, like one of those temporary things. But it's not. I know it's not. I really need your help."

He points at the bag in my hand. "You lost your memory but had time to shop?"

I look at the bag too. "I had some cash on me and thought I'd buy a few things." Buy some stuff in a mall. Be normal. Part of trying to not throw up into the nearest trash can.

He points at the floor now. "Set it down."

I do.

He crouches and opens the bag, then raises an eyebrow. "Is there anything in here that could harm me?"

"What? No." The way he's looking at me, like I'm a criminal, makes my skin crawl.

"You're sure?"

The ache behind my eyes becomes a burn, a hot spike narrowing to the bridge of my nose. It doesn't feel like a normal headache, but maybe I don't remember what a normal headache is. I take a shallow breath and rub my eyes while C. Lyle paws through my bag. He pulls out a red bra I spent forty dollars on.

"You lost your memory but had time to go bra shopping?" he says.

Someone bumps into me from behind. I step forward instead of lashing out with an elbow, which for some reason is my first instinct. C. Lyle isn't quite looking at me; he's looking up at the pale patch of skin between the straps of my black tank top.

"I have a lot of time," I say. "Like I said, I don't know where I'm supposed to be." I'd be content with a lie, a few comforting words. *Everything will be okay, Miranda.*

He sees the rest of the stuff is clothes, which I bought so I'd have something to change into. If I was going to be a fake shopper, I might as well buy fresh jeans.

He stands up and dusts his hands together like they're dirty. "Get out of here. I'm not here for you to play with. Or I can walk you out."

My mouth opens a little. I don't understand. I just told him I don't remember anything, and he's trying to shoo me out of here like he's got something more important to do.

"Please," I say. "I don't know what happened to me." If I knew, maybe everything would be fine. Maybe knowing would fill some of the emptiness inside. Or maybe I could lose the headache.

He drops his hand on my shoulder. And squeezes.

It's like a piano wire is running from the top of my head to the bottom of my feet. The wire breaks. I clamp both hands onto his arm and hug it to my chest. My black boots squeak on the floor as I pivot into him, still holding his arm, and set my back against his front. I pull his arm across my body and pop my hip against his thigh. He flips over me, legs kicking like he's on an upside-down bike.

C. Lyle lands hard on his back, blowing out an explosive, spittle-laced breath.

I stand there stunned. One thought flashes like a neon sign—*I'm in trouble*.

His face mirrors mine. Except for the area directly around us, life carries on in the food court. The line at Charley's grows. A kid spills a drink, and his mom shakes a finger in his face and shouts. Someone balls up a wrapper and shoots for the can, misses, and leaves it on the floor.

C. Lyle fumbles with his stun gun, trying to unbuckle the strap.

I have to stop him. I have to show him I didn't mean it. Because it's true; I have no idea why I did that. But he has the snap open now, and his fingers close on the stun gun. I stop thinking.

I thrust my hand forward, palm out. "*Wait!*" As I say it, the pain behind my eyes returns, stronger than ever. I squeeze my eyes shut, but it doesn't stop. My brain has been replaced by a huge glowing coal. And somehow, the pain and heat radiate *outside* my head. I can feel them spreading around me, moving outward in waves, even though it's impossible.

C. Lyle freezes on the floor, hand clenched on the stun gun. His eyes bug and his whole body begins to tremble. Thankfully, his hand spasms too violently to pull his weapon. People around him back away rather than help, then they freeze too.

Then they run.

C. Lyle flops over onto his belly. He gets a leg under him and tries to stand but slips and falls flat again. The fire in my head keeps spreading, releasing pressure with each pulse, granting me a fraction of relief with each passing second.

People flee from me, from us. Pounding feet rattle my eardrums. The pain blurs my vision with tears, but my eyes automatically search for an exit on their own. They find no escape route, just faces with open mouths and wide eyes—deer eyes, panicked.

Fear. Of what? I spin around, looking for someone sane, someone who will tell me everything is fine. Instead I see a man running, head turned over his shoulder, blind to the silver railing in front of him. He hits it. His feet leave the ground and he topples over. His shoes go upside down as he drops, soles pointed at the ceiling. The screams don't drown out the thump of his body.

I clap a hand over my mouth. It happens again. A woman flips over the railing. Her beige purse flies into space, coins and keys shooting out and flickering in the bright light. I focus on that, the purse pinwheeling through the air. I watch it disappear under the floor's edge.

More people fall, so I fix my gaze at the skylights framing the bright blue sky. A little boy calls for his mother. His voice cuts through me and pulls my attention back to the hysteria. He yells again—"Mom! MOM!"—but there's too much noise, too many bodies blurring past to find him. My numb feet carry me to the edge, where I clamp my hands on the cold metal tube that's supposed to protect people. Bodies sprawl far below, twisted and still.

I push away and spin back to the court, swallowing hard against my gag reflex.

Even the people who didn't see me flip C. Lyle—they run too. Like a spreading wave, the wave from my head, the people farthest away stiffen, then take off in no particular direction. Many of them scream. Some cover their mouths to keep the screams in, like me. I only catch snippets of their words—*help me what is this Mom where are you please please someone!*

C. Lyle staggers to his feet like a drunk, belt jangling as he lurches to the escalator. He almost trips over two men tangled on the floor. The last two. I watch them break apart and roll away from each other. They breathe in heaving gulps. One gets up and runs down the escalator. The other crawls, dragging his right leg. My last image of him is a work boot scraping over the ridges on the top step.

Somewhere in the food court a tray falls. A drink splashes over the floor.

At first the court seems empty, except for the bags and food trays people have left behind.

But I'm not alone.

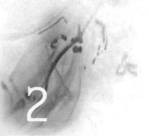

2

A guy about my age sits in the middle of the court amid scattered and overturned tables and chairs. A plate of mango chicken from Ruby Thai sits in front of him. He's lean, with the most intense face I've seen so far. A staring-contest face. His black hair is thick, a little long, curling slightly at the neck. His white T-shirt stretches over a body pared down to just muscle and skin.

He waves at me, like everything is fine. I stand there for a moment, frozen. Finally he turns his hand around and makes a *Come here* motion.

He knows who I am; he has to. No other reason he'd be sitting there instead of running. He could know why I can't remember; he could know what just happened; he could know why those people fell, why they're probably dead; he could know if it's my fault.

I make my way to him, stepping lightly over upended chairs. Part of me wonders if I should be moving in the opposite direction. My eyes keep flitting up to him, tracking him, and that's why I step in a puddle of Coke. My right foot makes a squeak with every step until I reach his table and fall into the chair across from him.

"Hello," I say, trying to play it cool. I don't know what I'm more afraid of—finding the truth, or not finding it. I fold my hands in my lap to keep them still.

Behind and below me, on the lower level of the mall, people still run and shout. Their panic echoes off the ceiling.

"Hello," he says. His blue eyes are startling. Fake, almost. Like bright blue paint.

I smell him then, his sweat and soap, but something else. Flowers? Not just flowers—roses. Now that I recognize the scent, I realize it's been there since the pain in my head started. "Are you wearing perfume?" I ask.

"It's the psychic energy. Messes with the limbic system, so for some reason you smell roses."

I don't say anything. He waits for a reaction, but I have no idea what to say. He lost me at *psychic energy*.

"It's . . . we smell it and they smell it, people the energy affects. It's just a weird byproduct. How's your head?"

"It feels like it's on fire," I say.

"It's running hot, yeah."

We sit there. Like nothing's wrong. Somewhere glass breaks and tinkles over the floor. He studies me under two black eyebrows that aren't thick but aren't thin either. It's like he has two faces—from the nose down he's amused, but his eyes are lowered in a studying scowl.

"Is this funny to you?" I say.

He frowns. "It's the least funny thing I can imagine."

I'm starving, and I need something to do with my hands, so I pluck a piece of his mango chicken. It tastes like ashes. For the first time, I begin to wonder if any of this is real. If a doctor in a white coat walked over and said I was experiencing a psychotic break, I'd probably buy it.

"Tell me what happened," I say.

"I was hoping you could tell me."

"No idea." I see it all again—the pumping legs, flailing arms. The people falling. The woman's purse in the air. "Those people . . ."

He shakes his head slowly. "This wasn't your fault." But his face says it is. He appears calm, but his mouth is tight. He's trying to hide his horror, that much is plain. I know now, for sure, the panic was my doing. All of it. Somehow.

"This wasn't your fault," he says again, like he's trying to convince himself.

"No?" My cheeks are wet now. I smear tears away with my fingertips.

He leans forward, pulls his tray back before I can grab more chicken. "How's your memory?"

He knows. But how? An excited trill cuts through me at the thought of an answer, numbing all the unease for a moment.

"Gone," I say, voice paper-dry. I suck in a breath and hold it, willing my hands to stop shaking.

"I figured."

"Did you?"

We sit there some more. The mall is silent now, tombish.

"Do you have a name?" I ask, harshly, since he doesn't seem willing to offer up information.

"Peter."

"Peter..."

"Just Peter for now," he says.

The insanity of the situation finally sinks in. Not the madness from before, but how I'm sitting here now, with "Peter," and he's talking about memory loss and psychic energy. I feel a kernel of something awful pop in my stomach. The truth is near and I don't know if I'm ready for it.

"My name is Miranda," I say. I lay my hands on my thighs and squeeze to keep from fidgeting.

"I know."

"What happened?" I say.

He scrubs his face with his hands and runs one through his hair, then leans back in his seat. "You released a burst of psychic energy that affected the brains of everyone in the mall, specifically their amygdala and prefrontal cortex. The energy incited base panic in the minds of everyone, freezing all other functions until only pure terror remained. You were able to control it before you forgot how. So when you felt threatened by the cop, your response was automatic."

"Liar," I say. I can't think of a more absurd explanation. I don't even understand what he said. But if I didn't believe him, I wouldn't be frozen on this plastic chair. If I'd woken up in Boston, I wouldn't be here listening to this crazy boy tell me these crazy things.

He gives me a patient blink. "I can explain more later, but we need to go. Now."

I stand up, the chair screeching under me, too loud in the big empty space. "Why can't I remember?"

"Because you haven't been taking your shots. Or your shots weren't actually shots."

My shots weren't actually shots. The boy who smells like roses named Peter comes around the table and takes my arm. I shrug out of it and almost punch him in the chest, but hold back. My body is humming again; I feel like I did the second before I threw that cop.

14

He holds my gaze until I look away. "Relax," he says. "We're friends."

"How do I know that? I lose my memory and you're just waiting for me, brooding over mango chicken?"

He shrugs like it doesn't matter. He starts to walk away, calling to me without looking back. "We're leaving, Miranda." The scent of roses gets fainter, as if it's coming from *him*.

I stand there a moment longer. Wondering if I should trust him when I don't trust myself.

But I can't stay here. If he knows more about me, there's only one option.

"If I come, will you tell me what happened?"

"I'll tell you everything," he says. He steps onto the escalator and descends out of sight.

I could stay here and get no answers, or I could take my chances with the crazy fearless boy.

Not much of a choice at all.

3

The bodies slide into view as the escalator takes us down. Five of them, spaced evenly across the floor. The woman's beige purse is next to her head, sitting in her halo of blood. The first man who fell, his arm is bent under him, bruised face pressed against the floor. None of them stir.

The escalator pushes at my heels but I don't want to move yet. Not until the wash of dizziness passes. A few blinks don't clear it. Peter keeps walking, scanning the environment like I did when I first came here.

"We just leave them . . . ?" I say, more to myself than him.

Peter sees I've stopped, and he comes back and grabs my arm gently. I jerk out of his grasp and walk toward the bodies.

He grabs my arm again and lifts it high. "You can't help

them." He's wrenching my arm upward, holding me in place. His midsection is exposed; I could hammer him and get away.

His harsh look falls for a split second. His forehead wrinkles and he squeezes his eyes shut, as if the idea of leaving the people is physically painful. When he opens his eyes, his face is clear, the flicker of emotion so brief I wonder if he felt any of it.

"I'm sorry, but we have to go."

I nod, unable to speak. Part of me, the cowardly part, is glad he's pulling me away. The other part hates him for it.

We walk fast through the empty mall.

"So, Peter, who are you, exactly?" I try to make my tone light, but my voice is on the verge of cracking.

"I'm a friend."

"Yeah, sorry if I don't buy that right away."

We break into a light jog. "I think you do buy it," he says.

"Why?"

He's pulling ahead. "You're following me, aren't you?"

He runs, and I match him easily. The storefronts whisk by us, some vacant, some containing refugees, who cower and huddle together. I catch glimpses of scratched faces. Hear hushed whimpers. I want to go to them, but Peter will just grab me again. A pang of guilt hits me—if only I could tell them it's all right. It's over now. The malignant psychic energy is gone. I step around a teenage boy lying on his side, groaning and clutching his arm.

"Where are we going?" I ask, since my first question got a three-word answer.

"Away from here first. One thing at a time."

I stop running. He makes it a few more steps before turning around and throwing up his hands. "What now?" he says.

"You can't just expect me to come with you. Tell me where we're going, or I walk."

"We're going home, Miranda. Do you remember where home is?"

"No..."

"I didn't think so. Now come on."

Not like staying behind is an option. I blow out a sigh, then hurry to catch up.

We go out through a sporting goods store. As we step into the failing light of the afternoon sun, a police cruiser screeches around the corner, heading right for us.

The parking lot is scattered with people who escaped this way; they mill in between the cars. The man closest to us blinks rapidly and rubs his eyes, squinting at the sky. The rest look like they're coming out of nightmares, with terrible hangovers.

The cop rams to a stop a few feet away. Of course he picks us to talk to. Maybe standing right next to the entrance has something to do with it.

Peter turns to me, that half-amused, half-deprecating look on his face. "Nice job, North."

"It was your idea to come this way," I say.

The cop flings his door open and steps out. I imagine the call for help didn't give many details, so he doesn't know I'm the culprit. Still, his hand is on his gun, back stiff and feet planted. "Stay right there," he says, even though we weren't moving.

He reminds me of my old pal C. Lyle.

"What happened?" he says.

A nightmare.

Instead of that, I say, "I don't know. Everybody freaked out and ran away. I think some are still inside."

"Is anyone hurt?" he says.

Yes. Because of me. And not just hurt—broken. Dead.

It stings, but I keep my face placid. If Peter can do it, so can I.

"I don't know," Peter says. "We hid until it was clear. We don't know what happened."

The cop nods a couple times, his mouth a thin hard line. "Okay. I want you to wait here. Wait here by my car. I'm going inside to look."

"No problem," Peter says.

The cop steps around us and goes inside. The door sighs shut behind him.

Police sirens wail in the distance, growing louder. We have another twenty seconds, tops, until they arrive. There's no reason a cruiser would be traveling away from a crime scene another was just called to. But trying to leave on foot is riskier; depending on what the emergency call reported, they may want to stop us.

"You wanna drive?" Peter says.

"Sure, why not," I say. He doesn't seem worried at all, so I pretend like I'm not.

We move to either side of the still-running cruiser and climb in. Peter closes the dash-mounted laptop and unplugs the wires from the back.

It smells like old coffee and sweat. I pull the shifter into gear, not positive I remember how to drive until I do, and put my foot on the gas.

We make it out of there okay, looping around the mall and passing the other cops from a distance. Thankfully, none of them peel off in pursuit.

Peter says, "Make a right out of the parking lot," and I do.

We're south of the city, in a suburb. I try to remember how I made it here from downtown, but I can't. My short-term memories aren't becoming long-term; things seem to float around in my mind, then gradually fade.

Without warning, Peter reaches over and jabs me with a

syringe, pushing the plunger down halfway. While I'm still driving.

"Ow!"

I take my left hand off the wheel and slap him across the nose, then reach down and pluck the syringe out of my arm, giving the lemonade-colored liquid a full second of my attention. Next second, I drive the needle into his leg and push the plunger. All while adjusting the wheel with my knee and maintaining speed.

"I already had my shot," he says through hands cupped over his nose.

"What shot?" My voice cracks. I'm more shocked at how I've stuck him with the needle while driving. No idea where that came from. It's another action foreign to me, like when I automatically scanned for escape routes and enemies in the mall. No thought involved, only movement, which is scary when you think about it. I don't know what it means, *or* how it's possible. Or what the hell was in that syringe.

Blood runs down Peter's wrist.

"You didn't break my nose," he says.

"Too bad."

"No, that's good," he says. "Because I would've broken yours."

"You'd hit a girl?"

"We fight all the time." Peter wipes his bloody palm on my

thigh, then rolls his window down and spits a red glob that arcs out and jets behind us at light speed.

"I wanted to get the medicine in you quick, without having an argument. You would've argued. And it tastes terrible in a drink." He wipes his nose again.

"What medicine?" I say, feeling a little bad that I hit him. I make a right; I'm not sure why. Traffic is light, and the sky is bright blue. It reminds me of the mall skylights, the people flipping over the railing. The little boy's voice calling for his mom. I focus on the double yellow line instead.

"The kind that helps us remember. I'm like you, Miranda. We're the same."

I want to believe him, but I still don't know what it means.

After a few minutes of driving and silence, Peter points to an alley between two worn-out buildings. The bricks at street level are stained with years. "There is fine," he says.

"Fine for what?"

"Fine to pull over."

I turn the cruiser into the alley, crushing a wet cardboard box with my right tire. I hope it wasn't someone's house. We get out, scraping the doors on the brick. He walks to a rusty ladder bolted to the building.

"Now what?" I say.

"We climb before someone sees us. Then we'll talk, I promise."

When I don't move right away, he grabs one of the rungs up high and leans against it. "Please. If you don't like what I have to say, we climb back down and go our separate ways. Deal?"

Fair enough. I don't think my curiosity would let me walk away if I wanted to. If you can call the need to know who you are curiosity.

I meet him at the ladder. While I climb, questions bubble up and fight to be asked first, but I can wait a little longer.

The roof is covered in gravel. Vents and ducts poke up. I shield my eyes and look north, see the city in the distance and the lake behind it. Now, away from the action, a familiar calm settles in. I feel safe up here, even though I don't fully trust Peter.

The stones scrape behind me. Peter sits down, wrists on his knees, back against the three-foot ledge. Half his face glows red in the sun, the other half in shade. He pats the roof beside him with his right hand, posture a little deflated, like he was staying strong to get us out of there, but now the reality of what happened at the mall is sinking in. He presses the first two knuckles of his left hand between his eyes, then blinks a few times and tries to smile at me. Like smiling around a sore tooth.

I shiver and rub my bare arms as a breeze cuts over the roof. I tug my tank top down and walk over to him. When I sit, it's closer than I intended. I feel his warmth next to me even though we aren't quite touching. I don't know how, but I still smell roses when I'm near him.

"What am I?" I say.

He doesn't sugarcoat it.

"Your brain has been engineered to emit waves powerful enough to affect the brains of people around you. Specifically, the centers responsible for controlling and responding to fear. You are a high-tech version of crowd control. When you were two, a doctor drew your blood. It revealed an abnormality that allows you to survive the gene therapy needed to become a Rose. That's what we call ourselves, because we don't have a name."

My hands are shaking now. I clasp them together and squeeze, but it does nothing. His words bounce around in my head—*waves powerful enough, crowd control, gene therapy*. I should've stayed in the mall and let the police take me. I should be in a jail cell, or better yet a dungeon. A place where I can't hurt anyone ever again. I don't know what I expected to hear, but it wasn't this.

Peter takes my left hand in both of his, which are warm and dry and a little rough. His calluses tickle, and a chill shoots up my arm and down to my stomach.

24

He continues speaking in calm tones, giving me time to process each idea, even though I can't. Not the way I want to. I try to accept each idea as fact, but with each one I want to stand up and scream *No!*

"A side effect of the therapy is memory loss. Our brains have so many more connections, and our axons are thicker than normal. Which means we run hotter than ordinary people, about a hundred and three degrees at rest. To keep from damaging our memories, we take shots. The medicine protects our cerebrum before all the extra energy flying around can fry it. Now that it's in your system again, you'll keep new memories."

He lets that sit for a spell. The words jumble around in my head, new ones added to the pile. *Axons. Cerebrum.*

"Will I get the old memories back?" I say softly.

He is silent for a moment. "I don't know." Better than *No,* I guess, but it still leaves me feeling heavy. Another stretch of silence. I can almost hear him wondering if I can handle more.

"Someone tampered with your shots. We know who. Two of us, two of our friends, left. They ran away. We *don't* know why. And now they're gone. Dr. Tycast thought you left with them, but I didn't believe it. I had a way to track you, and I did it."

Suddenly it's too much—gene therapy? Memory medicine? Friends running away, friends I don't even *know,* whose faces

25

I can't recall?—and I have to get up. My hand tears free of Peter's grip.

"Who is *we*?" I say. "Who is Dr. Tycast?" They aren't the only questions I have, but I figure the answers will be the easiest to handle.

"We . . . we is the four of us. Me and you, Noah and Olive. And the people who teach us. That's who *we* are."

"You know that doesn't mean anything to me," I say. Back in the mall I wanted answers. Now I'm not sure I do.

Below us, cars squeal to a stop at the mouth of the alley. Car doors open and shut. The cops probably tracked the stolen cruiser with GPS. But we're safe up here, I think. I assume they wouldn't expect a car thief to climb the building right next to the stolen vehicle. The commotion becomes faraway and unimportant.

"What's the point?" I say. "Of us. Of everything you're telling me."

Peter closes his eyes, like he's considering his words carefully. "Imagine being dropped into a war zone and scaring everyone into surrender. No death. No bloodshed. With enough of us, you could bring an entire city to its knees." His own words seem to startle him, like he got them from somewhere else and only now realizes how false they are. *No death? No bloodshed?*

I stand facing away from him, hands on my hips, that same breeze ruffling the fine hair on my arms. It doesn't make sense. I saw the panic in the mall. On a larger scale? Death and bloodshed.

Bullets and bombs are the alternative to my power.

Which is worse?

4

The cops shout to each other down below. Feet pound the pavement.

"Where are my parents?" I say.

Peter licks his lips, looks at the gravel around his feet. "They gave you up. For the greater good, I guess. So did mine."

"Did I know them?"

"No. You were too young."

For the greater good. I imagine faceless parents handing me over for *gene therapy*. Like everything so far, it doesn't make sense. The hollowness inside my chest is back.

"How do you know these people didn't just take me? They could've kidnapped me."

"You knew this before and you accepted it. You have to again."

I don't think I have to do anything; it's clear anyone, even Peter, would have a hard time forcing me to.

"We're your family," he says. "We have been for years. Since we were kids."

We. The four of us. Family, he says. You don't forget your family.

I turn away. My eyelash catches a tear and I blink it free. The muscles in my stomach are tight. I put a hand on them and try to relax, breathe through my mouth. It takes a few minutes, but I pull myself back to earth. I have to accept what I hear as truth because I've seen proof of it. I saw that mall empty itself. What I felt in my head can't be coincidence.

"Will I get my memories back?" I ask again.

Peter doesn't say anything. I turn around to see my answer on his face.

I try to play it off like it's no big deal, but the gap inside me widens, threatening to swallow me. "I guess I don't know what I'm missing, right?"

"It'll be okay, Miranda."

Exactly what I wanted to hear. If only I could believe it.

His face holds no deception I can see, no clue that will tell me he's crazy, or I'm crazy, or we're both crazy. There is only this steady calm, his unflinching eyes.

"Will you come home with me?"

So he asks me.

But, like before, there's not much of a choice. Not if I want to know more.

I believe and don't believe what he says next.

"We're going to jump across the rooftops."

I believe it because I don't see another way out of here, and I believe it because physically I seem pretty capable—but I don't believe it because, well, it's insane.

He smiles at my apprehension. "I'll go first, then."

So he does. He runs to the edge of the roof, plants one foot on the lip, and launches himself over the alley. He skids a few feet on the next roof, then turns and waves me forward. He made it look as easy as jumping across a puddle.

Anything he can do, I can do better. I hope. The only way to find out what happens next is to let go. Swallowing fear and reason, I sprint to the edge of the roof and leap. Keep my eyes forward, feet skating over an invisible pond, wind in my ears, then I'm down, feet planted on the next roof. And I don't stop. We run, opening ourselves up. I find it effortless. We leap from rooftop to rooftop, trading the lead, heading in a direction we both seem to know. Any fear and doubt I had before is just a memory, and a faded one at that.

My pulse is in my eyes and ears by the time Peter slows.

Some of the crushed rock he kicks up peppers my shins. He skids to a stop and I almost crash into him. I steady myself with a palm on his back. Instantly I want to take my hand away, but he pretends not to notice, and I don't want to be awkward.

"Here," he says.

Dusk has fallen, the purple sky milky with thin clouds. I peer over the edge into the alley below. Far, far below. The piled black garbage bags are disgusting M&Ms from this height.

"Can you make it?" he asks.

"What do you mean?"

He vaults over the edge and makes contact with the brick wall opposite us, five feet down. His hands and toes touch it, then he pushes off, gliding back to the wall of the building I stand on. He's barely made contact when he does it again, bouncing back to the other side a few feet lower. I watch him continue back and forth while he grows smaller and smaller. At the bottom he crashes into a mountain of garbage bags.

He rolls off them; one splits open, spilling trash into the alley. I see his white grin from this far away. "Your turn!" he shouts through cupped hands.

I sigh. The fear is back, but my guess is it'll evaporate as soon as I start. Besides, the self-doubt has a new companion—a strange and welcome balance in the bottom of my stomach. I like it. I don't know who I am, but I might be a badass. I plant my hand on the ledge and toss myself over. I hit the opposite wall like Peter did, latch on for an instant, then push off and sail back across the alley.

I misjudge the distance. I drop too fast and my heart flies into my throat. Peter shouts something at me. I hit the wall, hands and feet scrabbling at the brick. The window rushes past my face, and I slam my hands down on the sill, digging in with my fingers so hard they bleed. I cling to the side of the building for a moment, fingers aflame.

"Nice save!" Peter shouts from below.

I risk a look down. Still *way* too high up.

"Hey, there's a ladder down here!" Peter shouts again.

"Really?" I say.

He laughs. "No. Keep going."

So I do. I swallow the doubt packed around my lungs and breathe again. "I can do this," I whisper, then push off into space and twist around. I grab the next window down, and the next. Pretty soon I'm at the bottom. I fall into the same trash bags as Peter, then roll out of them and stand up. There is no trace of worry or fear in his eyes—he had complete confidence I would make it down okay.

"How did I do that?" I say. "Or more important, *why* can I do that?"

Peter shrugs like it's natural. "They want us to be more

than capable. Giving us this power wasn't enough—we need the ability to take care of ourselves in a hostile situation."

"They. You mean our teachers."

He nods slowly. "Yes. Our teachers."

I want more—some explanation for my existence, some hint of my past. It makes me sick again, and suddenly I'm grateful for all the running and jumping. It's hard to dwell on a terrible thing when your only focus is movement and precision.

Peter must see the look on my face; his smile fades with the light. He slides his arm around my shoulders, then guides me down the alley, holding me close. "Come on, Miranda. Let's go home."

If only I knew where home is.

I learn soon enough—home is the forest.

We find a Cavalier with the keys still in it. Peter says Cavaliers are good to steal because nobody looks twice at them. I pause when I realize that stealing the car doesn't make any moral objection rear up inside me.

In the car, I ask Peter why I don't feel bad.

"Your training taught you to take what you need to complete a mission. Our mission is to get home safely."

So that's that, I guess.

He drives us south, away from the city, until the roads

narrow and are lined with trees instead of rugged buildings. We pass a few cows, some cornfields. Soon the trees are dense, suffocating the road. After another ten minutes, Peter leans forward and watches the forest. "There," he says, when we come across a nearly invisible dirt trail leading into the woods. The Cavalier rocks over stones and bumps and depressions for a mile. At the end of the path, the forest appears whole again. It's not. Peter drives the Cavalier around the illusion into a darker trail that goes back another mile. We don't talk much—I just stare out the window and watch the trees. Until his hand moves off the shifter and brushes my thigh by accident. I jump like he's stung me.

"Jumpy much?" he says. He smiles at me, and I know he's trying to make light of the whole situation.

"Just nervous, I guess." And I am, with nothing to back his words up against. It could all be a trap. For what, I don't know. But Peter doesn't give off any signals he's lying. No shifty eyes or fidgeting hands. It doesn't mean I trust him, but it's enough to keep me inside the car.

Our home is a plain one-story building made of concrete and painted to match the forest. The top is covered in vegetation to keep it hidden from planes or helicopters. Peter pulls around back, and I see the building is actually a garage filled with a few cars and motorcycles. On the roof, an unmanned turret follows us, tiny motors whirring inside it. The twin

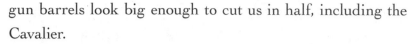

gun barrels look big enough to cut us in half, including the Cavalier.

"We live underground," he says.

"Oh. I thought we lived in the cars."

He doesn't offer a courtesy laugh, and heat creeps up my neck. He should not be able to make me feel embarrassed. "That was funny," I say.

"I know. But I've heard the joke before. I suspect I'll have to hear all of them again."

That stings. He must notice, because he adds, "Not that I mind."

We step onto a square cut into the metal floor. "There are worse things," I say.

"I know," he says, as white bulbs in the square light up. "Hands inside the border, please."

The square descends smoothly. Once the walls surround us, Peter turns to me and cups the back of my neck. He tilts my head back so I have to look him in the eye.

"I don't know what's going to happen down there," he says. His fingers burn hot on my skin. I am stuck between wanting to pull away and wanting to stay in his grip. I don't know why. I wonder if I *could* pull away, if I'm as strong as he is.

"What could happen?" I say.

"I don't know. You went off the grid. I tracked you through a chip you have under your skin."

A chip under my skin? I doubt I consented to that. I may not know myself, but I don't seem like the type who agrees to be watched. He found me, though, that's the important part. I could still be wandering around that mall, hurting people.

The elevator continues its descent. We have to be a few floors underground by now.

He runs his thumb over my ear and releases me. Sweat prickles the back of my neck; maybe putting myself in a hole wasn't the best idea.

"You could've told me earlier," I say.

"Would you have still come with me?"

Good question. "Yes. I don't know."

"With Noah and Olive leaving how they did, Tycast might suspect you. Stay calm. I'll be with you the whole time." Peter offers me another smile, but clearly he's worried too.

The elevator slowly reveals a thick metal door, then stops. Our breath echoes around us. Too late to turn back now. The surface is just a dim square high above.

The door clanks, followed by a scraping metallic sound that lasts two seconds. Then another clank.

The door slides open from right to left, and many, many guns are pointed in our direction.

5

The scarier part of my brain takes over. The part that makes my body react first and think later. All I see is the threat—

Four men, all in black, with armored vests and metal helmets. For all I know they could be robots. The helmets resemble motorcycle helmets but smaller, without the padding. Narrow black visors cover their eyes. Each carries what I recognize as H&K UMPs—these squat, ugly submachine guns.

The fact I know what they are startles me. "Peter, I remember something."

He sidesteps in front of me, blocking their line of sight. In the middle of the four helmeted men is an old man. He doesn't wear body armor or a helmet. Instead he has on a white lab coat, the pockets weighed down, rippling the fabric. Fine gray hair is combed back from his forehead. He's wearing a thin headband, like the workout kind, but made of black plastic instead of cloth. I don't know this man, but I feel a rush of affection for him.

"What is this?" Peter says. "Doctor, it's Miranda."

The doctor raises his hands, palms out. The men flanking him might be statues. "She left the reservation, Peter. This is a precaution. You expected this, I'm sure."

Peter stands stiff for a moment, then nods slowly. He steps back to put his shoulder next to mine again.

The doctor steps into the elevator. "Miranda, my name is Dr. Tycast. Do you remember that?"

"No."

He nods. "We have to detain you. Will you come peacefully?"

"Yes," I say. What choice do I have? I doubt I could escape at this point anyway.

He raises two fingers, and half the men behind him split off and leave. Their boots thunk down the hallway.

Dr. Tycast drops his hand on Peter's shoulder. "Thank you for bringing her back. Go to your room, I'll be there shortly."

"Sir," Peter says, "with all due respect, I'm staying."

Dr. Tycast's eyes crinkle when he smiles. "With all due respect?"

Peter holds his gaze for a few more seconds. "Sir—"

"Good night, Peter."

Peter sighs and walks out of the elevator. His left hand is clenched in a fist.

My heart pounds. Even if I didn't trust him before, I trust him a lot more than anyone else here. I feel naked without him.

Dr. Tycast sees this. "Relax. You'll see him again. You might not believe this, but just a few days ago you trusted me implicitly. Come with me."

He takes my arm and guides me from the elevator. The men with the UMPs and creepy helmets fall into step behind us. The hallway is cramped and featureless, gray, with tiny lights embedded in the floor, showing us the way to wherever we're going. The entire narrow ceiling is a light panel, glowing uniformly, illuminating every square inch.

The first right is my holding cell. A cell, because we are immediately locked inside. The big metal door shuts and a bolt rams into place, followed by a too-loud buzz.

Dr. Tycast pulls out one of two chairs at a metal table. "Sit," he says.

I wait just long enough to let him know I won't jump at his commands, not even if I used to. Then I sit.

A long mirror takes up the wall behind me and makes it impossible to not feel watched. Behind *him* is a wall that's different from the others, like it's covered in a fine film.

He clasps his hands together and looks at me across the table. The chair is cold and sucks heat from my legs and butt.

"Can I take this headband off?" he says.

"Sure. It isn't very fashion forward."

He breathes a laugh through his nose. "You're not one for making jokes when you're uncomfortable, Miranda."

"I guess I wouldn't know that." My curiosity gets the better of me. "What's the headband for?" I ask, even though I think I know the answer.

"It blocks the psychic energy you emit. Not as well as the helmets, but well enough. One develops a tolerance after so much exposure. But for those not used to it, being around a Rose is enough to cause discomfort, given enough time. Residual energy and such. But you're not going to use your power on me, are you?"

"No."

"Good." He takes the band off and sets it on the table. It contracts into a circle small enough for a pocket. He keeps smiling this familiar smile. My shoulders relax a little. Taking off the headband was a gesture of trust. He's vulnerable now.

"What do you remember?" he says.

What do I remember? Good question. I remember waking up on the bench. I remember meeting Peter, who makes me feel safe even though it's obvious I can take care of myself. I remember the mall. The people and their screams. The little boy's voice. The man who fell. The blood and broken limbs.

How will the survivors explain that? When they are themselves again, what will they say?

Who will speak to the families of the dead?

I swallow hard again, fighting the urge to vomit. I don't want to talk about what I remember.

"Let me help you," Dr. Tycast says.

Behind him, the wall sparks to life. It's a screen. A massive screen playing a video. It shows a room, narrow but long. At the far end is a big steel door. Halfway into the room, bunk beds are stacked along the walls to the left and right, one set on each side. Two small trunks sit at the foot of each bed. There's open space between the beds, but set farther away from the door, closer to the camera, is a big table ringed with chairs. For surveillance footage, the video is perfectly clear.

I wait for something to snap into place, some hint of recognition. But it's just a room. There's a brown rug between the beds. Each morning, it must have been the first thing my feet touched. I don't know if it's coarse. Or if I feel it with bare feet, or if I sleep with socks on.

In the video, I lie on my side, on the bottom bunk to the left. A boy kneels next to me. At first I think it's Peter, but he's too slim. Not smaller, just leaner. And instead of midnight black, his hair is wheat-colored and shaved close to his head. He has one hand on the side of my face. I bring my own hand up and tap the tip of his nose with my finger.

He leans in and stops with his lips a centimeter from mine. He hovers like that until he finally smiles and I lean forward to give him a peck. We both laugh silently because the bed above me and the bed across from me are occupied by still forms. Then we really kiss and his mouth travels from my lips to my chin and down my throat to the hollow between my collarbones.

I swallow as I watch, feeling heat bloom in my stomach and spread out.

The boy gives me a final kiss, goes back to his bunk, climbs to the top, and slides under the covers. On-screen, I squirm around, pulling the blanket up to my neck.

The video fast-forwards over our motionless bodies until, four hours later according to the video, the boy climbs down from his bunk slowly. He pads over to me. He places a hand on my cheek and I open my eyes.

"Who are you?" I say in the video.

He puts a finger to his lips. "Shh. Miranda, it's me. Look at my face."

I stare at him for a few seconds, then slowly shake my head. "Where am I?"

"I want you to come with me," he says, easing me out of bed.

He leads me from the room. Minutes later, a girl with black hair climbs down from my bunk and tiptoes over to the form that must be Peter. She jabs something into his neck, and he bolts upright but falls down almost immediately. She kisses her fingertips and presses them to Peter's temple. Then she leaves, and the room is empty except for Peter.

The video pauses.

"Do you remember leaving with Noah?" Dr. Tycast says.

Noah. The boy who kissed me. I replay the image of my head tilting back to give him better access to my neck. I don't know what to think. I can't remember any of it. I can't remember what his lips feel like, or what his skin smells like. Or what I feel when our eyes meet.

"Miranda?" Dr. Tycast says.

"I'm sorry. No."

He takes his glasses off and rubs his eyes so hard I wince. "That's because he'd been altering your memory shots for days. I assume Peter filled you in on most of this."

"Yes."

"Yes, well. You're on them again, so you'll be able to keep new memories. And though I can't be sure, I'm afraid what's lost might be lost forever."

"It doesn't matter," I say.

His eyes widen. "No? Why not?"

"Because I can't change what's already been done." I don't

know if I mean it; the words come automatically. But I hear the truth in them, however hard it is to accept. I *can't* get my memories back. It makes me feel cold. Helpless.

He smiles a tired smile. The smile of a father. "Very true. You always were the one to deal best with change. The others, they would hold on to what was, rather than embracing what is."

I absorb that, try to glean something about myself from it. "Doctor, why can I remember some things, and not others? Why do I know what a mall cop is, but I don't recognize myself in the mirror?"

Dr. Tycast nods while I talk. "There are different kinds of memory, Miranda. The memory shots you take counteract decay in a portion of your long-term memory. You remember your name, but you don't remember how the others celebrated your fourteenth birthday. You don't remember the first time you put your martial arts instructor on his back."

I have nothing to say to that. We sit in silence that might be amicable under different circumstances.

Dr. Tycast puts his glasses back on. "Noah and Olive took you from your home. They put one of my men in a coma to do it. If you remember anything, I want you to tell me now."

"I don't. I wish I did."

"Noah was your boyfriend," he says.

"Yeah?" I say, almost a whisper. I don't want to believe it.

The wall-screen snaps on again. Video-me sits at a desk, staring into what must be a webcam mounted on a laptop. My fingers dance over the keys, then come up and tug on my lower lip. Behind me, Noah reaches over and pulls my hand down.

"Stop doing that," he says. He's beautiful. My eyes trace his hard jawline to his lips. I try to remember what they feel like on mine, but again, there's nothing. He looks into the camera, at me sitting here in this cold chair.

"This is Miranda and Noah, and we're doing an after-mission log," Noah says.

"Yes," I say, "because we're too lazy to do one by ourselves."

"And so we combine them," Noah says, grinning.

We talk about some training mission where we split into teams and had to find a snow globe by following clues across the city. Neither of us was impressed with it. Noah, our team leader, makes a few cracks about Peter, leader for the opposite team. There are only two people on a team, and we make a joke about that. We beat Peter's team. Noah mentions the name of the black-haired girl—Olive.

I don't know how I could have no memory of him.

The video ends abruptly and I flinch.

"We think he was trying to keep you safe somehow. He took Olive, but kept you out of his plans, whatever they are. He thinks something is coming."

"What's coming?" I ask.

45

Dr. Tycast shrugs. "That's your mission. To find out. Go see Peter. I'll brief the both of you tomorrow morning." He spreads his hands flat on the table. "What happened in the mall was not your fault. For now, I need you to put it out of your mind. We will take care of the families. Do you understand?"

Hearing the words doesn't help, but I nod. Dr. Tycast begins to stand.

"Wait," I say. "Tell me what this place is all about. Tell me what I'm for. Really."

He studies me while he considers his words. "You're part of an experiment. To attain peace through chaos. You are the hope for a better tomorrow."

"Sounds kind of cliché, Doctor."

He nods. "Very. But that's one of the sacrifices we make."

He leaves the cell, which is now just a room.

The door stays open.

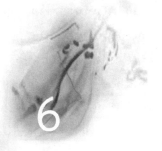

6

I t's raining. No, *pouring*. Sheets of rain. A dark alley. Behind me, a sharp *twang*. I throw myself to the ground and feel something pass over me, tugging at my hair. A spiderweb made of wire is plastered on a brick wall twenty feet away. They're shooting *nets* at me.

I'm on my feet again and running. Another *twang*. Throw myself left. The net passes me, still coiled. It unfurls in midair and catches a window. The window shatters and glass bites at my clothes.

I open my eyes.

The alley is gone, replaced by an underground corridor. The door to our quarters is just ahead.

I stand there for a moment, bracing myself on the wall with outstretched fingertips. A memory? Tycast didn't say it was impossible for them to return. I'm almost mad it couldn't have been a quieter moment, about the people in my life. It had to be some stupid training mission.

A training mission that felt real. Or at least the fear was real. But I guess that's the point of training.

The images have faded by the time I reach the big steel door, which is painted with a large rose, fully four feet tall. At the bottom, Olive signed her name in overblown, swirling script.

I open the door to find the room from the video. A chessboard sits on the big round table, the white pieces tipped over, but otherwise it's the same, just a reverse perspective. At the far end are a refrigerator and four small dressers, and an open door leads to what I assume is the bathroom.

The camera is mounted high above the fridge, pointed right at me. Only now does it really hit me that it recorded me and Noah kissing. Or making out, or whatever. I guess we just . . . didn't care.

In the bottom bunk on the left, Peter is passed out on his back, one arm draped over his eyes. I watch him for a while, feeling the carpet under my feet. It's smooth, not coarse. Peter has a tiny scar on his chin, a little white line. I stop myself from reaching over to touch it. Part of me wants to wake him up and ask about the nets, the dark alley, and the rain.

I shake my head and climb into my own bed a few steps away. I pull the sheets over my face and wait for sleep.

When I sleep I dream. Noah is in my bunk and we're quiet because the others are asleep and we both know this is against the rules. I feel his fingers trace lazy circles on the bare skin of my back. His breath is hot in my ear and he asks if we can but of course the answer is no. He gives a disappointed groan and kisses the soft spot under my ear.

"How long are you going to make me wait?" he says.

The room changes before I can answer. Now I'm playing chess with Olive. She leans over her pieces, biting her lip. Noah and Peter spar halfheartedly in the space between our beds.

"Don't worry about it," I say to Olive. Although I don't know what I'm specifically talking about.

"It was a stupid mistake," Olive says. "No wonder I'm always fourth place."

"Hey, I'm always third. That's one from four."

Olive scrunches her face. "You're always second. Don't act like Noah is faster than you. Or smarter."

I grin, moving my bishop into her half of the board. "Well, he cries if I don't let him win."

"I heard that," Noah says, ducking under one of Peter's kicks. "And of course our fabulous leader has to be the best at everything." It's a joke, but there's an edge to it. Some hint of accusation.

Peter chuckles. The room changes again, morphing into one of the stone corridors. The four of us round a corner and pull up short. Phil stands there, arms folded over his barrel chest. He has a red goatee but his head is shiny and smooth.

"Where do you think you're going?" he says.

Olive steps in front of us. She always had the most pull with Phil. She isn't the strongest fighter, but she's the best listener. "We were going for a walk, *Sifu*." Only Olive calls him *Sifu* regularly. Chinese for master, or teacher.

"It's midnight," Phil says.

"We just want to go outside," Olive says, giving her most dazzling smile.

Phil tries to hold the hard look, but he steps aside. "Be back before the sun comes up, or Tycast will have my ass in a cast." Phil always uses that phrase, which summons a disturbing mental image. "We have a mission tomorrow morning, so no sleepy faces."

Mission makes us groan in unison, but really we're excited about it. We train nonstop, or have class, but every once in a while Phil has us go on scavenger hunts in or around the city. I love getting out, stretching my legs, seeing the sky.

Noah pats Phil on the chest. "Don't tell me you're afraid of the good Dr. Tycast."

Phil shakes his head and grins. "The man is terrifying."

The corridor changes. We're in a train yard, later in the same night, running alongside a moving train. We jump onto the end of the last car, then climb to the top and ride through the muggy night, lit only by the white moon. Pure exhilaration.

The scene changes again. I'm in a classroom. The four of us are learning calculus, then history, then economics. Phil is our teacher. There are four chairs, four desks, four students. It's always this way. Class is about learning the material fast, so we can get back to physical training. There is no talking, just lecture and tests. Phil horrifies us by saying civilians go to school for more than seven hours each day, and learn less. We get it done in three hours.

Suddenly I'm in a gym. Phil demonstrates a throw on Olive, then we practice on each other until our breath is short.

Another change. I'm in an all-night diner. The four of us in a booth. Noah and I hold hands under the table. It's the same night we rode the train just for fun.

A couple kids eat burgers and fries in the booth across from us. One whispers a joke and they all laugh and steal glances at us, until I make eye contact with one of them. They stop.

"You ever wish you were normal?" Olive says, popping a fry into her mouth.

"What's normal?" I say.

Olive shrugs, elbows Peter in the ribs. "What's normal, Fearless Leader?"

Peter laughs, shaking his head. "I wish you guys would stop calling me that. I didn't ask for anything."

Noah drinks until he hits the bottom of his Coke. "No, you just can't help being the strongest and fastest."

Peter grins. "Do you want to arm-wrestle again?"

Noah makes a low moan in his throat. "No thanks." He rubs his arm. "My shoulder still hurts."

It's not even funny, but we're all loopy with the rush of sneaking out, so we laugh. Although Phil saw us, so it doesn't really count as *sneaking*. Noah squeezes my thigh under the table.

"You guys ready to go back?" Peter says. "It's almost dawn."

"Maybe a little longer," I say.

I never see what comes next.

When I wake, I feel empty and full at the same time; the memories fade but remain inside me. The little glimpse of my past leaves me wanting more.

So I grab at one again, the last memory in the diner. I'm there in the booth, but I can't remember how I felt. I see Noah and Peter and Olive, but they're just people. Noah holding my hand, I liked that. I'm sure I did.

It doesn't answer the question of who I am, but I have a better idea now. And I guess that's something.

But at the same time it's nothing. The fragments didn't come with an understanding of the people within them. They came and went, too fast to truly experience, or to truly keep as my own. It was just a movie of someone else's life. How much can I learn from a few snapshots?

Maybe if more pieces come, I'll get a better picture. If enough pieces come, maybe I'll be able to claim them.

I sigh and toss the covers off and sit up in bed. Getting a few memories back was supposed to make everything better, but all it does is confirm there was most definitely a life here that used to belong to me.

My sweaty T-shirt sticks to my stomach and back. I swipe some of the hair off my face and tie it into a loose ponytail, then realize I'm dying of thirst. My eyes adjust to the dark by the time I'm in the bathroom.

A light flicks on. Peter leans against one of the stall doors, wearing jeans and nothing else.

He startled me, so I'm a little demanding when I say, "What are you doing in here?"

He shrugs, which is awkward with his shoulder against the stall.

"Just brooding in the dark?" I say.

"I couldn't sleep."

He tries hard not to, but his eyes cut over my bare legs before settling back on my face. My greater willpower allows me to hold his eyes, not the lines of his hips disappearing behind the waist of his jeans. He scrubs at his black hair with one hand. I try to remember how I looked at him in the dream, if I felt anything when I did, but I can't.

"I had a dream. A memory of Noah—of all of us. It was a memory."

"A phantom," he says. "You might have a few."

"Could they come back clearer?"

He looks away. "No."

"But earlier you said you weren't sure."

He shrugs. "You're right, I'm not."

"Then why did you—"

"I just don't want you to get your hopes up." There's something off about the way he says it, like he's leaving something out.

Maybe more will come, in time. And maybe they won't come attached with borrowed emotions.

Maybe.

We stand there barefoot on the cold tile. Neither of us knows what to say. I fill the silence with something.

"Don't worry about where my hopes are." I pause. "Or I'll put your ass in a cast."

Peter's mouth drops open. "You remember Phil."

I nod. "A little."

"He's around. I don't know why he hasn't come to see you yet."

"Maybe he's afraid I won't recognize him." It's a joke, but then I think about what this must be like for everyone else. They know me, even if I don't.

My arms are folded. I feel weird standing in the middle of the bathroom, so I walk to the stall and lean against it too.

"You were really just standing here in the dark?"

"I was stretching. It helps me sleep when I have nightmares."

"What kind of nightmares?"

He walks to the sink and fills a glass with water, totally ignoring me. Two sinks side by side, two mirrors, four toothbrushes. His back is to me. A thick red scar runs horizontal from shoulder to shoulder; it bulges when he lifts his arm to drink. I wonder how he got it, then realize I probably knew. Just a few days ago, I knew.

Nightmares are a sore subject. *Check.* I try something else.

"I'm taking this pretty well, don't you think?" Or I'm faking it well. I still feel like I could crack at any minute, like I'm being held together with brittle glue.

"Like I said, you're trained. You adapt. And as much as you've forgotten, you still remember our way of life. We've been here for years. Last week we played chess out there, me and you. I won but I think you let me. And you never let anyone win."

When he turns around, his eyes are red. It must be the light; he didn't sound upset at all.

"We've been friends for a long time," he says.

"I'm sorry I don't remember."

He shrugs like it doesn't matter, but it does, and we both know it. "We'll make new memories."

I watch him leave, wishing I had something better to say, something to show him I'm the same girl he remembers, even if I don't remember her myself.

He left his cup on the counter, half full. I finish it and go back to sleep.

7

W e wake to knocking on our door. Dr. Tycast comes in with a little pushcart. Two trays on top carry our breakfast—an unlabeled protein bar, egg whites, and orange juice. And two syringes filled with the flaxen liquid.

"I thought I'd brief you here, so you can leave as soon as you finish eating," Dr. Tycast says.

We sit at the big table, the chessboard between us and the doctor. I was able to sleep, and I feel better. The bed felt and smelled familiar. Even though I don't recognize the things around me, it *feels* right, and that's enough to get by for now.

Dr. Tycast folds his hands together and leans on the table. "We're working with limited time here. It's not my usual practice to keep things from you, but with Miranda's recent, ah—"

"Let's call it an incident," Peter says, elbowing me. Heat pricks the back of my neck—how can he joke about it? But then I realize he's trying to make me comfortable, to make it how it was. Assuming we joked around before.

Dr. Tycast sees my reaction isn't negative. "All right, incident. As I was saying . . ." He takes off his glasses and rubs the bridge of his nose. He still has sleep bags under his eyes. "I know you have secrets. I know *Sifu* Phil trained you differently, Peter, as leader. He's not here right now, but if you have a way to track Noah and Olive, I want you to do it. Can you?"

"Yes," Peter says, chewing on a bit of protein bar. While Tycast was talking, Peter uncapped both syringes and administered both shots. No alcohol swab, just a quick sting in my arm and it was done. I didn't complain because I didn't want to seem like a baby. He slid the other needle into his forearm, pressed the plunger, then set both syringes on the tray and picked up his protein bar again. Total elapsed time—six seconds.

"Then find them," Tycast says. "Keep Miranda on a tight leash."

"Hey," I say. He said it casually, but that doesn't mean I want to think of myself as a liability. Plus, I'm not a dog.

Dr. Tycast holds up a hand. "Were you yourself, young

lady, you would agree with me. You are . . . unreliable. For the time being, at least. I'm keeping you in play because we need you. Understood?"

"What about all those guys with guns?" I say. They seem reliable.

He smiles. "They haven't spent over a decade training with Peter. Peter knows you. And we need to see what you can and can't do. So you go."

"Yes, sir," I say automatically, no smart-ass undertone.

He claps his hands together, eyes flitting from me to Peter and back again. "Good. Fantastic. Please return them home. Don't come back until you do."

He leaves us alone. The door shuts as I take my last bite.

Peter stands up, all business, wiping the corners of his mouth. "Get dressed."

At first I'm confused because I'm already wearing clothes. Then I open my dresser and see what he's talking about.

My uniform is made of two parts.

The first layer is body armor. A black one-piece that reminds me of a wet suit with scales. The fabric is woven with something Peter doesn't want to elaborate on. He just wants me to put the suit on so we can get moving. So I do. In the bathroom. I slide my limbs into the stiff but still flexible fabric, feeling somewhat like a cyborg. It covers my feet and ends at the top of my neck, leaving my hands exposed. The suit contracts slightly, hugging my bare skin.

That's the first layer.

The second is a pair of regular jeans and a black long-sleeved T-shirt. Once they're on, it's impossible to see the suit underneath. I have a pair of soft black leather boots under my bed, with socks stuffed in them. I slip them over my armored feet while Peter grabs a shirt like mine, only dark blue.

"Weapons?" I stop. Putting on the armor made my thoughts go there automatically. Suddenly I'm excited about *weapons*.

Peter tugs the shirt over his head, smiling. "You remember something?"

"No, I . . . This is weird."

"Good weird?" He sits on his bunk and laces up his boots.

"I think so."

"Just wait," he says.

We enter the corridor and follow the glowing ceiling back to the elevator, passing no one. The place feels empty, like a crypt. I'm giddy by the time we're in the elevator. I don't know what comes next, and it excites me. I feel like I was made for this.

"I hope you remember how to ride a bike," Peter says, once we reach the garage.

Two motorcycles sit in the corner, tucked behind a massive olive-green Humvee. They follow the black motif. The labels have been removed, but somehow I *know* they're Ducati Superbikes. I fight the urge to share with Peter every time I remember something.

Faint rubber marks stain the concrete next to the bikes. Two are missing.

Peter passes me a helmet. "If not," he says, "you can always ride with me." He doesn't look at me when he offers.

"I'm sure I remember." Not that the idea of riding behind him is completely repulsive, or repulsive at all, just ... I don't know. I can ride my own bike.

I pull my hair back into a quick ponytail and push the helmet over my head. Peter starts his bike and its growl fills the small building. He pulls a chunky watch out of his pocket and buckles it onto his left wrist, then messes with it while the bikes fill the garage with the sharp tang of exhaust. Finally, he puts it in gear and I do the same.

I follow him into the gray morning, down the bumpy path to the main road. The ground is uneven but I dart around the depressions easily; apparently I was really good at this too.

Peter turns right, to the south. He talks to me through a speaker in my helmet. "I've been tracking Noah and Olive. They rode west for a while, to Indiana, but they stopped in Indianapolis. Should take less than five hours to get there."

"Why?"

His voice crackles through again. "Why did they stop?

Who knows. Maybe they're tired. Or maybe they found the tracking devices I implanted and took them out."

He swerves around a Mustang and cuts back in before a truck coming the other way can obliterate him. I keep pace, enjoying the wind pushing against me and the way the bike moves with simple corrections of my body.

"The same device I have? Why track us?"

He looks over his shoulder at me, but I can't see his face through his helmet visor. "In case one of you gets lost in a mall."

We ride on, only stopping to fill up our tanks, or to grab a quick meal. The five-hour trip will be closer to four; we can't help racing each other when the road is clear and straight. As we near Indianapolis, silence reigns. I know he's thinking about what we'll find in the city. So I'm left alone with my thoughts, and one thing in particular just doesn't fit with what I've been told so far.

At the next gas station, I sit next to the pump eating a hot dog. Peter stands next to the bikes, watching the road like he's expecting company.

"Peter?"

He keeps looking down the road. "Hmm?"

"You said before we were meant for good, to end conflicts without bloodshed."

He shoves the last of his hot dog into his mouth, rubs his hands on his jeans. "Yeah," he says through a full mouth.

"I mean, I'm not an expert or anything, but the mall was pretty chaotic. People got hurt." My throat is dry and dusty. "People died." I don't add, *because of me*.

"It's better than bullets, right?"

I stand up. "Yeah. But how do we know we'll be used for good?"

"That's like anything. Anything can be used for evil. A gun can be used to murder, but in the right hands it can also protect."

I straddle my bike, feeling the heat from the engine seep into my thighs. My back aches from being hunched over. "I know. I just . . . I feel like a weapon."

Peter drops his hand on my shoulder. "I trust Dr. Tycast. He would never let someone use us. Whatever Noah and Olive are up to, we'll know soon enough."

It's enough to calm me. Again, I'm calm because he is. But I doubt anything will completely erase the worry chilling my skin.

We start our bikes and take the road back to the highway. Indianapolis comes into view soon after.

Once we're in the city, Peter is stricter with the rules of the road. We obey the speed limit. We ride around construction.

The police officer directing traffic eyes us the whole time. I lift my visor and smile at him. After a second, he smiles back and returns his attention to the cars.

Peter lifts his visor just to roll his eyes.

The signal leads us to a Holiday Inn on the edge of downtown. The building is four stories of pale brick, boring, the perfect place to hide, I would guess. Not too cheap, not too expensive.

Two bikes identical to ours share a space in the back. We park in the next space, hidden behind a huge van in case Noah and Olive are watching their bikes from a window. Peter lifts the seat off his bike and pulls out two small semiautomatics —Walther PPKs. He tosses one to me; I snatch it out of the air, then snug it against my lower back. I pull my shirt over it.

"They're loaded," he says. "I hope you remember how to shoot."

"Me too." The confidence isn't there, not yet. It always comes the second I discover I *can* do something.

We enter the hotel like we belong there, not acknowledging the desk clerk. Really, I'm just following Peter's lead; all I can think about is the hunk of metal pressed against my spine. Hoping against hope I won't have to use it.

In the elevator, Peter checks his watch again, which he's clearly using to track them. My hands shake. I don't know if

I'm afraid, or if I'm nervous about meeting Noah and Olive. The anger is a sure thing, though, thanks to Noah. I still can't believe the boy I kissed in the video is the one who took away my memories.

Peter leads me to room 496, and checks his watch a final time. He stands off to the side, holding his gun against his thigh, then nods to the other side of the door. I take up a similar position, listening for any signs of life over the pounding of my pulse.

He knocks three times.

8

Nothing, no response.

Peter knocks three more times. "Room service," he says. We share a grin despite the situation. "C'mon. Noah, Olive. Open the door." After a few seconds, Peter sighs. "All right, I'm coming in. Don't shoot."

Neither of us has a key card, so Peter raises his foot and kicks above the doorknob. It sounds like a gunshot. The door swings open and bangs off the inside wall. It bounces back to hit us, but Peter shoulders his way through, gun up, muscles tense. I follow a second behind him, and take in the room at a glance—

Bed. Small desk. Tube TV with a bulging screen. Wooden

dresser on the far wall. Window overlooking a section of down-town. A dark opening to my left, the bathroom.

Peter, frozen with a gun to his left temple.

"Drop it," says the person holding the gun.

I recognize him immediately from the video. Noah. The boy I kissed.

His eyes flit toward me. "Miranda?"

Right then, as we make eye contact for the first time, anger flares inside me, white hot.

Peter makes his move. He tries to knock the gun away with his left hand and punch with his right, but Noah is too fast. He swings the gun down and bounces it off Peter's forehead. Peter stumbles a few feet and slams his hip against the desk, hand pressed above his eyebrow. Blood rolls down his cheek and drips off the end of his chin.

"Don't try it," Noah says to Peter.

"Thanks for the advice," Peter says, leaning against the wall.

I still have my gun up through sheer power of will, and I point it at Noah. Not that it's heavy, just, I know I shouldn't be pointing it at him. This is *wrong*, any way you cut it. We're supposed to be a team. His eyes widen; I know he wants to swing the gun from Peter to me.

He doesn't. And I know why. I sense movement in the

dark bathroom to my left. Before I can process it and decide to switch targets, a gun barrel nestles in my hair.

"Drop it," a girl's voice says.

Behind me, the main door shuts, closing us off from the hallway. "You've got to be kidding me," I say.

"Don't drop it," Peter says to me. "She won't shoot."

"Shut up," Noah and the girl say.

It must be Olive. I see her hovering in my peripheral vision, on the edge of darkness. The only detail I can make out is long black hair.

We stand like this for thirty seconds—me aiming at Noah, Olive aiming at me, Noah aiming at Peter, and Peter really just holding his head. Finally Peter blinks a few times and raises his gun at Olive.

"I guess I'll complete the figure eight," he says.

"Lower your gun," Noah says calmly.

Peter shakes his head. "Guys, just listen. For a minute."

He waits. We haven't moved. I study Noah at the end of my sight. He's taller than he looked in the video, as tall as Peter. Sweat beads his forehead and he has this look on his face. I recognize it.

Suspicion.

He thinks *we're* the ones up to no good. It takes everything I have not to start giggling like an idiot. And not a *ha-ha* giggle, either. Definitely a *Get this girl to the crazy house* giggle. I'm looking at this guy who used to be my boyfriend, and something is definitely there. The Ghost of Feelings Past, maybe. But the idea that he suspects us when he's the one who left the way he did...it's so ridiculous that I doubt everything I've learned about myself so far. I believe we were together; I just don't understand how. Plus, that whole part where I'm pointing a gun at him doesn't make things any clearer.

"If you have something to share, please do," Noah says. His eyes keep cutting to me, searching for something. Recognition? He won't get it. Maybe if he hadn't altered my shots or whatever the hell he did...The anger I first felt has shrunk slightly, like turning down the flame on a stove. It's no match for the emptiness in my chest, which seems to gobble everything moments after I feel it.

Peter takes a deep breath. "A few days ago we slept in the same room, ate our meals together, took turns using the showers. Trained together. Had class together. Do you all remember this? I mean, except Miranda."

He smiles at me—his brilliant smile, the one that needs a trademark. Noah seems disgusted, but whether for me or himself isn't clear.

"I remember," Noah says.

"Me too," Olive says from the shadows.

"Okay then," Peter continues, "is it reasonable to talk about this minus the guns?"

"It is," Olive says.

"Shut up, Olive," Noah says.

"*You* shut up," she replies. "Who made you boss?"

"You did, when you followed me."

In the hallway, someone opens and closes a door. Kicking in that door wasn't quiet, and I wonder if we'll have company soon.

No one wants to make the first move, that much is clear. Fine. Let the girl who has the least reason to trust any of them show she's willing to talk. "Okay," I say. Slowly, I lower my weapon until it's next to my thigh again. The grip is slippery with sweat.

"That's my girl," Noah says.

"Item one, I'm *not* your girl."

His growing smile disappears like it was never there in the first place. He keeps his gun on Peter, who keeps his gun on Olive, who keeps her gun on me.

"Guys," I say, "I just lowered my weapon. Good faith, anyone?"

Peter lowers his too, slowly. Noah and Olive don't move.

"Now," I say, "you two have the guns. Why don't you tell us why you left? Why don't you"—and now I'm speaking to Noah—"tell me why I can't remember a goddamn thing."

Noah swallows; I watch his Adam's apple go up, then down.

"I saw something," he says, keeping his gun on Peter.

"What?" Peter asks.

"Don't play dumb, you *know* what I'm talking about."

Peter's jaw clenches. He squares to Noah. Noah aims the gun, I don't know, *harder* at Peter. Before I can stop myself, I walk forward. If Noah won't stop pointing his gun at Peter, maybe he'll stop pointing it at me. One hopes.

I slip my gun into my jeans, then reach out and put a palm on each of their chests. Both are warm. I feel the scales of their armor underneath the fabric. It shouldn't be possible through the armor, but I feel their fast heartbeats thrum against my palms.

I try to make my voice as calm as possible. "Either we talk to each other, or we shoot each other. Pick one."

I should've done that in the first place.

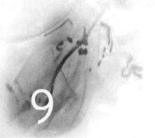

9

N oah tells us a story.

He was snooping in Dr. Tycast's office last week, searching for pain pills. He'd hurt his back during a training mission. It was my fault, apparently. He was only allowed so many but the pain was flaring up, so he wanted to see what the doctor had in his desk.

We tell him to get to the good part.

Noah closes his eyes and seems to fall into a kind of trance. "Just . . . stay with me," he says. "This is what happened."

Two seconds after finding the pills, he heard Dr. Tycast in the hallway and slid into the small closet Tycast keeps some personal stuff in. It was already late, and he figured the doctor would be in and out. Instead, Dr. Tycast sat down and something vibrated on his desk, like a cell phone.

Dr. Tycast said, "On-screen," and a video appeared on the far wall, like it had in the holding room for me.

Noah didn't see who was on the screen—the door to the closet was shut, with only a sliver of light coming through. But he heard the voice just fine.

"Are you alone?" the voice said, which was female and familiar.

"Aren't I always?" Dr. Tycast said.

"I mean physically, Brett."

"Yes. Go ahead."

"We're moving ahead with the dry run."

"I know."

"No, I mean now. Two weeks."

"You said I had another year with them."

"I did."

"I told you they won't be at full potential until then."

"You did, yes."

"And you want to test them why?"

"Because our buyers want them now, and they demand a test."

"Who are the buyers?"

"I am not at liberty to say."

"Why do I have a feeling it isn't our government?"

"Because it's not our government, Brett."

"They backed out again."

"Yes, they did."

"Do they know about the children?"

"No, they do not."

There was a long pause here, like Tycast was thinking hard.

"When you say dry run, you mean—"

"What we talked about, Doctor. You said you were okay with it."

"I said we could talk about it. We had a year to talk about it."

"And now we don't have a year. The Beta team will move into the facility and you can have the extra year with them. Beta team will take part in the dry run to make up for the power Alpha lacks. The longer we wait, the higher risk we never recover a cent from this project."

Another pause.

Finally, Dr. Tycast said, "Hundreds could die. Thousands. We don't know how far it will spread."

"Hence the test, Brett."

"We can do this indoors. We can simulate—"

"We have a buyer locked in. A deposit has been made. But they have requested a real-world demonstration. We voted today, unanimously."

"These are good kids. They won't go along with it. You know this."

"We have ways of convincing them. You know we won't deliver them to their buyers without security measures."

"Security measures," Dr. Tycast repeated. "The tattoos."

"Yes, the tattoos. You're on board, Doctor."

"Are you asking me or telling me?"

"I'm asking. Come on, Brett."

"I want to know where they're going. After the dry run, I want to know."

"Of course. They're your children as much as they are mine."

"Right."

Noah pauses here. He lays his palms flat on either side of his head. He says he wants to get the words right. It's important. It's why he's here. Why he did what he did.

"There's one more thing, Doctor," the woman said.

"Yes?"

"The rogue."

"You've found him."

"No. Not yet. We last tracked him to Indianapolis, but lost him. He might be hiding there. Or he might be back in the city."

"You think Rhys will repeat his actions."

"I don't see why he wouldn't. You saw the aftermath of his escape. Four Roses dead in a matter of minutes."

"You should've let Rhys go! You knew he was stronger than the others."

"Yes, well, we're trying to keep him away from the teams. He'll either kill them, or try to use them against us. In that situation, I hope he chooses the former. If you understand."

"He can't get in here."

"I hope you're sure."

"I am."

"Good night then, Doctor."

"Good night."

The light from the screen went dark. Dr. Tycast pounded his fist on his desk and swore softly, like he'd hurt himself. After a minute, Noah heard him crying. He sobbed for five minutes before pulling himself together, sniffing back tears and snot. Finally he left. Noah went to his desk and tried to find the video in his files, but it was gone.

He didn't know exactly what was going on, but he knew enough. They were going to sell us, make us hurt people. A lot of people.

"I wanted you safe," Noah says. "I switched your memory shots until the drug was out of your system."

He wanted me safe. Those people in the mall are dead because he wanted me safe.

"I took you away, and . . . There's no excuse, I know. I just needed you safe."

Everyone is looking at me.

He brushes a hand over his short hair. "Then I went to find the rogue. This *Rhys* they talked about. He could change everything. He could help us."

"Or kill us," Peter says. "Sounds like he kills Roses for a living."

Noah raises his hands and spreads them wide. "Yes. Roses. Plural. More people like us. I had to know if it was true. And I knew if I found the rogue, there was a good chance he'd kill me outright, including Miranda if I brought her with me."

Leave me at home, and I'm sold off as a weapon. Take me with him and risk death at the hands of someone who's already killed four separate Roses. Yeah, I get it now. But it's the furthest thing from right I can imagine. He took away my choice.

Oh, and there's one flaw in his argument.

"It was okay to risk Olive?" I say.

Olive holds my gaze. "I don't agree with what he did, but no one risked me. I came because we have to do *something*." She licks her lips, sighs. "By the time I knew what Noah's plans were, it was too late to stop him."

"And did you find the rogue?" I ask Noah.

He opens his mouth to speak, then closes it. Shakes his head slowly.

"You had no right," I say, feeling more empty than angry again. It's tiring to attempt understanding. "Why did you leave me downtown if you wanted me safe?" I can't even begin to wrap my head around Dr. Tycast's betrayal. If he's up to something, I can't trust anything he said to me last night.

Olive and I sit at the foot of the bed. Peter leans against the wall with his arms folded, looking out the window, holding a red-spotted towel to his forehead. Noah paces, occasionally reaching up and lacing his fingers behind his head.

"I didn't leave you downtown. I took you to Columbus," he says.

"I woke up in Cleveland." I must've traveled, forgetting along the way. Heading home even if I didn't know it consciously. Still, that's a long way to be unaccounted for.

He shakes his head. Keeps pacing.

"You're an asshole," I say.

He stops pacing. "I know. Miranda, I did it because I—"

"Stop! Don't say it. I don't want to hear you say it."

"I have to say it," Noah says.

"No, you *don't*." If I hear him say the word *love*, I don't know what I'll do. I still have my gun. Maybe one day I can forgive him, but all chance of that goes out the window if he claims he did it for love. If you love someone, the idea is you respect them enough to trust them. Not take away their freedom. Their life.

And if he says it, that opens up a whole new line of questions. Like, Why are you in a hotel room with this girl instead of me? If you really love *me*, why take *her*?

Noah shakes his head once, not meeting my gaze. "It was wrong. I know. *I* was wrong. I don't know what else to say. I could say I'm sorry a million times."

"So you were wrong," I say. "Why not let me help? Do you think I'm an idiot?"

"No, of course not! I just couldn't risk your safety. As lame as that sounds now, that's what it was all about. Once we learned more, after we figured out who we could trust, I was . . . I was going to come get you."

"So I was just some distraction you needed to hide until you had time to deal with me."

He doesn't say anything because there's nothing he can say.

"You could've done anything else, anything but take away my memories." I feel my blood beating faster, making me vibrate. Dull heat under my skin.

The room becomes very quiet. I hear air whir in the vents, and the electronic tone the TV makes even though it's off.

Noah says, "I don't expect you to understand right now. And I know 'sorry' won't cut it."

"But why Peter?" I say. "Why leave him behind?"

Noah stops pacing and turns to Peter, who raises his eyebrows as if to ask, *Well?* "I couldn't be sure," Noah says. "He was always Tycast's favorite, not to mention our leader. If he knew, or was involved, asking him would've given me away."

"I don't blame you," Peter says. "I've been involved the

whole time." For the slightest moment, the room slides under my feet.

It takes Noah a second longer to get it. He shakes his head slowly.

"Bad joke," I say, knowing Peter didn't mean to upset us. Any irritation I feel is eclipsed by Noah and his actions.

Peter laughs at Noah's scowl. "I'm kidding, you dick. But yeah, I get it. What I can't forgive is what you did to Miranda." I meet his eyes. For the first time since the mall, I feel like I might not be alone.

Everyone looks at me again, probably expecting some reaction. They won't get one. I might be a shattered mess on the inside, but outside my face is placid. I give Noah nothing, because that's what he deserves.

"I'm sorry," Noah says to Peter. "I should've trusted you. I just didn't know what I would find. What Rhys would do if I found him. I wasn't thinking clearly. I..."

Peter holds up a hand. "Don't worry about it." He points at Olive. "Now, *you* I expected more from." He laughs, and so does Olive. Noah cracks a careful smile, staring at the floor. It's like I'm watching us stitch ourselves back together, but where I fit in, I'm not sure. Suddenly Olive turns me around and wraps her arms around my ribs, hugging me tight. After my initial shock fades, I hug her back. An idea flashes through me, burns me from the inside—I'm hugging a stranger.

"I didn't want him to do it," she says. "I didn't know until it was done."

From behind me, Noah says, "Oh please, Olive, I don't need her to hate me more, all right?"

Olive pulls back, and I see her tear-streaked face. "It's *true*. I only followed you because..."

"Because why?" Noah says.

Olive shakes her head and turns away. I can't look at Noah without putting a glare on my face. It might be physically impossible.

Us...together? In love, even? Maybe in a different life.

Before I can figure out what to say next, someone pounds on the door.

"Police! Everything okay in there?"

10

"Everything's fine," I say automatically. While Noah was telling us his story, I wedged the broken door back into its frame. The cop just needs to push a little harder to get it open. From the outside, it must not appear broken.

The cop's voice is muffled from behind the door. "Miss? Please open the door."

"I'm not dressed, can you give me a minute?"

"We don't hurt the cop," Peter whispers.

"I'll give him a small burst?" Olive says.

Noah moves to the window; it's too high to jump, and there's no balcony we can scale down.

This is the perfect opportunity to see what it's like when I *intend* to strike fear in someone. If the fear isn't under my complete control, it needs to be. I can't let it sneak up on me again.

Hopefully the cop prefers a burst of fear to one of us choking him out.

"I'll do it," I say. The idea brings cold sweat, but it's the best way. I hope.

Noah shakes his head. "Wait."

I don't wait. It's either fear from one of us, or we risk hurting the cop physically. I check the peephole and see one distorted man—blue uniform, badge, gun, baton—but his backup could be hiding to the left and right.

Olive gives me a small nod, so I close my eyes and face the door.

The heat is immediate, blooming to the inside of my skull. It narrows, pressure building behind my eyes again, and I release it. Don't ask me how. It feels like capping a hose with your thumb, and letting just a bit of water jet out. After a calming breath, the pressure in my head seems to decrease, but not completely.

Through the door, I hear the cop make a choked cry. The others tense behind me, something I feel instead of see. With the energy swimming in my head, my senses seem to be heightened. I swear I *hear* the carpet compress when Noah steps toward me. Or it's my imagination, and the already-familiar headache is messing with my mind.

Muffled by the door, erratic footsteps travel away from us, to the left. He sounds alone.

"How big was the wave?" Noah says, worried.

I chew the inside of my cheek, nervous that it might have been powerful enough to affect the other hotel guests. "Not big," I say.

Is this why he wanted to leave me behind? Because I'm reckless? *Am* I reckless?

He shakes his head and tries to walk past but I open the door first. The cop is gone. His radio is on the ground.

Peter checks up and down the hallway—we're alone.

"Time to go," Olive says, flipping her hair over her shoulders.

The four of us move down the hallway and get on the elevator.

"Where are we going?" Noah says, somehow managing to pace inside the elevator even with all of us crammed in it. "We can still find this Rhys guy. We should be looking right now. He might know the truth. He might help us."

Peter sighs as the doors shut. "We're heading back to base. I'm pretty sure Tycast plans to flog you. When we get there, we can talk about what you heard. If we don't like what he has to say, we leave together." Peter looks at each of us. *"Together."*

"Flog?" Noah says.

"Yeah. He's that mad."

Olive snorts and covers her mouth. I smile involuntarily, and she laughs louder. She's pretty, with almond eyes and tan skin. Peter laughs then, and Noah is left trying to frown. Before we reach the bottom floor, we're all laughing. I may not remember my friends, but right now I see into the past—

The elevator changes. I'm in a white room with vents in the ceiling. Massive fans churn inside them, exchanging the air. Olive, Noah, and Peter are in the room with me. They look younger, fourteen or fifteen.

Dr. Tycast is telling us how to control the fear. He stands off to the side with his headband on, watching.

"When you turn inward, what do you see?"

Noah raises his hand. "I don't know what that means."

Olive crosses her eyes. "I can see my brain."

Tycast raises his eyebrows; it's enough to make us fall silent. "Imagine there is a flame in the very center of your brain. Like a stove, you can turn a knob to increase or decrease its intensity. You are in control."

We spend a few minutes trying to focus on the heat. The room fills with the thick scent of roses.

"That flower smell," Tycast says, "is all in your head. Ignore it." He's sweating; he keeps adjusting his headband. "Ignore the pain, too. It feels like pressure, but your shots protect you. You're not in danger. Okay, that's enough."

I let the pressure fade from behind my eyes, relaxing as it drains out of me.

Tycast frowns at us. "Remember control. Your power is dangerous. You don't just incite fear, or panic. With enough exposure, a person can go mad. Rage comes to the forefront. Insanity. So it is not to be played with, understand? This is more than a loaded gun."

I raise my hand.

Tycast nods at me. "Yes, Miranda."

"Why can we do this?" I say.

Tycast licks his lips. "You just can. And that's good enough for now, right?"

Peter nods. "Yes, sir. Alpha team, fall in." We line up and stand at ease.

It feels good, snapping into formation. The four of us, we're part of a whole. A unit. Together, we're unstoppable. Sure, the adults are vague about our uses, but they make us feel special. Important. And they never keep us apart.

But Tycast's words echo in my mind—

Your power is dangerous.

Rage comes to the forefront.

This is more than a loaded gun.

The white room morphs back into the elevator.

"The doctor will be madder when we confront him," Noah is saying. "We should make Tycast come to us. He's not going to let us leave the base, not once we tell him we know about the dry run and his intent to sell us. How could he?"

My spirit drains out from the bottom of my boots. The memories that made it so we could laugh like this, a tense moment snapping into something fun and light—I'll never have them again. Because even as I make these new memories, it can't be the same as before. I'm the new girl on the team, any way you look at it. It can't be undone.

Now the heat in my brain is from anger, not energy. I can't decide which is worse.

Before I know it, I'm punching Noah in the mouth and Peter and Olive are pulling me back. So I kick. He's not defenseless though. He cocks his fist like he's going to punch me, but he holds it back.

"Do it!" I say. "Hit me!"

"What is your *problem*?" Noah says. Peter still has my right arm held back and Olive is blocking my legs with hers.

"I don't know who I am!" I scream, and it feels good. The tightness in my chest is still there, but I've said it out loud now.

The elevator doors open, revealing a cop. He has a radio at his lips. He sees me red-faced and huffing, the others restraining my arms. He lowers the radio.

"What's going on here?" the cop says.

Just a little family dysfunction. Last time I told a cop I

couldn't remember who I was, I accidentally incited mass panic and got people hurt. *Killed.*

I'm thinking of what to say when Peter darts out from behind me and grabs the cop's shoulder. The cop tries to pull away but freezes, as the rose scent returns.

"Come on, it won't last," Peter says.

Noah is still grumpy. Olive looks tired. Peter leads us to the bikes parked in the corner.

Noah gets on his first and backs it out of the space. It hums to life.

"I miss you guys, I really do. And I'm sorry. And maybe you're right about all this." He pushes his left foot down, putting the bike into gear. "But I'm not going back yet. Not until I find the rogue." He twists the throttle, pops the clutch, and rockets toward the exit, the front tire coming off the ground slightly.

"Son of a bitch . . ." Peter says as I start my bike.

I put it in gear, vision turning red. If Noah thinks he can do what he did and keep running away, he's wrong. I tear after him, wind filling my ears and tugging at my hair. I fly onto the street and lean hard to my right, almost touching my knee to the blacktop. A car blows its horn but I barely hear it. Noah is up ahead. He sees me over his shoulder, and turns left down an alley, cutting in front of some cars heading the opposite way.

The cars pass; more horns blare. I turn down his alley,

twisting the throttle until the engine screams under me, deaf-ening as it echoes off the tight alley walls. I guess I should be surprised by how natural and unafraid I am on the bike, but it feels just that—natural. My tires crush wet cardboard and newspaper. Zipping around a Dumpster, I manage to catch up to Noah, who has to slow down before the next street.

A final twist of the gas and I leap forward, knocking his back tire with my front one. His bike wobbles, tires chirping as they struggle for traction, and he rams into the left wall and goes down. The bike slides past him a good ten feet, throwing up a trail of orange sparks as he skids after it.

My back tire rises when I squeeze the brake, tilting me forward. The black, pebbled ground rushes under me. The rear tire falls with a bang. I put my kickstand down and jump off my bike and run toward Noah as he begins to stand up. He has one leg under him, but I send him back down with a punch to the face. He falls against the alley wall, holding his cheek, looking up at me with hurt eyes. At the other end of the alley, I hear the twin buzz of Peter and Olive catching up.

"Jesus, Miranda…"

I grab a handful of his shirt and lift him up, staring into his eyes. My words come out in a hissing whisper.

"You did this to me, to us. And now you're going to own it. You're coming back with us, end of story. Maybe you're right about finding the rogue, maybe you're right about everything,

I don't know. But I do know that Tycast has the answers, and we *know* where he is. So let's not waste any more time in getting them."

"Tycast won't let us leave if we go back," Noah says flatly.

"Like anything could stop us," I reply with more verve than I feel. I might not have the confidence by myself, but I bet the four of us together is a different matter. If we want to leave, we will find a way to leave. I have to believe that, otherwise Noah would be right and we would be the foolish ones.

Peter and Olive stop behind where I left my bike. Maybe the three of us can convince Noah to cooperate, or at least not flee.

He smiles as the bruise grows on his cheek. "Well, when you put it that way," he says. Then he does the last thing I expect. He rises up and presses his lips against mine. I feel his kiss for a whole second before I break off and slap him across the face. He slumps against the wall again, but his grin shows through whatever pain he feels.

I try for something biting and scathing, but there's nothing. Just a flood of sickness coursing through me, like I don't know *what* I should be feeling. Anger? Not quite. Annoyance? Definitely. But there is something familiar about his lips, something right.

It disappears the second I remember everything he did. I

make sure my face shows no chink in my armor, nothing that says he can break through to me again. Hopefully he didn't notice the *something right* part.

Peter and Olive are next to us now, staring down at Noah, who measures our faces in turn. A child searching for the parent who will go easiest on him.

"What?" he says.

Peter walks back to his bike, throwing his hands up in disgust.

Olive sighs. "Come back with us. Searching for the rogue was an idea, but we can't find him. Let's go home and get the answers we should've had all along. Let's be a pack again."

She has a nicer way of putting things, I'll say that.

Olive and I reach down at the same time; Noah takes our hands and we pull him up.

At our first gas stop, Noah wants to argue pros and cons again. We're all pulled up to the same pump, straddling our bikes.

"I feel a little coerced," Noah says, as he finishes filling his scraped-up tank. "We could be leaving our best chance behind."

"Don't you want to know the truth?" Peter says.

"Of course we do," Olive says. "What Noah is *trying* to say, is that he's worried about going home like we never left."

"Who said we're going to do that?" Peter says. "We'll go home, carefully, and find out the truth from Tycast himself. Like we should've done in the first place."

Noah touches the bruise on his cheek, then quickly lowers his hand. He is very interested in the gauge cluster above his handlebars. "I'm just saying, what if we're making a mistake?"

"Okay," I say. "It's clear Tycast was upset about the situation. It's possible he'll help us once he realizes we know the truth. How were you going to find the rogue, anyway?"

Olive shakes the last few drops into her tank and passes the nozzle to Peter. "We were getting to that part," she says. "Checking out places *we* would hide. If he's a Rose, he should think like us."

"Sounds promising," I say. "Go in search for a guy who kills Roses, on the off chance he'd help us." At the same time, I can't help but worry Noah is right. Maybe Peter is a little too trusting of Tycast.

Peter holds up his hands. "So here's what we do. We go back and explain that you never went rogue. We explain to Tycast what you heard, and he'll have no choice but to come clean with us. We don't even have to go into the base, that way no one can make us stay if we don't get answers. And the first thing we ask him is what the dry run is supposed to be. Is that fair?"

Noah turns his bike on. We all do. The combined growl echoes off the canopy overhead.

Noah says, "If Tycast jerks us around, I'm gone. I'll find the rogue on my own if I have to."

Peter nods. "If Tycast jerks us around, we'll go with you." He pauses, then almost smiles. "How many memory shots did you bring, exactly?"

Noah's cheeks turn scarlet. Even if they brought a ton, I doubt their supply is self-replenishing.

One corner of Olive's mouth goes up. "We're . . . low. We'd have to come back for more soon anyway."

Peter laughs. "It's settled, then."

Noah nods. "For now."

I toe the shifter into first and pull into the street; the others follow in a warbling harmony of engines.

We don't say more than a few words the entire way back.

I think we're afraid of what we'll find at home.

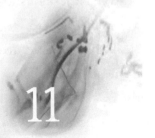

11

Home is not as we left it. I smell the smoke from a mile away. Not normal smoke, either. A chemical smell rides the surface. Peter signals us, and we pull off the road, still a ways from the forest entrance.

"Is that what I think it is?" Noah says.

Peter sniffs the air. "Smells like H9. A lot of it."

"H9?" I say. My vision flashes—a white brick, melting before my eyes, bubbling and popping, glowing orange. Spreading into an all-consuming fire.

Peter inhales again. "You remember?"

"Yeah. Like plastic explosives that..." I recall the image again, see another flash of orange. "It burns through anything."

Peter nods. He seems happy I remember something, even something as awful as H9.

Noah climbs off his bike and interlaces his fingers behind his neck. "I don't like this."

Olive shakes her head. "You think any of us do?"

Noah kicks a rock into the tree line, but says nothing.

Peter starts his bike, twisting the throttle a few times. My blood quickens. This little pill of dread hit my stomach when I first smelled smoke; now I feel drugged. Like my life is about to turn upside down again.

"We still need more shots," Olive says. "We have to go home no matter what."

"That's definitely H9," Peter says. "Let's get in and get out. If we find Tycast, great. Agreed?"

"Agreed," Olive and I say together.

"Finally, a decent plan," Noah says, swinging a leg over his bike.

Peter pulls away and we follow him, Noah hurrying to catch up.

We turn down our narrow green road. The smell thickens. I see the tension in Peter's body; he's scared, which makes *me* scared. We stop just outside the clearing and climb off and drop into crouches.

A fire burns where the garage used to be. Only it's burning

from *under* the ground, the flames licking up a few feet. Like the garage disappeared. We step closer and see melted metal and concrete in the hole.

"Tell me there's another way out. . . ." I say.

Peter breathes heavily. "There isn't." He pushes against his forehead with his hand. Noah bursts into the clearing alongside Olive. Peter and I follow, walking to the massive collapsed rectangle. The fire bakes my face until I have to step back.

Noah cups his hands around his mouth. "TYCAST!"

Peter lunges at him, but not before Noah screams "DR. TYCAST!" again. Noah pushes him away and Peter's feet slide in the dirt.

Olive grabs Peter's arm to hold him back. "Let him yell, Pete. Everyone's dead." Her eyes shimmer with tears.

"What do you care?" Peter says.

"Peter," I say. We can't point fingers now. This changes everything.

He shakes his head. "I didn't mean that."

Olive says, "I know."

Noah calls out again, this time for Phil. He takes a big breath and bellows, *"SIFU* PHIL! PHILLIP!"

Olive is silent, head bowed. I can't tell if she's crying. I can't tell if I'm supposed to be crying.

The family moment in the elevator is gone. Whatever

training I have didn't include the right way to handle this. Danger could still be near.

I can't take my eyes off the flames. The hole looks like it leads straight to hell. "No one thinks this is strange timing?"

Noah turns around. "What is?"

I swallow and drag my fingers over my cheek, wiping away a cold tear. I'm crying after all. Feeling something besides emptiness and anger is welcome. "That this happens while we're gone? I know I'm new to the group, but no one thinks that's odd? We could've been inside."

Peter looks at Olive. "Do we have weapons?"

Olive nods and slinks away to the trees.

I try to imagine a reason someone would do this, and can only think of one.

"Don't you see?" I say, and now Peter is watching me intently. "What if Dr. Tycast decided not to go along with the voice in his office. He sounded upset, right?"

"He was crying," Noah says.

"Were the men here loyal to Tycast?" I ask both of them.

"Everyone was," they say together.

Peter scans the trees behind me. "We don't know if anyone is dead. Maybe whoever did this burned the place and took off."

I shake my head. "We talked to Tycast *this morning*. Why would they do that?"

"Let's be clear on *they*," Noah says.

"Whoever you heard Tycast talking to," I say. "Obviously she's not alone."

"Nothing is obvious," Noah says. "He could've done this on his own, or helped them."

I want to fire back with something, but he's right. We can't be sure of anything.

The fire is lower now, just an orange glow reflecting off the dirt walls. The ground beneath my feet is warm through my boots. I crouch down and press my palm on the grass.

When I look up, Peter stands over me. "Take off your boot," he says. His eyes are blurry with tears, but maybe it's from the billowing smoke.

"Why?"

He kneels. Grabs my laces and tugs.

"What's wrong?" I say.

"You're right about what happened here," he says. "We're not safe. And we won't be until no one can track us."

Noah is next to him. "What are you doing?"

"Removing her tracker."

"What tracker?"

Peter takes my sock off and finds the seam in my armor with his thumb. He splits it along the top of my foot and rolls it halfway up my shin, holding my foot in his dry hand. My toes are painted a burnt red color, kind of like my hair. I don't remember painting them; it doesn't seem like something I would care to do. My bare foot in his hand makes me feel a little exposed, and I don't know why.

Then Peter pulls out a knife.

I see something in his eyes. Pain. But not for our burning home. Because he's about to hurt me?

I bite my lip.

"This won't feel good," he says.

Noah reaches down and grabs the wrist holding the knife, but Peter elbows him in the chest. "Back off," he says. "I'm saving our lives." To me, he says, "This is where I put the tracker. I thought I was the only one who could use it, but I don't know if that's true now."

I nod. The knife goes in just behind my ankle. I bite my lip harder to keep from screaming. He twists the blade and a little red pill shoots out and falls into the grass. I taste blood and blink my vision clear.

"You should be able to stand," Peter says.

Olive comes back carrying four long sticks in her arms. Slim combat staffs. I smell a gym mat, hear the thwack of a staff hitting bare skin. Another phantom, this time without images. I shake my head to clear the sensations.

"No guns?" Noah says. Peter disposed of the two Walthers

in a storm drain before leaving Indiana. He didn't want to risk getting pulled over with them. After some grumbling, Noah and Olive did the same.

Olive shakes her head. She's smeared dirt across her cheeks and brow. With her dark hair and black suit, she blends in with the shadowed tree trunks perfectly. I feel like a road flare in comparison, with my red hair and pale skin.

Peter wipes the knife on his shirt, smearing my blood. "Who's next?" he says. He rolls the armor down my leg and pushes the seam together. The pain fades a moment later as the armor acts like a bandage over the wound.

I put my sock and boot on while Peter removes trackers from Noah and Olive. Noah calls him an asshole for keeping tabs without his knowledge, but Olive just shrugs like it all makes sense. I get why he did it—we wouldn't be here together if he hadn't—but I'm not sure I like that he didn't ask. Still, from what little I know about him, it seems like the idea was for the right reasons, not to spy on us. Our situation kind of proves that.

I practice walking around. My ankle is tender but feels like it's already healing, if that's possible. The fire from the H9 has died down even more. It's just a smoking pit in the middle of the clearing, and none of us look at it. We know we shouldn't stick around, but I think we're afraid to leave the hole behind. It's our home. Not remembering doesn't change that fact.

Olive offers me a staff, and I give it a few experimental twirls. It rolls over the back of my hand like I've been twirling staves my whole life, which I probably have.

When she turns away, I tap Olive on the shoulder with the staff. "How good was I with one of these?"

"Almost as good as me."

Her eyes are red-rimmed and wet, just like Peter's and Noah's. I try to drag up some memory of my home, some phantom, but there's nothing. I can't remember anything I've lost the way they can. That's almost enough to make the tears return. I find myself glaring at Noah again, and he notices.

He opens his mouth to say something, but then we hear the helicopter.

12

We all freeze, but only for a second. We break as one, sprinting for the trees with our staves. Peter is in the lead, followed by Olive then Noah then me. I look over my shoulder every few seconds at the thin column of smoke curling above the trees. The leaves rustle as the helicopter passes over our heads. We keep running. The trees thicken till we come to a narrow path of moist dirt and roots.

I skid to a stop. The others keep running silently, growing smaller. Noah realizes I'm missing first and shouts, "Hold up!"

Peter and Olive stop farther down the path. They run back to me, but I'm not looking at them.

I'm looking at Dr. Tycast propped against a tree.

The front of his white coat is bloody and torn. The lenses in his glasses are cracked. His lips and nose are smeared with dried blood.

"Miranda..." he says. I crouch next to him and touch the side of his face lightly, afraid to cause him any more pain. He manages a weak, shaky smile, showing blood on his teeth.

"What happened?" I say.

"You have to go. Beta team, they're still here. They... aren't your friends." His voice is so quiet and wet. I hear the others standing behind me. Peter crouches down and balances himself with a hand on my shoulder.

He says, "We have to move him. We can carry him. Doctor, did anyone escape with you?"

Tycast shakes his head. "I was in the garage when they dropped the H9. It collapsed, and I barely got out." He looks up at Noah, standing behind me and Peter. "You were right to flee. You were right." His face crumples and he coughs for a few seconds. "How did you know?"

Noah's voice is soft. "I was in your office. You received a call from a woman. You—she talked about buyers and tests."

"I expect that left you... a little confused."

"Yes, sir," Noah says.

"Who is she?" I ask.

"Part of the people behind all of this. Everything. The

creators of this project." Tycast's eyes roam over us and he smiles again, warmer this time. That missing piece inside me is filled, maybe temporarily, but enough to make my eyes ache.

Another helicopter—or is it the same one?—zips overhead. The branches sway and green leaves spin to the forest floor.

Tycast takes a deep breath. "You belong to one another now. But they will hunt you. You have to . . . be ready. You have to . . . stay together. They raised you for a purpose. All of you."

Tycast begins to slip off the tree trunk.

Peter reaches out to hold him in place. "What purpose?" he says.

"You are all aware of your power," Tycast says. "There are people in this world . . . who would do anything to own you. To control you. The people who made you the way you are, they want to, to . . ."

"To what?" Noah says.

"To test you. In the city. A dry run to prove your worth. They will use you to terrify the city until it can't function, until people flee and nothing is left but empty buildings and streets."

"And those who die trying to get out of the way," I say.

Tycast nods. "I'm sorry. I am. I thought I could change their minds. Even if you evade capture, they'll still use the other Roses."

Peter says, "You knew we'd be sold all along. . . . You *knew*."

His jaw is clenched. It's like he's fighting the urge to feel betrayed. We all are. But there's love in Tycast's face, even if I can't remember it.

He fights the pain with clear eyes. "I did. Yes. But I was unwilling to let you go. And now it's happening without me...."

Noah says, "That's what I heard. That's why we left."

Tycast says, "I should've sent you away. Sooner. I was a coward. Didn't stop it."

"Until now," Olive says behind me.

"Too late, my dear," Tycast says. "I said I would have no part in it, so they destroyed all my work...our home. They must've known you four were out. They still want to use you. You are worth so much."

Peter shakes his head. "Even if they capture us, they can't make us cooperate. They can't break us."

Tycast's white eyebrows go up. "All they have to do is deny you your memory shots. Then you won't know what side you're fighting for. And there are other ways, too."

A freezing hand reaches inside me and grips my stomach. Olive gasps. I guess the thought of future shots wasn't on anyone's mind, including my own.

Noah is huddled next to Peter and me now. "Where can we get more shots, Doctor?"

"There is a place," Tycast says. "I made a secret cache for

emergencies. I sunk it, in the lake. Off the third pier downtown. Red paint. Third pier. I'm sorry. I failed you. There's
enough to last. Get it, and hide. Don't fight them. Don't..."

He's fading. I squeeze his shoulder, trying to keep his
attention. Maybe he can hold on. But even as I think it, I
know these are his last moments.

"This Beta team," I say. "Who are they?"

Tycast grimaces, but it's not from the pain. Disgust or
shame, it seems. "They are just like you," he says.

Just like us.

Noah asks him another question.

"Rhys," he says. "The rogue. Who is he? Will he help us?"

Noah asks something else but I don't hear it. I'm too busy
watching the light fade from Dr. Tycast's eyes. They shut halfway but stay cracked, like he's slowly waking from a nap and
adjusting to the light.

For a few moments, none of us moves or speaks. I can't
read their minds, but I'm guessing we all ponder the same
question—did Tycast betray us? He knew what was coming,
but that doesn't mean he was powerless to stop it. I want to
believe he meant what he said—he wouldn't leave us, or use
us. I know the others do, too. But as usual, I don't know what
to think.

Eventually, Peter stands up and walks away from us,

gripping his forehead with his palm. The rest of us watch him, waiting for orders, I guess. We should be moving. Standing here makes the bottom of my feet itch. Or maybe that's the blood still leaking from my ankle, pooling under my foot.

Noah puts his hands on his hips. Sweat glistens in his short brown hair. "We need to get that cache of shots," he says to Peter.

Peter doesn't face us. "Don't you think I know that?"

"Then what are we standing around for?" Olive says. She's so quiet, but her presence is reassuring, maybe because she isn't loud about it. She's like Noah's opposite. Especially now with the dirt on her face, and the way she seems to hang a few steps back, watching us rather than taking part. There's something feral about Olive. A strange light in her eyes that seems more than human.

I want to know her. I wonder what I've forgotten.

Peter finally turns to us. Behind him a squirrel skitters over the dirt path and up a tree. The helicopters still drone in the background, far away.

"We need to stop this dry run," Peter says. "If what he said is true . . ."

We all know it's true. I spin my staff around and hold it behind my back.

"That's not our priority right now," Noah says. "Our priority is making sure we don't lose our memories."

"Like I did?" I blurt.

It hangs in the air between us, my stupid reminder that I'm still the wild card.

"Miranda—" Noah begins.

I shake my head. "The dry run needs to be just as important. You know what we can do, so imagine it happening in a city. You weren't there in the mall with me. When people couldn't get out of the way fast enough." I swallow thickly, wishing the scene was part of my forgotten memories. "We'll get those shots, but we have to stop *them*."

Them. Wish I was a little more clear on who the enemy is. It's hard to fight what you don't know.

I bite the inside of my cheek again, feeling the raw flesh against my tongue. More leaves tumble down as one of the helicopters passes overhead. I focus on the taste of blood, if only to focus on something.

Peter rubs the bruise on his forehead. "Tycast once told me we can only create the fear waves during our teen years. After a while the density of our brains will decrease until they resemble a normal person's. That's why we've been training since we were kids."

Olive says, "He told me that too. So they need to use us soon, or not at all."

Peter nods. "Precisely."

"Will we still need our memory shots?" I say. "After the powers fade?"

Peter shrugs. "I don't think so, but I can't be sure. There was only so much Tycast shared with me."

Noah holds up his hands and steps between me and Peter. "Planning for the future is fine, but we need to deal with the *now*. Let's get to that cache before it's too late."

Noah is about to say more, but he's staring at Peter funny. Then I see it—something is sticking out of Peter's neck. Peter reaches up to touch it, then his eyes roll back in his head and he collapses onto his back. His head thumps against the dirt.

"Cover!" Noah says.

I react instantly, backpedaling and curling around a tree, crouching low, holding my staff at my side. Noah and Olive have disappeared. I breathe slowly through my nose and let my eyes scan the trees for any threat. They keep straying to Dr. Tycast's body against the tree trunk a few feet away.

And Peter—oh God. The initial reflex has faded, and now I see him with the dart in his neck. It could be poison; he could be dead. I fight to keep my breath even. I can't lose it now, not out here, with all of us under attack. My scan of the trees just shows leaves and more leaves.

Noah grunts. Then I hear the sharp crack of wood against wood. I burst from my hiding spot and step onto the dirt path with my staff held close. Noah stands ten feet away. In front of him, between us, is someone wearing a black bodysuit identical to ours, down to the little scales. A cowl covers her head. I can only tell it's a girl from the shape of her body.

Behind Noah is an exact clone of the first black suit, a male; since he's facing me, I see his scaled face is featureless except for two smoked lenses over the eyes. Both suits hold staves like Noah, only theirs have knives on the end. Why do we have the low-end model?

Noah parries a front attack from the girl, then takes an unblockable hit in his back from the male. He groans, stumbling forward. Olive bursts from the tree line, her staff a spinning blur. I'm on the black-suited girl, who's had her back to me all along. My staff comes down on top of her head and she screams behind her mask.

The cheap shot doesn't slow her, apparently, because she spins toward me, sweeping her staff low over the ground to take out my legs. I jump as it passes under me, and since I'm already in the air I plant a semisolid kick on her chest. She staggers back, knocking into Noah, who engages the other black suit with Olive. The continual crack and slap of wood rings outs like a drumroll. The girl trips over Noah's leg and falls into an awkward somersault.

If this is the Beta team, why are there only two? I watch Olive thrust the end of her staff into the male's chest; he goes down with a violent grunt. The girl takes a whole second to stand after her tumble. Against the three of us working together, she has no chance.

I want to laugh, but something isn't right. It shouldn't be this easy. I glance over my shoulder to check on Peter, and see it isn't.

Two more black suits stand over him, another guy and girl. I catch a glimpse of eyes before the guy's lenses darken. I remember those eyes. Pale blue, too blue—almost fake. Before I can remember anything further, both of them are on me. I snap my staff from side to side, picking off their thrusts and blunt slashes, but they're as fast as I am. One of them reaches out, holding a dart identical to the one in Peter's neck. I jerk my head back before it can prick me, but the movement throws me off balance. A blade cuts through my jeans, scrapes the side of my knee.

I'm falling.

Noah catches me. He doesn't hold me for long, just enough to break my fall. Then he slashes back and forth again, driving the black suits away. Olive sneaks in behind them and heaves Peter up. She wrestles him over her shoulder and slips into the forest. Behind me, the first two black suits stagger upright, dazed. The girl clutches her head.

"Noah, come on!" I don't wait, just sprint into the trees and run and run and run. Noah's feet pound the dirt behind me. Our only chance is to lose them. A dart pierces a tree trunk five feet ahead of me. I flow around the trunk without losing speed. The forest is a green blur, and the only sound is our feet landing lightly on dead leaves and dirt. I zig and zag and Noah keeps pace and I know we have to escape together. I think we're losing them. A few more twists. Whatever I am and whatever we're supposed to do, it doesn't end in this forest. It can't.

The river roars up ahead, and I coax a little more power from my muscles. I'm not even breathing heavily. Part of me feels alien because I don't know what I'm fully capable of. My body seems to have its own memory, one still intact.

The speed burst carries me through a tangle of branches to open ground that ends at a gray-brown river flowing right to left. With the next step, I leap from the bank and soar over the river, straightening my body into a dive, thrusting my hands out in case the murky water is shallow. I cut into the rushing water and submerge. I'm lucky—no bottom found. The current tries to push me to the surface, but I pump my arms and legs, fighting to stay under. The cold water stings my eyes and nose; I can't see anything but brown.

A hand closes over my wrist. I try to jerk away, then see a T-shirt through the murk.

Noah.

I blow out my air so I don't bob back to the surface and

reveal our location to the suits. Noah keeps his hand tight around my wrist. Bubbles surge around me. My chest grows tight. It's so much harder to hold your breath when there's no breath to hold.

Noah orients himself over me, and we scrape along the bottom. I open my eyes and see him through the haze of dirty water.

I have to go up.

I *have* to break the surface and fill my lungs.

But I don't know how far we've traveled. Maybe not far at all. If we surface now, they might see that we didn't cross the river. I should have kept running.

I jerk in Noah's arms. I'm drowning, I know it. Can't hold my breath any longer. I pull free, fighting and clawing at him, anything to make him let me go. I have to reach the surface. But his hands hold me tight, and for one sick moment I think he's trying to kill me. A rock on the bottom scrapes my neck hard, and as my lips part to gasp, Noah puts his mouth on mine. He blows his hot breath into my mouth just as I inhale. Just in time. My lungs still burn, but not as badly, and I can take it. Here, scraping along the bottom of a river, lips on my once-boyfriend who gives me his air, I realize I'm not going to drown, not yet. Our lips stay sealed, allowing me to give a little back. Then his mouth isn't just on mine, it's moving. He's kissing me. And I'm kissing him. We forget about breathing.

❊   ❊   ❊

A phantom memory hits me—

I unlace my shoes on my bunk. We've just finished a workout, a run followed by thirty minutes of sparring. A layer of chilled sweat covers me. Noah stretches on the floor in front of me, shirtless. His muscles are lean and hard, more compact than Peter's. The ridges in his abs make sharp shadows.

I'm tugging on my laces when Noah grabs my leg and pulls me off the bunk. I catch myself with my hands before my butt hits the floor. He pulls me on top of him.

"You're all sweaty," I say.

He has a bruise on his cheek from where I failed to pull a punch. Peter and Olive will be back soon. Our relationship is still secret. We hide it from them because everything the four of us do, we do together. We aren't ready to change things. Noah is patient. Tension grips both of us because Peter and Olive could come in at any second. He pulls me down for a kiss and I taste the sweat on his upper lip.

"I wanted to tell you something," he says.

"Oh yeah? What's that?"

"I'm in love with you. I love you."

I stare at him for a moment, this boy who grew up as my brother. We watched each other grow into weapons, into something so honed we're afraid of what our bodies can do. Every moment worth remembering was spent with him.

And now he says he loves me, and I know I love him too. So I say it.

"I love you too."

The memory fades quicker than it comes, and we're still underwater. Even as panic threatens to overtake me completely, I have time to feel the loss. The love I felt in the phantom stays with me. It's real. And yet . . .

He took it away. He *threw* it away.

So why can't I leave the feeling behind?

This is the first memory I feel like I can claim. I've accepted the other phantoms as true, but this is different. Heavier.

The air is gone now, enough of it escaping that we're left clutching at each other, on the verge of drowning. Mindless panic swoops in. I have to get free. I break away—he lets me go this time—and kick once to the surface. Cold air hits my cheeks as Noah splashes up beside me. I spin around, gasping as we float downriver, swallowing great lungfuls of air that taste so good. The banks seem clear, no black suits in sight. But no Peter and Olive, either.

I sink lower in the water, hiding the parts that don't breathe. I taste the dirt in the water, Noah's breath and kiss. I'm afraid to look at him.

We drift. Neither of us says a word.

We pretend it's in case the black suits are still near.

13

We don't talk after we're out of the water, not right away. We're on the bank, hidden by an outcropping of rock. A kind of cave that's open to the sky. I strip off my long-sleeved tee and wring it out, shivering, until the sun warms me through my armor. Water beads on the scales like glowing pearls.

Noah stands at the edge of the rock shelf, pretending to scope out the banks upriver.

Before I can stop, I say, "You know, if you hadn't stolen everything I am, we would still be together."

Noah stiffens but stays quiet. I watch the tendons flex in his jaw. I'm not sure why I said that; I don't have to punish him. At the same time, it feels good to see his regret. His doubt. He can't take back what he did. So what's a little hurt feelings over my lost memories?

"You're still you," he says, now looking the opposite way down the river. "Same old Miranda. Your memories don't make you who you are."

I search for a comeback, but end up sitting with my knees against my chest. I reach behind me and squeeze water out of my hair. It feels gritty and slick with river mud.

My mind keeps going back to how familiar his lips felt, how I recognized his kiss. And I can't help wondering exactly how familiar he is with *me*. I don't know what it was like to be with him all the time, or what we've done together. The kiss didn't stir up forgotten memories for him; according to just about everyone, we were together a week ago. It was probably *normal* to him. I find myself jealous; he has that over me, he can know everything about our past, and I can only have glimpses.

So I ask just before I chicken out, "Did we have sex?"

I feel myself blushing as the seconds pass.

Finally he smirks. Not exactly what I want to see at the moment. "No. Phil said it was forbidden."

Suddenly I remember the dream-memory of Noah in my bed. I told him no, but can't remember why.

Noah looks pained for an instant, just like Peter had before digging out my tracker. Peter. Here we are trading barbs instead of searching for Peter and Olive.

Noah crouches, keeping his eyes on the tree line upriver. His voice is quiet.

"Phil taught us most of our hand-to-hand combat skills, some swordplay too. He said our power came from within, that sex would diminish it, and also ruin whatever relationship we had as a team. Shaolin monks figured out the power thing a long time ago. He was probably just saying that to keep us in line, but we were too competitive with each other to risk it." A pause. He pivots on the balls of his feet, half facing me. "Not that you didn't want to."

My neck prickles with sweat. I look away. "Well, I don't now."

"You remembered," he says. "When I kissed you under the water, you remembered a little what it was like with me. I could feel it in your lips."

"Whatever I felt doesn't matter."

"Yes it does."

"No, because whatever was between us is reset. I don't know you." I stand up, fighting to keep my voice down. "Why did you do it, Noah? Why did you think you had that right? We grew up together. You *knew* I could take care of myself. You *knew* I'd want to stand by you guys and figure things out together." I can only assume that last part is true. If it's how I feel now, it's how I would've felt then. I would've wanted that chance, the choice to fight beside them.

He stares at the rock under our feet, unfocused, like he's trying to decide something. He rises from his crouch and walks to me.

"What is it?" I finally ask.

"What if I said . . . what if you gave me permission? What if I'd asked you, and you'd said yes?"

"Said yes to erasing my memories?" No. No way. He's lying.

He takes my hands and rubs his thumbs over the backs of my knuckles. I want to pull away, but I don't. He's closer now, only a foot between our faces.

"Remember?" he says. "You have to. Try to remember. We were on the train. Do you remember the train?"

I picture a train in my head, the one we surfed at night. Nothing else comes. I want him to be right, but I don't see it.

"I asked you a question. If I had to do something, something you wouldn't like, something you'd disagree with but I believed would keep you safe, and me safe, so we could stay together. I asked you that, and I said, *would you trust me?*"

Finally, falling into his eyes, the memory comes.

We're in a train yard, on top of an old rusted car off the tracks. We snuck out again. To my right, a train rumbles past, wheels scraping down the rails. The metal vibrates under us. I'm nestled in the crook of Noah's arm, on our backs as we look up at the stars. He's been distant tonight, distracted.

I turn in to him more, draping my arm over his chest. His hand strokes my hair, tracing a line around my ear.

"What's wrong?" I finally say.

"Nothing."

"Noah," I say.

After a while, he sighs. "There's something I have to do."

"What is it?" My right ear is over his heart. I hear it pound a little faster.

"It's something awful, and unfair, and selfish. But I think it might be the right thing. For us."

"Okay. So tell me."

"I can't tell you. I can't."

I get up on one elbow, looking down at him. He tilts his head toward me. I lean down and give him three slow kisses. "You can tell me anything," I say.

"I can't," he says. "But I need you to trust me. I need to know if you can trust me to make a decision. A hard one. I guess what I'm asking is, would you trust me?"

I kiss him one more time. The train disappears down the track. The rumble fades with it.

"I trust you," I say.

❊　❊　❊

Back in the present, tears run down my cheeks.

"If I'd known . . ." I say. The memory ended abruptly. I have no idea what happened after. If I just agreed, or if I pried for more information . . .

Or if I trusted him, exactly like I said.

"You trusted me," Noah says. He wants some sign of forgiveness or understanding, I'm sure. And part of me wants to give it to him. I just don't think I can yet, or what it'll mean when I finally do.

I wipe the tears away. We can't do this now. Our friends are out there, who knows where, and they need us. A trip down memory lane doesn't make our problems go away.

"You made your choice," I say with as much finality as I can muster. And he did. Trust or not, I never would have agreed to stripping my identity. But remembering what happened, it's harder to be mad at him.

He looks upriver again. The banks are still clear, and I'm done waiting to be found. I run to the edge of the rock and jump onto the bank, throwing my damp shirt over my shoulder. My jeans stay on in case we make it back to civilization.

The stones shift and clap under my feet, too loud. I pick my way along the shore, hoping I can find my friends before the sun goes down.

"That's what people do when they're in love," Noah calls after me. "They make crazy decisions. They do what they think is best, and sometimes it turns out to be a mistake. Miranda."

I stop. And turn. He stands on the rock above me.

"Just tell me you won't hate me forever. Tell me it's not over between us."

I want to say the words. I even think them. *It's over.* Because how could it not be? But all I can say is, "I don't know. Please," before starting up the bank again. The sadness is in my chest and the only thing I can do is walk. I slip into the trees for cover. Eventually Noah catches up and we walk side by side in silence.

He finds something else to talk about. Something obvious. Something that saves us from discussing any memories or declarations of trust. "You know, we don't have much time left on those shots."

"So I've heard," I say. "You didn't happen to snag any when you left the first time, did you? Because that would be really convenient."

"I did . . ."

We make it another ten steps without him elaborating. I duck under a low branch.

"But," I say.

"But I lost them in our escape. We had to fight one of Tycast's security. My bag, it . . . well, it spilled, and . . ."

My mouth falls open. "So if Peter hadn't found you, you guys would've lost your memories too."

Noah's hand brushes mine on the forward swing, but I can't tell if it's intentional. "We would've come back before then. But the shots we brought gave us time."

"And you didn't invite Peter because..."

"I told you why."

"But you trust him now?"

It feels like we're wandering, but we're not. We're taking a roundabout route, back the way we came; considering how long we were in the water, we know Olive and Peter have to be in this direction. I wait for Noah to answer while my eyes flit over the trees. Dead leaves coat the forest floor, crackling underfoot.

"Noah," I say.

"Sure. I trust him."

I look at him. He stops and I stop. The corner of his mouth turns up in a forced, uncomfortable smile. Then his eyes narrow, and I feel it too.

A fear wave. It's weak, but with the now-familiar scent of roses. And it seems like I can feel what direction it's coming from.

"They're close," I say, picking up the pace.

"How do we know it's not the other team?"

"We don't."

"They could be trying to lure us," he says.

"Then we'll be careful."

I take off at close to a sprint, trying not to crunch the leaves under my feet. The scent seems to grow, so either it's getting stronger or we're getting closer. Branches whip my exposed face, scratch at my armor and yank my hair. I know it's Peter and Olive, I can feel it.

"Slow down!" Noah hisses behind me. A branch snaps under his foot like a gunshot. I see a break in the trees up ahead. A person with long black hair tied into a ponytail. I burst through and stop, raising my hands.

Olive holds the end of her staff in my face.

Noah stomps to a halt behind me. "Olive, what are you doing?" he says. Next to Olive's feet is Peter, still unconscious. Olive breathes heavily through clenched teeth. She doesn't take her eyes off me except to check on Noah. The hovering wood in front of my face makes my eyes cross.

"Prove it's you," Olive says. I'm so confused I take a step forward, and Olive thwacks me hard in the chest. My suit absorbs most of it, but I still lose my balance. Noah steadies me with one hand.

"I said *prove it's you*."

"Look at our clothes," I say. "The others didn't have them."

"You could've taken them," Olive says, but I hear the doubt

in her voice. A bright red scratch bisects the dried mud on her right cheek.

"Olive, it's *us*," Noah says. "What are you talking about?" I watch Olive study him as he says it. She slowly lowers the staff away from my face and holds it at her side.

"What happened?" I say.

Olive looks down at Peter, who twitches in his sleep. The tiny wound on his neck is bright red. "One of them caught up to us. She was alone, I . . . I fought her. I dropped Peter and I fought her, and I won. I knocked her out. She fell against a tree and I was going to grab Peter and run again, but I had to know who it was. They wear the same suits as us. The exact same. And I was thinking about what Tycast said . . ."

I swallow, tasting the river in my throat. "About the Beta team being like us."

Olive's eyes lock on mine, go a little wider.

"They *are* us," she says. "The girl beneath the mask, it was me. Exactly like me, like a twin, or a clone, or whatever. It's *us*."

"Impossible," Noah says. He's standing next to me now, his shoulder to my slightly lower shoulder.

"Is it?" Olive says. Her voice cracks; she's trying her best to stay calm, and so am I. "Because I know what I saw. I even pulled up her eyelids and she has the same eyes. Same *teeth*, Noah. God. There were four of them, right? Four of us. Two teams."

I think about the mall again. The mayhem I caused by myself. Add seven more like me and repeat in a major city.

We cannot be caught.

I walk over to Peter slowly in case Olive gets staff-happy again, then crouch down and feel his strong pulse on my fingers. His skin is burning. Wind cuts through the trees, thrashing the leaves. We freeze, listening. No helicopters this time.

Olive lets her staff fall to the ground.

"And then you released a wave so we could find you," I say.

She nods, tries to smile. "It's a risk I had to take. We have to stay together, like the doctor said. Like Peter said."

Noah turns a full circle, scanning the trees. "Then we need to move. If we could track you, what's stopping the other team?"

Olive shakes her head. "Distance. I carried him for a half mile, and Beta was sweeping the forest in the opposite direction. I could hear them moving away after I knocked out the … girl."

"Wanna bet your life on it?" Noah says.

The wave *did* feel subtle. Possibly short-range. Still, we shouldn't linger.

I stand up and put my hand on Olive's shoulder, tentatively, as I would with a frightened animal. She relaxes under my grip. I slowly pull her into a hug, and she wraps her arms around me. It feels strange because I don't really know this girl. I just have to trust in my past, that we were once close. When she saw me in the hotel, she seemed so relieved, but that doesn't mean we were friends growing up. Teammates, for sure, but there's a difference.

I wish I knew you, I think. *I wish it was like before, when we were a family and there were no outside problems, when we didn't have to run from ourselves. Literally.* The other Miranda, the other Peter and Noah. I wonder if they have the same names. If they're like us, or our opposites, or somewhere in between.

"I'm fine, really." Olive pulls back with an awkward look on her face, like she's surprised I hugged her. I admit I don't seem like the hugging type. I nod and say nothing more.

I crouch again and sling Peter's limp arm over my shoulder. "You guys want to help me with him?" I say, grinning up at them. I have something to grin about—we're still alive.

Olive grins back, wiping at her nose, and after a moment Noah smiles without his eyes. We each hold a part of Peter to carry him through the woods.

14

We head south for a few miles before trading the forest's cover for a road. Cars and the occasional truck pass, but we need something that can carry us and also keep us hidden from prying eyes.

It takes an hour.

A white van rounds the bend, and I step from the tree line and wave my arms, keeping my eyes peeled for Beta, though it's unlikely they tracked us this far. I'm wearing my black long-sleeved T-shirt again. It's damp but less conspicuous than the scaled armor. The van slows and I put on a big smile. At first, with Peter still unconscious, I worried about trusting whoever stopped for us, but with the three of us? We'll be fine.

The van pulls off the road slightly, crunching the crumbling blacktop under its tires. A decal on the side says MORTON'S PAINTING. The driver rolls down the passenger window. I curl my hands over the window frame and smile at him. "Hi!"

"Hey," he says, smiling back. "What's up?"

I make a show of looking over my shoulder, then back at him. "Me and my friends were hiking, and one of them fell. He's okay, he's not bleeding or anything, but he passed out. We just need a ride. Could you help us?"

Is that a helicopter I hear again, or just the wind? I step away from the door and check the narrow ribbon of sky above the road. The day is nearing dusk; the strip is purple-blue to the right, orange-red to the left. My stomach growls, and I realize I've never been hungrier. All the fighting and running and swimming have caught up with me.

"You okay?" the man in the van says. The name tag on his paint-slashed shirt says MICHAEL.

"I'm fine. Can you give us a ride? We can pay you." I have no idea if we can pay him.

Noah pops up on my left; I didn't even hear him coming. "Hey!" he says brightly. "There's only four of us. And the fourth is asleep. He had a little too much to drink."

At first I'm pissed, thinking he's an idiot for changing the story, but then I realize it's perfect. It looks like I tried to cover up Peter's unconsciousness and Noah isn't afraid to say he's passed out drunk. Just some kids screwing around. Both explanations are better than "He got stuck with a poison dart."

Michael furrows his brow while he studies us, but must decide he likes what he sees. He takes a swig from a bottle of raspberry tea. "Hope you don't mind riding with paint," he says.

All four of us get in—we kind of heave Peter onto the floor—and Noah gives Michael an address I don't recognize. Which doesn't really surprise me. I don't know if it's somewhere I've been before or not. Michael asks us questions, occasionally looking in the rearview mirror at us sprawled over ladders and other paint equipment. I answer as best I can, being friendly but vague.

The sun has almost set when the van stops in front of a house. Noah passes him some money, but Michael waves it away until Noah presses it into his palm with a handshake. "You're a lifesaver," Noah says. I smile at Michael before we get out.

The van chugs away from the curb. The house is two stories of gray brick with a Mercedes in the driveway. The neighborhood is upper class—plenty of space between houses, huge and sprawling front lawns, lots of dense trees to hide under if the helicopters return.

"Where are we?" I say as we carry Peter up the driveway.

Peter's arm is looped around my neck, and his head lolls into mine. I wince. This stuff better wear off soon.

"Just let me do the talking," Noah says. "Dr. Tycast had all of us make contacts in the city, places we could fall back on. Maybe he knew we'd need them someday. This house belongs to a girl whose parents are always out of town, and who won't ask too many questions."

"A girl?" I say, ignoring the way my stomach flips. Really ignoring it.

Noah looks over his shoulder. He has his left arm wrapped around Peter's legs. "Yeah."

I don't ask any more questions. We get to the front door and Noah rings the bell. I count to ten before the door opens. A gorgeous blond girl stands in the opening. Or not a girl—she's definitely older than us, maybe early twenties. She's wearing a white tank top and peach-colored shorts that barely cover her long tanned thighs.

Something twists behind my breastbone; it's a pang of *jealousy*. My mouth drops open. I don't even know what I'm jealous of. This is some girl Noah knows—big deal.

"Noah East," she says. "What are you doing here?"

Noah East? It strikes me that I don't know anyone's last name. Not Peter's or Olive's. I tuck that away for a less awkward moment.

"Hey, Elena. Nice to see you too."

"What are you doing here?" Elena says again.

"I need your help," he says. He turns toward us, letting his ragged team into the circle. "We need your help. Obviously."

She hasn't fully opened the door. Her eyes cut between Noah and Peter, and then to Olive, who has this scary dead look on her face. I try to imagine being in her position, seeing and fighting another version of myself, but I can't.

"Is he okay?" Elena says, raising her chin at Peter.

"He will be," Noah says. "Just let us inside before someone sees us."

Elena steps aside and we carry Peter into the house. The house feels fake, like no one lives here, as if its only purpose is to appear catalog-perfect.

Noah points up the steps. "There's a spare bedroom up there. Lay him down. I need to talk to Elena." He tries to make eye contact, but I turn away and help Olive drag Peter up the steps.

"Watch the mud," Elena says. Peter is streaked with it. I ignore her.

The bedroom is like the rest of the house—preserved. We get Peter into bed and arrange him on the comforter. I pull his T-shirt over his head, easing it over his ears.

"You okay?" I say to Olive, tossing the filthy T-shirt into the adjoining bathroom. Olive works on his jeans and together we strip him to his armor. I touch the back of his exposed hands, feel their dry heat.

"No," she says.

I leave the blankets off. A wet piece of Peter's longish black hair sticks to his cheek, and I push it away with the edge of my thumb. His face burns under my fingertips. I imagine a future where he doesn't get better. We can probably get the shots on our own, but we'll need Peter to stop the dry run. He'll have a plan. I don't know where Olive stands, but Peter knows it's our responsibility. Noah says he wants to find the rogue, or at least get the memory cache first, but I doubt he's keen on fighting back directly. Because if we get caught, it's over. Before they strip our memories, we'll wish we had run and hid.

Which path is right, I don't know. But we can't do nothing. I remember the mall once more, the blind panic, a miniature dry run in its own way. People concerned only with flight, not who might get hurt in the process. More people will die if we do nothing.

Olive paces away from me, folding her arms, hugging herself, fingers clenched around her biceps. I sit on the bed with Peter and watch her. She's agitated, mouth drawn, even though we should be safe here. The dirt has flaked off her face. The scratch on her cheek has begun to scab.

"You okay?" I ask her again, before her unease infects me.

"I don't know who we are," Olive says. "Ever since we were kids, none of us thought to ask. We accepted our way of life because it was what we knew, you know? We were together, all of us, with our parents—"

"Our parents?" I say.

"Yes," she says. "I remember that, I think. Your mom was there, and Peter's dad."

I stand up. "Was *where*, Olive? Where were we?"

She's blank-faced for a moment, then shakes her head. "I don't know. I don't remember."

"Then maybe you're remembering our parents wrong. How can you be sure?"

"I can't." She shakes her head again and presses her fingers to her forehead. "I have to lie down."

She's about to say something else, but stops.

"What is it?" I say.

"It's just good to see you, Mir. What Noah . . . what we did was wrong. I didn't know what he was doing until it was too late."

"Why couldn't you trust Peter?" I say.

Olive considers it. After a while, she shrugs. "I don't know. Noah had me convinced we couldn't chance it. We always planned to contact Peter after we were safely away, because if he wasn't on our side there wasn't much he could do. Or so we thought." She flexes the ankle her tracker was buried under.

"Hey, when we first got here, that girl said 'Noah East.' Is that his last name?"

Olive nods slowly.

"What's yours?" I say.

"I'm Olive South."

I don't understand. These aren't our real names. They have to know that.

"And Peter—" Olive begins.

"Is Peter West," I say.

She nods again.

"No one thinks that's weird?" I say.

"I guess so. We never really thought about it. Just another normal thing to us." She turns to leave.

"Wait," I say.

She freezes in the doorway, like she's been caught. Caught doing what, I'm not sure.

Maybe it's because I don't buy Noah influencing her over Peter. Or maybe it's something else, an old memory or an intuition, but I ask a question that surprises me as I say it.

"Was there something between you and Noah? Is that why you left with him?"

She looks at the floor for several long moments. "Noah was always yours. I never got in the way of that, and neither did Peter." When she lifts her eyes, they're narrow with pain.

"You left with Noah because you wanted to go with Noah."

Her eyes on the floor again. Seconds pass.

"Do you love him?" I say.

Finally she meets my gaze.

"Yes."

It feels like someone swings a hammer into my chest. I open my mouth; no sound comes out.

She sighs. "I don't blame you, or hate you, Mir. I can't. You're my sister. But when Noah came to me and told me what he knew, I had to go with him."

"He stole my memories," I say, like she didn't already know that. I don't mention the memory of the train, when I said I trusted him to do what he thought was right.

The light catches a tear on her eyelid. She wipes it away. "I know. It was selfish of him. Of me, too, for still following him. But I trusted him, and I still do." Her eyes fall to Peter on the bed. "Peter is our leader, since we were kids. It always made things different between him and us. You included." She looks at me again. "He couldn't act the way Noah could with us. Tycast and *Sifu* Phil wouldn't let him. I know they pounded into his head that the team comes before the individual. Peter is one of us for sure, don't get me wrong, but . . . I'll always choose Noah first. And you."

"I understand."

She wrings her hands together. "Can you forgive me?"

I nod, unable to speak.

Olive says, "You won't say anything to Noah, right?"

I shake my head even though part of me wants to. I don't feel anger toward her. Something else. She's upset about Noah and the situation, but she still remembers who she is. Jealous, then. I'm jealous she has her identity and I'm just scraps of a person stitched together.

"I know what you're thinking," she says. That would be a neat trick, because even I don't know. "You think I'm happy Noah gave you up."

I try to laugh; it sounds like a choked cry. "Is it true?"

She holds my eyes. "No. Because even after he did it, I knew his heart would always be yours. He thought it was the right thing, even if now he'll regret it forever."

"I wish you had stopped him," I say, suddenly feeling very tired.

"Me too," she says, and I believe her.

She leaves before I can say anything else. I sit on the bed next to Peter. Some of his dark hair curls around the back of his neck. I reach down to feel it, hoping it wakes him, but also just wanting to touch his hair. His breathing is even and slow, and his skin is cooler than before. Mud streaks his face and neck. I watch him for a long time, trying to process everything. Olive and Noah. I wonder if Noah knows, and feels the same way.

I wonder if I care.

I press my hand against the side of Peter's face. His lips

are parted slightly. I remember the feel of Noah's lips, but also the taste of the river, the pain in my chest as I struggled for air during the final seconds underwater. It all feels muted looking at Peter. I rub my thumb over the white scar on his chin.

His eyes snap open. He bolts upright, curling his hand into a fist. I get my arm up to block his punch. He tries again but I grab his wrists and pin him to the bed. He blinks until his eyes focus on my face.

"Miranda," he says. And his expression breaks apart into equal parts horror and relief. "You're okay. I didn't mean—"

"It's nothing." I ease my grip on his wrists so he doesn't bruise, but still hold him down. My face is close to his, our chests pressed together.

"Noah and Olive," he says.

"They're fine, everyone's fine." My hair slips from behind my neck and trails along his cheek. Peter twists his left wrist and suddenly he's free of my grip. His warm fingers slip around my neck and bury in my hair, making me gasp. The whole movement took a half second.

I drift closer; he's not pulling me, just guiding. Right before I close my eyes I see his widen. I pull back.

"What's wrong?" I say.

"I'm going to be sick." He releases the back of my neck and the warm imprint of his fingers fades away. A shiver runs across my shoulders. I don't understand what he means, because I'm still thinking about the shape of his lips and wondering if I looked at them before, when I was still me. Then he rolls off the bed and runs into the bathroom, slamming the door behind him. Oh, sick.

I sit at the edge of the bed and almost laugh. Pretty sure I was about to kiss him. Yeah, I was. Maybe he saved us both from that. I rub my gritty palms over my face. "Get a grip, Miranda," I say.

Especially when I kissed Noah only a few hours ago. Yes, I didn't kiss him on purpose, it kind of just turned into that. And yes, I'm almost positive I was about to kiss Peter willingly. Still. The last thing I want is to confuse both of them; I'm confused enough for all three of us. But it's not my fault—*Peter* was the one who grabbed the back of my neck. I had been holding him in place, with no plans of lip contact. His fault.

Which doesn't explain why I'm trying so hard not to smile.

Peter opens the door, disrupting my thoughts, looking like he saw a ghost. He hovers in the bathroom doorway. "Don't ever let them stick you with whatever . . . Don't ever get stuck with a dart. Okay?"

"Yes, sir." I snap off an awkward salute.

"Don't call me that," he says. He crawls back into bed and pulls the covers over himself, moaning. "I feel hungover."

Flash—

*   *   *

The four of us at the table in our room. A mostly empty bottle of something called Jameson. It burns our throats but we're too drunk to care. We're playing Monopoly, but only because we don't feel like sneaking out again. Olive has a lot of hotels. Noah is broke. We laugh and laugh and then I stand up suddenly and run to the bathroom. I get the lid up just in time to puke. I stagger back to the room and lean in the doorway.

Olive says, smiling, "You should stick to juice boxes."

Peter laughs. "Or maybe just light beer."

I give them both the middle finger and stagger to my bunk. Fall into it.

A glimpse of the next morning...

"Yeah," I say, back in the present. "Hungover."

In the bathroom I splash water on my face. After being in the river, I've seen enough water to last a lifetime. But the bathtub does look inviting. All sorts of expensive oils and soaps line the shelf above it. Who *are* these people? A brief image surfaces of the metal shower stalls we used at our base. It's possible I've never had a bath.

I take a washcloth from the tub and wet it in the sink, wring it out. Staring at myself in the mirror, I drag the cloth over my neck. My lips are chapped, on the verge of cracking. The skin under my right eye is purple. I run water into my hands, try to smooth the tangles and dirt out of my hair, then whip it into a quick ponytail. Nothing keeps me from smelling like the river. My eyes look lighter in the mirror. Before they were... I don't know what they were before, but now they're ... pink? I lean closer. The whites are perfectly white, but the irises are a reddish pink. I tilt my head and the effect shifts, revealing a hint of green. It must be the light.

I look away, still not recognizing my face or my lank auburn hair. I rinse out another washcloth for Peter and take it into the bedroom. His eyes are closed but he opens them when I sit on the bed.

"How did we escape?" he says.

"Olive carried you. It was her."

He nods. "What happened?"

I tell him nearly everything. About Olive's meeting with her other half. He can't think of anything to say. I leave out the part about me and Noah trading air under the water. He listens to it all while I wipe the cloth over his face and neck, cleaning the dirt away. He takes my hand at one point and winds his fingers through mine. We look at them folded together.

"Peter..." I begin, even though I have no idea what I'm going to say.

I see movement to my left. I know I'm semi-safe in this house, but that doesn't keep my heart from speeding up. Noah stands in the doorway, leaning forward with his hands gripping the door frame on both sides. He's not looking at us; he's looking at my hand wrapped in Peter's.

"Hey guys," he says.

"Hey," Peter says.

Noah steps into the room and holds up his wrist, taps it like he's wearing a watch. "You ready to recover those memory shots? I don't want to rush anyone, but the clock is ticking."

15

The kitchen table is covered with bags and bags of Taco Bell. We sit down and dig into food Elena was nice enough to pick up for us. Noah and I inhale tacos, but Peter can only stomach one, and Olive looks dazed. I'm curious how she feels about Noah's blond mystery girl.

Since Peter is woozy, Noah seems to take over leadership duties. I wonder if it was always this way, with Peter and Noah calling the shots while Olive and I hung back. It feels normal.

Noah paces next to the table, taco in hand. Elena is nowhere to be seen, meaning Noah probably told her to get lost. How well they know each other is still a mystery.

"This should be fairly simple," Noah says. "Tycast didn't give any indication that the other team knows about the cache.

So we check the pier out. If we can confirm it's not being watched, we recover the shots."

"And what happens when we need more?" I say.

Noah scratches his head. "We worry about that after we survive the next few days. But there should be enough to last us. What good would it be for Tycast to make a half-assed cache?"

Olive says, "And when our powers fade in a few years, the memory loss is supposed to go with it."

I remember them saying that before, but this time it sparks a phantom. The way my vision wavers into something new is familiar by now.

Weird. For a girl who isn't supposed to get her memories back, I've been remembering a lot lately.

If only I could choose what comes back.

My heart races in anticipation of more memories about the others, but I only see a cold white room, Dr. Tycast at my side. He holds a syringe filled with the lemonade-colored liquid.

"How much longer do I have to take these?" I ask him. I don't like the shots. Not because they prick, but because of how often I take them. They make the inside of my elbows sore. Noah sometimes mixes them with a drink to avoid the shot, but it's not as effective.

Tycast holds the syringe up to the light, flicks it with his finger. "Not long." He smiles down at me, takes my arm gently in his warm, dry hands. "When you fully mature, your brain will atrophy to a normal level. Maybe atrophy is the wrong word. It will *thin*. Now, when it does, the strain on your cerebrum will end, and it will begin to heal. You will, for all intents and purposes, be an ordinary woman."

"And then what happens to us?" I say. I don't want my brain to thin.

He's studying my arm, probing for a vein with his thumb. I watch him, but he never answers.

I blink.

"Are you okay?" Peter says. Some of the color has returned to his face.

I blink a few more times, shaking my head to clear it. "I'm fine." He doesn't look convinced, so I try my best smile. It feels like a grimace.

Olive polishes off another taco. "How much time do we have? Before memory loss sets in?"

Noah turns toward me and opens his mouth, then shuts it.

"Go on," I say, fully back in the present now. "Say it."

He rubs his nose. "Uh, based on Miranda, we should have about eight hours before we notice something's wrong. Or at least you and me, Olive. I don't know when Peter and Mir took theirs."

Peter grabs the last taco. "We better get moving."

We do a check of the house for anything we can use. Olive finds binoculars. Noah gets Elena to lend us her car, when she returns from wherever she was.

While we search, I toss out a random question. "So this dry run. Why not test us in a controlled environment, on one or two people at a time? Why reveal us to the world?"

Olive stops her inventory of the top shelves in a closet. "Remember what the woman said in Tycast's office? About a buyer being locked in? I bet they want to see our true capacity. Like firing a gun at the range, then firing one in the field."

Noah stands in the doorway to the garage, having checked over the Mercedes. "Good point. If we're talking about the kind of money Tycast hinted at, the buyers will want a guarantee that we work."

"We can't let them win," Olive says.

Noah smiles with more surety than I feel. "We're not gonna."

Something passes between them, but I don't know what. It feels private, enough to make my cheeks burn. But it's not like I can get jealous when half an hour ago I almost kissed Peter, if I was even going to. Noah definitely shies away from Olive's gaze, stepping back into the garage.

I turn away before Olive sees I noticed. And find two polished katanas resting on the mantel above the fireplace. My eyes trace the curve of the sword, and something primal stirs within me. I want to feel the grip in my hand. I pull Elena over and point at the swords. "Are those real?"

She stares at me. "Yes. My dad likes to collect Japanese stuff. Why?"

"You mind if I borrow them?"

"Uh..."

"Awesome. I promise to bring them back." I go to the mantel and lift the swords up. I hear Elena huff a sigh and walk away. When I turn around, Noah is standing in front of me. "You scared me," I say.

"No I didn't."

I hand him a sword. "You know how to use one of these?"

"Not as well as you."

Experimentally, I lift the sword over my shoulder and let it point down my back. It sticks to my armor, through my T-shirt. The scales layered on my back are magnetic.

"Nice feature, huh?" Noah says. He's trying to be nice, or something. "So, about Elena..."

"I don't care, Noah." The response is automatic, and maybe a little untrue.

"What?"

I pull the sword from my spine, test the weight with a quick twirl, then put it back. "I don't care how you know her."

"Yes you do. She's a friend, that's it. I made these contacts before we were together."

"I said *I don't care*. She's been very helpful."

He holds up the keys to her Mercedes. "Yes, she has."

We drive downtown two hours before midnight. The looming threat of memory loss is at the front of our minds. I don't have much to lose, I guess. Two days of memories? But as soon as I think it, I realize I'm wrong.

I have everything to lose.

I'm back with my friends, my family, and we have a purpose. I'm closer to finding out who I am with every passing moment.

But the others, they'll have to go through the same confusion and despair I did. At first it doesn't seem so bad, until you realize what's missing. The more you learn, the more of your life you see is lost. The worst part—if we all lose it, there would be no one to explain what happened.

We go over the plan in the car while Noah drives. Peter and I will watch the pier. Once we say it's clear, Noah and Olive will move in and search the water. Simple enough.

We drive into downtown Cleveland and I lean against the window and watch the people and lights and cars. I imagine them plunged into invisible terror, running from whatever horrible images their minds produce. I imagine cars overturned,

people trapped inside, fires raging. I hear a siren, thinking it's
in my head, but an ambulance passes us going the other way.

Noah stops next to a building of crumbling brick and broken windows. Far off, I see the blackness of the lake. I force
myself to shake off the imagined destruction; we're here now,
and without our shots we won't be helping anyone.

Noah hands me a small radio he must've taken from Elena's
house. I try to grab it but he holds on until I meet his eyes.
"We'll be hidden," he says. "When it looks clear, let me know
on this. Channel two."

I take the radio and he grabs my wrist. Peter is already out
of the car. The dome light makes Noah's face ghostly pale. "Be
careful," he says. "And watch for Rhys. He could be anywhere."

The rogue's name makes me shiver. He could be an asset
if he was on our side. But until we know more, he's definitely
classified as dangerous.

From the back, Olive says, "Noah, she'll be fine. We all
will."

He lets go of my wrist. "I didn't mean to grab you."

"Don't worry about it." I can still feel his fingers through
my armor. It wasn't exactly a nice touch, but I'd rather he didn't
touch me at all; I don't need to be any more confused about
what *was* between us, and what is.

Noah pops the trunk, and I make sure we're alone before
pulling out the sword. A breeze carries the lake's dead fish

smell. Down the street, the pier juts into the water. It's peaceful near the shore, darker and quieter. Noah drives away to stash the car somewhere before sneaking to the pier.

Behind me, Peter puts his hand on my shoulder. I jump. "Easy," he says.

"I am."

He smiles at me in the dark and tilts his head back, taking in the building. "You think the elevator still works?"

We climb the stairs of what was once a warehouse, all seven floors. Our boots crunch in the dirt and refuse left behind from whoever last called this place home. It's almost pitch-black— the only light is filtered through the broken and boarded-up windows. At the top, I put my shoulder into the rusted door and it screeches open. The sky over the lake is black. From here I see the pier perfectly. The third one, the one Tycast told us about, is the closest. It's streaked with red paint, just like he said. A small dark boat is moored to it.

Peter settles onto his stomach at the edge of the roof, and I lie down next to him. A little closer than I meant to. Through the binoculars I can see the imperfections in each wooden plank making up the pier.

Peter activates the radio. "Clear so far. How long do you want to wait?"

Noah's voice crackles through the tiny speaker. "Not long. The bad guys either know about this place or they don't."

We fall into a weird, tense silence. Our eyes are on the pier, but I can't ignore Peter's shoulder touching mine. It would be awkward to pull away now, but not moving says something too. It's like my mind has been cut in half when I really need it whole.

Peter clears his throat. "So are you and Noah back in the swing of things?"

"I don't know what you mean by that."

"You know," he says, taking the binoculars from me. "Back together. Like that."

"No," I say.

"No?"

"No, why?" I tuck my chin over the roof's edge and look down. I remember running with Peter over the rooftops, leaping into space with no fear. My pulse races just thinking about it. I turn on my side to face Peter. The faint light from the city is reflected in his blue eyes, making them appear lit from within. He stares back at me, binoculars drifting from his face.

"No, why?" I say again.

The radio in my hand crackles. "Guys. Guys, he's going over," Olive says.

On the pier, Noah looks around with his hands on his hips.

Across the street, Olive holds the radio and the sword. She crosses and stops in front of him. They argue, but their voices don't carry this far.

"Idiot," Peter mutters.

"He's showing off," I say. But it looks clear, and I'm ready to get this over with so I can sleep.

Noah turns away from Olive and walks to the end of the pier. Olive watches the street with the sword hidden behind her back. She lifts the radio to her lips and we hear, "What an idiot."

Noah dives off the end and slips into the water with barely a ripple.

Peter puts his hand on mine and squeezes the radio with my fingers, then leans close. "You might need to help him if it's too big to pull up."

"I hope it is," Olive replies.

Time passes. Olive paces the width of the pier.

She spins around and freezes, watching the boat.

"What happened?" I say into the radio.

Olive brings the radio to her lips after a few seconds. "Just thought I heard something."

My thoughts turn to the rogue, but it could be anything.

I take the binoculars back from Peter and watch the water. "He should've surfaced by now," I say.

"We used to have competitions when we were kids," Peter says.

"Yeah?"

"Yeah. See who could hold their breath the longest. Noah always won. One time I even passed out trying to beat him. He's fine."

It doesn't seem that way. Olive keeps staring at the boat. And if Noah is searching the bottom it doesn't mean he can't come up for air. Unless he's trying to impress us by staying under. My eye twitches. I take a breath and hold it.

Olive raises her sword. From this far away I hear her shout, "Come out of there! Show yourself!" at the dark boat.

In the water, bubbles break the surface.

Shit.

Peter and I stand up at the same time. We whirl around and prepare to sprint for the door.

The door that is now shut. Two people in black scaled suits stand in front of it.

The other Peter and Miranda.

16

They both hold shimmering silver staves. Shimmering because tiny tendrils of electricity crawl up and down their lengths. Suddenly I miss the knife-tipped version from the forest. At the same time, seeing the electricity makes my brain scream DANGER, which keeps me focused, blocking the stun of seeing myself staring back at me. Something I definitely need right now.

My other version leans on her staff a little, smiling. It's the smile you make when you're happy to see someone, maybe someone you haven't seen in a long time. Even their hair is identical to ours; the boy's matches Peter's longer black curls, and the girl has her reddish brown hair cut to the same length as mine.

"I'm Grace," she says. She drops a hand on the other Peter. "And this is my teammate Tobias."

Grace and Tobias. I thought they'd have the same names as us—but that wouldn't make sense. I almost smile at the thought; no words come because I can't speak. It's like walking into the bathroom in the mall and seeing my face for the first time all over again. I must make the same facial expressions. My voice has to sound like hers.

"What's so funny?" Grace says. She steps to her left and Tobias steps to the right. The space widens between them, but there's no way we can make it. Another step, widening the circle to come in from the outside. I reach up and wrap my fingers around the hilt poking above my right shoulder. The katana comes off easily. I twirl it once before holding it out before me.

"Give me the sword, Miranda," Peter says next to me. I haven't taken my eyes from our twins.

"You don't have to protect me, Peter."

"I'm not. Just let me try first."

Tobias and Grace continue their slow circle toward us.

"Are you better with a sword?" I say.

"Well, no, but—"

"Then I got it." I raise my voice a little so Grace and Tobias can hear. "You don't seem surprised to see us. But we're just learning about you."

They trade a look. Tobias—who has an aura of menace Peter lacks—has a strange gun on his hip; there's a spool of cable connected to it.

"Do you know what they're trying to make us do?" I say.

Peter shifts his feet on the gravel beside me. They've stopped moving toward us, offering an alley between them for us to escape. No doubt they hope we'll run for it, and why wouldn't we try, when they've got electro-staves and we've got a sword between us. The door behind them is shut all the way. I know the effort it takes to push from the inside, so I'm guessing it'll be just as hard to pull. I'm so tempted to run, but I can't trust Peter will follow.

"Many people will die," I say. "You're aware of this?"

Grace shakes her head, halfway confused. "It's not our place to question."

That's when I know something is wrong with them. I point the katana behind me, back toward the city. "Look at those people down there. Look at the buildings filled with them. Imagine them fleeing in a mass panic, the chaos it would cause. All for proof of our worth. So we can be sold off to the highest bidder."

Grace's eyelids twitch. Her eyes are bright green, unlike my reddish brown ones. "It doesn't matter," she says.

It sounds like an automated response. Like she doesn't fully understand. Like her only goal is to bring us in, no matter what we say.

Tobias jerks his chin at Peter, as he slowly crouches, holding his electrified staff as a walking stick. "How's the neck?" he says.

"Good," Peter says. "Thanks for your concern." I see his head turn toward me in my peripheral vision. "I don't have any weapons, Mir."

"I'm aware of that," I whisper. "Just run. Make sure Noah and Olive are okay."

"I don't think so," he hisses back.

It doesn't matter, Grace said. These two can't believe that. If they have any part of us inside them, they wouldn't go along with the plan. It's almost like they're robots . . . programmed. If we're two parts of the same team—Alpha and Beta—how can we be so different? Then I remember our purpose, and the obvious question is—how can someone buy and truly control us? There has to be some kind of mechanism, or brainwashing, or *something* that keeps a Rose in line. Something to make us follow orders. Otherwise we're just loose cannons.

"Are we twins?" I say to Grace.

She shrugs. Whoever I'm dealing with is not me. I am no longer afraid. My only regret is I can't risk looking down at the pier behind me, to see if Olive and Noah are okay.

Grace moves in.

There are two ends to her staff and only one blade to my sword. I parry as fast as I can, whipping it left and right as she tries to smack me with one end and then the other. I don't have gloves like she does; the shocks from her staff travel down the sword and up my buzzing arm. With every hit I almost lose my grip. Grace sweeps the staff up between my legs but I thrust down and catch it, groaning against the pain in my arm. The blade sparks on the staff. Grace reverses and tries to come from above with the other end. I sidestep and the sizzling staff smashes onto the gravel with a burst of white sparks. I don't have time to counterattack. Peter is beside me, on his knees from a solid strike to the chest. He tried to block with his forearms.

"Just run!" Peter says.

Maybe it's my lack of sleep, or the shock. Whatever the reason, Grace is faster than I am. She hits me three times in the ribs, so fast her staff is a white, crackling blur. I stagger back—one step, then two. Three. I'm too close to the roof's edge. My foot slips and my arms pinwheel, keeping me in place an extra second. Grace is in front of me, reaching out to grab my neck. To stop me, or give me a final push? I grab her arm but her footing isn't strong enough. She slides over the gravel and I'm looking at the night sky. A strange end, to fall seven stories with your doppelgänger. Images flash in my head, more

phantom memories, too fast for me to decipher. Faces mostly—
Noah, Peter, Olive, Tycast. And someone else. Someone who
looks like me, but much older. It might be my mother.

A final flash—

I'm a child, my head not reaching my mother's waist. She kneels
down and looks into my eyes. We have the same auburn hair,
the same nose, same lips.

"I have to go now, sweetie." A man stands behind her. He
has a red goatee and kind eyes. "This is Phillip. He's going to
help teach you, okay?"

"Where are you going?" I say.

I never get my answer. I blink, and the woman's face is suddenly Grace, clutching me as the floors rush by. I try to count
them but we drop too fast. My body tenses, convulsing as it
tries to writhe away. If only I can orient myself, get my legs
pointed the right way. The surge of hope is dashed. Whatever
way I land won't be good.

Wind roars in my ears. I squeeze my eyes shut and brace
for the end.

Then the wind stops.

I jerk so violently that, for one awful second, I think my
neck has snapped. Something squeezes my stomach so hard
I can't breathe. I'm upside down, dangling ten feet above the

159

sidewalk next to the building. Swaying. I look *up* and see a long black cable connected to Grace's leg. Grace has her arms wrapped just above my hips, hands clasping her elbows. That's why I can't breathe.

I am strangely calm about everything. The cable jerks upward a foot. Grace grins at me, triumphant.

"Close one," she says.

"Yeah," I say, then punch her in the face. She grunts, grip loosening for an instant. I backflip out of her arms. My feet swing down, and I land crouched on the sidewalk below her.

She curls upward, a vertical sit-up. Tobias isn't standing on the edge; he's using the roof as a fulcrum. "Let me down!" Grace shouts.

I spare a glance at the pier—Olive and Noah are gone, and Peter is up there alone. I sprint through the door Peter and I first came through. My vision darkens as the blood rushes out of my head, but I keep it together, taking the stairs two at a time. I reach the top and burst through the closed door.

Then skid to a stop, carving furrows in the gravel.

Peter is on his knees. Blood runs from a cut on his forehead to the tip of his nose. Tobias stands next to him, staff in one hand, katana in the other. The sword's point nestles under Peter's chin.

"You should've run," Peter says. His shoulders slump.

"We only need three of you for the dry run," Tobias says.

"I could kill him, and it would be within my orders." That's why Grace held on to me, in case Tobias had already killed Peter.

I hear Grace come through the doorway behind me, but don't bother turning around. She kicks the back of one knee and I stumble forward and down, cutting my palms on the crushed rock. I settle into a kneeling position and put my hands behind my head. Peter stares at me like he's mad I didn't save myself. I shrug at him.

It's false bravado; inside I am shivering and shaking. We failed. I have no idea what will become of us now, or if Noah and Olive escaped.

And since there's no way we'll cooperate, they'll deny us our memory shots, erasing all the new ones I've made. It's the only possibility.

Peter smiles at me, shaking his head. Behind the smile I can see he's as scared as I am. Blood drips onto his lips. "You never did listen to my orders," he says.

I smile back. "Aren't you glad you'll have company?"

17

They cuff us. I can't feel my fingers by the time we reach the first landing. It doesn't seem real. We didn't come all this way to be captured by knockoffs. At the bottom a van waits with the rear doors open. My shoulder rubs against Peter's as they guide us to the van.

"They're going to make us like them, Miranda," Peter says. He won't look at me. Inside the van I see Noah and Olive, similarly restrained, and I breathe again. I'm torn between relief at seeing them safe, and dread because they're captured along with us.

"What does that mean?" I say.

But I know. Whatever they did to Grace and Tobias. The thought of being altered *more* makes my throat clench.

I close my eyes and try to imagine how they'll do it. Drugs? Brainwashing?

"It means they'll do something to make us play along. So we can't think for ourselves. We won't be ourselves."

He meets my eyes reluctantly. "If that happens, I want to..."

"Want to what?"

We're at the back of the van and he shakes his head. I step inside and sit down on a bench next to Olive. She smiles weakly at me. Peter sits next to Noah, across from us. Noah is soaking wet, water beading in his short hair. Grace shuts the door, and now the only light comes from a small bulb in the ceiling.

"Hey," Noah says to me, "that's you." He looks as sick as Peter, sick as I feel. He knows we failed, that there's nothing to protect the city now. Or us.

"I noticed that," I say.

There's a partition between us and the front of the van. I hear the doors open and shut. The engine starts. We sway in our seats as the van pulls away from the building.

"So what happened up there?" Noah says, eyes on the ceiling. He sounds a little slurred, like his tongue is swollen. Maybe someone punched him in the mouth.

"They had better weapons," Peter says flatly.

Noah nods at that. "Okay, fair enough, but seriously."

"Seriously *what*, Noah?" I say.

He leans forward. "Seriously, Mir. How. Did this. Happen."

Olive kicks his knee across the van. "You dove in before we decided it was clear."

"Yeah," I say. "Your fault."

Noah laughs. "They were waiting for me down there. I found the cache, though, so Tycast wasn't lying." In the dim light, I see him shift something into his cheek.

"Of course he wasn't," Peter says.

"What if they deny us shots?" Olive says.

"In that case," Noah says, "it was nice knowing you guys." He doesn't seem worried now. My skin burns, which I'm glad for because I'd rather feel angry than helpless. . . .

Then I realize Noah is mouthing the word *quiet*. He opens his mouth. Inside I see four tiny vials under his tongue, each filled with a lemonade-colored liquid.

While we talk without really talking, I pay attention to where the van is going. I count the turns and stops, trying to picture it in my head. Eventually I lose track, and so do the others. It sounds like we're on a freeway for a long time. Then more traffic lights. We turn and the van tilts down, like we've just entered an underground parking lot. We trade glances, priming ourselves for whatever comes next.

The van stops, and the front doors open and shut. A second

later Grace opens the rear doors and I blink in the bright light. We're in an underground parking garage, empty but well lit.

"Out you come," Grace says, waving us down.

"So who are you?" Noah says, smiling like an idiot at Grace. "Miranda two-point-oh? Do you have upgrades?"

Grace punches Noah in the stomach and he bends over, groaning. He can't catch himself because his hands are behind his back, so he goes down on one shoulder and rolls onto his side. "Same sense of humor," Noah says once he has breath.

They put bags over our heads, which is pretty useless since we could always find our way back from wherever we're going —a moving vehicle is one thing, but on foot I'm confident. The bag is scratchy and makes the air I breathe hot and moist.

"Alpha team has better bags to put on people's faces," Noah says. I hear Grace—or someone—hit him again.

The four of us sit on a bare concrete floor in a cell without a door. One wall is a smoked-glass window, the other three are white. They didn't remove our bags until we were inside. There was an elevator that went up many floors, a few short hallways. Other than that I have no idea where we are.

The first thing we all did was sit down and tuck our legs and squeeze the cuffs over our feet, to put our hands in front of us.

"At least we're together," Olive says, scratching at the

pocked floor with a nail. She sits across from me, next to Noah. There isn't much room, so her leg is resting on top of mine.

Noah stretches his arms over his head. "Maybe. Who knows for how long." He must have the vials spaced around his mouth, because I can barely tell his voice is different.

"You're always so negative," Peter says.

"Hey, c'mon leader. Lead us out of here."

"Noah," I say.

Noah holds up his cuffed hands. "You're right, I'm sorry." He holds a finger to his lips then pretends to scratch his nose. He's afraid they're watching us, which of course they are. Noah opens his mouth like he's yawning, and Peter sees the vials. Olive must know, because she gives me a sly smile.

The wall of smoked glass slides open. Four soldiers in black armor point rifles at us. They wear the same thin metal helmets worn by the soldiers at our base, with the same creepy narrow visor. Two come in and pick me up off the floor. I don't struggle. Peter does. He tries to stand but a soldier kicks him in the chest.

"I'm the leader. Take me," Peter says. They ignore him.

"It's fine," I say. "I'll see you guys in a minute." I will it to be true, even though it feels like I'll never see them again.

My team stares at me with blank faces. The glass wall slides shut.

The soldiers march me down a hallway. I consider building

a fear wave, but it won't do anything except give me a headache. Or burn me out, since we're cutting it close with the
shots. If it's after midnight, then I had my last shot yesterday
morning, before leaving on the bikes with Peter. No way to tell
how much longer it'll last, since I've used my fear since then.

The first door on the right opens to a small office, complete with a desk and bookshelves. Grace sits behind the desk,
and seeing her face again startles me. She points at the chair
across from the desk and the soldiers sit me down. At least it's
comfy. She nods at the soldiers and they leave, shutting the
door behind them.

We stare at each other.

"These cuffs are a little tight," I say. Just banter to mask
the unease, the creeping dread rising in my throat. We can all
talk the big talk, but I don't think any of us expects to leave
this place the way we came in. For now I have to fake it, even
if I can barely hold my head up. I have to show Grace I'm not
afraid.

"You know it's impossible to escape from here," Grace says.
"There are too many doors, too many guns you'd have to pass."

"My home was kinda like that."

Grace comes around and unlocks my cuffs. She tosses them
onto the desk and sits back down.

"Who's running the show here?" I say.

"I am."

"I meant, who is your Dr. Tycast?"

Grace smiles. "Dr. Conlin. Janet Conlin."

I rub my red wrists. "So why am I talking to you?"

"Because Conlin thought I'd be able to get through to you best, seeing as we share the same DNA."

I look up from my wrists. "Yeah, about that. So you're my . . . clone?"

"Who says you're not mine?"

"No one," I say.

"The truth is neither."

I swallow, wondering if I should believe anything she says. If I should allow her words to sink in as fact, or keep fighting them.

"Then what?"

"I know it's hard to accept at first," Grace says, ignoring me. And what's that in her face now? Compassion and under-standing, it seems. "I was like you at first. I didn't want to accept the truth. And I didn't. But they helped me with that."

"How?"

Her eyebrows scrunch together. She stares at some point over my shoulder. "I don't remember."

"Yes you do. What did they do to you?"

Grace shakes her head.

"How are they controlling you?" I say.

"It doesn't matter," Grace says, and for a single insane second I think she's going to cry. "They just do."

"Who is Rhys?" I say. If she's off balance, maybe I can keep hammering her. Push her over the edge until she tells me something useful.

"I don't know that name," she says.

"Do you like being controlled?"

I watch her face re-form into a cold, calculating look. Like a robot. This is what they'll do to me. Make it so I can't feel or think for myself. They'll have to if they want to test us on the city.

I picture the vials in Noah's mouth. There is still hope, however small.

Grace places her palms flat on the desk. "I don't mind it," she says. "It makes my job easier. And it will make your job easier too. There is a computer in my skin, Miranda. Every time I have a forbidden thought or desire, the tattoo purges it. Over time, you stop fighting it."

Tattoo . . . I remember Noah saying the word while recalling the conversation he overheard in Tycast's office. Before I can ask what she means, Grace grabs her hair and pulls it aside, turning so I can see the circuitry embedded in the skin at the base of her skull. It looks like a bumpy tattoo of a circuit board, just under the skin.

So that's why Beta team is so unlike us. And why we will soon be so like them.

My throat is too dry to swallow. "And you want to do that to us."

Grace nods. "Conlin worked on the tattoo herself, and we were the first to receive them. I am not ashamed to admit Beta team received them first, to make sure it wouldn't kill *you*."

"Me," I say.

"Alpha team. The darlings of Project Rose. Your team was always our creators' favorite, everyone knows it."

I lean forward and Grace tenses. "Creators? More than one?" I guess I already knew that. The voice in Tycast's office had said *We're moving ahead with the dry run.* Plural.

When I don't move any closer, her shoulders relax. "Well, someone had to make us, didn't they? And yes, more than one."

Make us. I stare at her blankly.

Grace says, "We were *grown*, Miranda."

"Grown."

"Yes. God. I can't believe we're related. We are clones, Miranda. Clones. Of one person. Copies. No mother. No father. Do you understand?"

I understand. I think I knew all along, deep down, somewhere hidden and dark, that there was more to us than gene therapy. Maybe that's where my emptiness stems from—not the loss of memories, but because I've been hollow from the

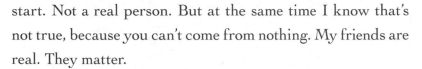

start. Not a real person. But at the same time I know that's not true, because you can't come from nothing. My friends are real. They matter.

But what she's saying, what I believe . . . it means we were never born. We never had parents to give us up. We never left behind old lives. It's always been this, from the first beat of our hearts.

Now isn't the time to dissect my feelings. I have to stay focused, on the slim chance Noah can get those vials to us. Maybe we can fake it.

"Why are you telling me this?" I say. Numbness spreads down my arms and legs, to the tips of my fingers and toes. I know the answer.

"Because in a few hours, you won't remember anything. Unless you agree to join us. Dr. Conlin has been ordered to proceed with the dry run immediately. With enough of us, we can provide a demonstration to the world that will never be forgotten. Eight Roses would be ideal, but we can get by with seven."

"You're prepared to be sold off as a *weapon*?" I say.

"I accept it because I must. The tattoos for Alpha team aren't finished yet, and won't be for some time. So we either take your memories, or you sign on without the tattoos. Forcing you to forget is something Conlin wants to avoid, as most of your experiences go with it. It renders you less valuable."

"It'll never happen," I say. "We will never help you."

Grace nods. "At this point I am instructed to persuade you."

The door to her office opens, and I half spin in my chair. Two soldiers march Peter and Noah in at gunpoint. The soldiers shove down hard on their shoulders until they kneel. Noah slumps forward a little, head hanging. His cheek is freshly bruised.

When I turn back, Grace smiles at me. "Different as you think we are, I'm going to guess we have some similarities. Tell me if I'm wrong, but hasn't it always been between these two?"

She pauses, drinking in the look on my face.

"And now you have to choose," she says.

18

Choose.

The room tilts, but I hold on to the armrests.

As far as persuasion tactics go, this is pretty awful. I made it clear we won't help them no matter what they do to us. They'll have to erase our memories if they want any cooperation, or give us those tattoos. But if I didn't believe Grace would really kill one of them, my heart wouldn't pound. My mouth wouldn't be dry and it wouldn't feel like I'm the one with a gun to my head.

Grace said they only need seven. But that doesn't mean they'd destroy something as valuable as a Rose. I have to believe that.

She stands up and leans forward, fingertips on the desk.

"Agree to help us. We can't just take your word for it—you'll have handlers. But cooperate and I'll spare both of them."

"Don't agree to anything," Peter says.

Grace ignores him. "Stand up, Miranda. Look at them."

I hold Grace's gaze a moment longer, as long as I dare, then push myself out of the chair and turn around. Peter and Noah kneel with assault rifles pointed at the backs of their heads. Both of them manage to smile at me. It fills me with strength, and something else . . . something warm. It keeps me standing.

"You should pick me to die," Noah says. "Peter needs to lead us." He says it blandly, like I'm choosing something to drink instead of someone to kill.

"Oh please," Peter says, taking on the same careless tone. "You love Noah. If you pick him to die, you'll regret it for the rest of your life."

Noah snorts. "Are you *kidding*? I saw you guys holding hands. I saw that shit. She hates me for what I did to her."

"I don't hate you," I say. I'm not sure what I feel, but it's not hate. The two helmeted soldiers behind them are statues. To them I say, "I'll remember you both, even if I can't see your faces." The one behind Peter tilts his head to the side, like a dog.

"You have five seconds," Grace says.

I turn around. "I'm sure I have more. You won't kill us."

Peter and Noah hid their fear, so I must do the same. I

can smother it with reason. The creators would gain nothing by killing us. Instead, they're about to gain four blank slates. That's just logical. You don't throw away a weapon this valuable to gain cooperation. They have other ways.

And yet . . .

Grace's eyes hold a crazy sheen, some glimmer of madness.

I was wrong. She's going to do it.

They don't care who lives and who dies, as long as they have their seven Roses for the dry run.

Peter and Noah's faces haven't broken, but this time it does nothing to comfort me. Give me a sign, I think. Let me know I'm doing the right thing. That everything will be okay. Don't make me pick.

"Okay, I'll choose," Grace says behind me. "Kill Peter."

Peter closes his eyes. Noah lets his head hang again. I turn around, ready to leap over Grace's desk, but she has a gun pointed at my face.

Behind me, a soldier fires.

It's so loud in the tiny office. Everything inside me dies and rots. I should have picked. I would have picked.

Who would I have picked?

"I wish you could remember this moment," Grace says. She jerks her chin to the boys behind me. I turn around and Peter has his eyes closed. Smoke curls around his head. On the floor, near his knees, is a smoking bullet hole.

They didn't kill him. Relief floods through me, making it harder to stand than ever before. I reach out and use the back of the chair for support.

Peter opens his eyes and they are tearless and fierce, revealing a glimpse of his true self. Pure animalistic strength. There was never any fear for him to hide.

"Take them back to the cell," Grace says. The soldiers yank Peter and Noah to their feet, then shove them roughly into the hallway.

She huffs a sigh and collapses in her chair. "Now we wait."

The soldiers pull me from the room a few seconds later, but our eyes stay locked as Grace slouches in her chair, grinning at me with big eyes. Her madness clearly hasn't faded. I don't look away until the door shuts.

Tattoo or not, I make a silent vow to kill her before this is over.

They toss us back in the cell. I stand in the corner, away from everyone, and listen to my pulse slowly ratchet down. The shot plays again and again in my head. My ears ache and feel packed with concrete.

Noah comes up behind me. He grabs my shoulder and turns me around. He takes his finger and tilts my chin up. I open my eyes.

"You did the right thing," he says. "They were never going to kill us." He leans in until our lips almost touch. I kiss him. I know he wouldn't kiss me right now for any other reason. My mouth opens and I feel his tongue slip over mine, dropping two of the small vials into my mouth. He pulls away and smiles without teeth, uses his thumb to brush some hair out of my eyes.

Peter stands in the corner, watching us. I shift one of the vials under my tongue and give him a glimpse of the other, a flash of the yellow liquid inside. I hold out my arms like I need a hug. Someone is watching us, listening. It'll look odd kissing Peter right after I kiss Noah, but it's the only way to do it without bringing the vials into the open. Better to look odd than obvious.

Peter stands in front of me. His shoulders are so wide I can't see Noah and Olive behind him. "I'm okay," he says.

I put a hand on his chest. "I know. Come here." I wrap my fingers around the back of his neck, pull him down to me. He kisses me softer than Noah. Goose bumps spring up along my arms and back. He opens his mouth and I pass the vial to him, slipping it in with my tongue. He pulls back the second he has it, but I find myself reluctant to let him go, moving forward to keep my mouth on his. Finally I break away, lips burning, vial secured under my tongue. He looks as confused as I feel.

We still have a job to do. I bite the cap off the vial and let the bitter liquid roll down my throat. Then I swallow the pill-sized container. The phantom I had of Tycast comes to mind —of remembering that Noah sometimes took his shots mixed with a drink, but how that made them less effective. If only we had access to a syringe.

I watch Noah give Olive her "kiss good-bye," and can't help but wonder what's going through her head. And Noah's. I wonder if he can feel her love in that one kiss. When they break, he stares into her eyes for a long moment. For the briefest second, confusion flickers on his face. From what, I don't know. Either because he felt something in her kiss, or felt something *for* her. *Stop. I'm speculating. You can't feel things in kisses;* but even as I think that, I know it's not true.

Noah turns away from her, to Peter.

Olive touches her lips with her fingertips, feeling his kiss. She notices I'm watching and quickly lowers her hand. I want to tell her it's okay in some way, but I don't know how.

Peter hugs Noah, but I see it's so Peter can whisper in Noah's ear. Noah nods almost imperceptibly and heads toward me.

How long the vials will last is a mystery, fine—but I can't deal with just hoping it's long enough. I need to be doing *something*.

Noah puts his arms around me and whispers in my ear, "We fake losing our memories. Go to sleep. If we can trick them into thinking we're wiped, they'll give us shots again. Be convincing. Now start crying."

Behind Noah, Peter whispers to Olive. I squint so hard my eyes water, then blink a few times to shake the tears free. I'm listening to him, but it's hard to focus when his arms are around me like this. After just kissing Peter, it's too much. I don't want to look at either of them.

"Say you're sorry," Noah whispers.

"I'm sorry. Noah, I'm sorry."

"Shh, stop. This isn't your fault," he says, in a normal voice now. He releases me and dabs at his eyes, too, but they're dry.

The cell door opens. Tobias stands there, flanked by two soldiers. He claps Peter on the shoulder like they're old friends. "Open your mouth," Tobias says. Peter does. Tobias shines a flashlight around, making Peter's cheeks glow red. I'm frozen, hoping everyone got rid of their vials fast enough.

He points at me. "Open." I do. He finds nothing. He does the same with Olive and Noah, makes them lift their tongues.

Noah coughs in his face. Tobias backhands him without a word and Noah falls against the wall, chuckling, until Tobias raises a fist.

Noah shuts up, and Tobias steps backward to the door. He appraises us one at a time. "You guys are pretty weird," he says.

"You have no idea," Noah says.

"Hopefully that goes away when you lose your memories."

"Doubt it," Olive says.

Tobias shakes his head in disgust and leaves the cell. The door shuts again, and the glass darkens.

We wait.

19

The desire to talk to them gnaws at me like hunger. We can't just sit here waiting; we need to fall asleep and wake up changed if we're going to convince these people. That's how it happened for me.

Peter rubs his temples and manages to look sad. I have to remember we're acting, we have a plan. "I'm sorry," he says.

"For what?" Noah says.

"I failed you."

"Stop," Olive says. "Don't put this on you. You don't get to do that."

Peter shakes his head, eyes unfocused. "They're really going to erase who we are."

"They'll do whatever it takes," I say.

We fall into another silence.

I make the first move. "Look, we shouldn't drag this out. It won't be much longer—I'm going to sleep. I'm going to fall asleep, and when I wake up I won't care anyway. We'll just make new memories."

Noah fights hard to keep the smile off his face. I go to each of them—Peter, Olive, then Noah—and kiss them once on the cheek. Then I walk to the other end of the cell. I lie down facing away and pull my knees up to my chest.

And wouldn't you know it? I actually fall asleep.

The cell door slams open and wakes me up. I roll over and blink at the fluorescent lights as groggily as I can, propping myself on an elbow. It doesn't require too much acting. There are no windows, but it feels like the middle of the night. The cell door is open but no one is there.

Time to convince everyone I don't remember a thing.

It's hard, considering the glut of emotions coursing inside me. So many things to consider, to worry about, and I have to pretend I don't have a care in the world.

Slowly, piece by piece, I clear my mind. I think about us in here, trapped behind enemy lines, and I wipe it away. I think about the people in the city, the pure terror they will soon experience, and I wipe it away. I think about Peter and

Noah. What they feel for me, and what I feel for them. I wipe it away. My friendship with Olive, if I can ever rebuild it. I wipe that away too.

Of course they don't really go away. How could they? Instead they vibrate in the background, humming, threatening to break though and cut my legs out from under me. But for now I can act the part. I know what it's like to not remember.

I let my gaze drift around the cell, taking in the others while trying to make my face blank. I add a slight furrow to my eyebrows, like I'm trying to solve a puzzle. The sound of clicking heels echoes down the hallway. In walks a short Asian woman with black hair in a bob cut and black-framed glasses. She has a white coat like Dr. Tycast wore.

I sit up. "Where am I?"

The woman smiles. "Hello, Miranda. My name is Dr. Conlin. You've all been in an accident. Do you remember?"

"What accident?" I say.

Peter and Noah look at me like they've never seen me before. Olive rubs sleep from one eye.

"How do you know my name?" I say.

Dr. Conlin licks her lips. No soldiers accompany her. The others make their best bewildered-and-slightly-confused faces.

Noah uses the wall to stand up. "Where are we?"

Conlin holds up her hands. "Relax. I'll explain everything in due time. Start with telling me what you remember."

I close my eyes. I open them. I shake my head. "Nothing," I say.

Conlin nods once, then holds out her hand. "Come with me."

I walk past the others warily, like I'm afraid they might lash out. The cell door slides shut behind me and sweat breaks all over my skin. I feel so alone without them. Naked and exposed.

"Where are we going?" I say. I try to recall those initial feelings in the mall, but they're fuzzy. There was confusion, but also acceptance. I can fake it the same way.

Conlin leads me back into the office, where my friends were kneeling not long ago. The faint scent of gunsmoke is still in the air. Conlin points at the chair in front of the desk and I sit down, wringing my hands in my lap. Then I stop— that might be too clichéd a gesture. I don't want to appear so nervous it draws attention.

Conlin sits behind the desk and folds her hands on top of it. "You were in a traumatic incident, Miranda. You and your friends."

"What happened?"

"The four of you are at this facility for special treatment. You have a rare memory disorder, and we've managed to cure it with a series of shots you take daily. We tried to boost the potency, and it failed in the process. Your memories are gone, but we believe they'll come back shortly, once we put you back on the old dose."

Okay, what would I be curious about next? I look over my shoulder at the door we came through. "I know those people back there? The two guys and the girl?"

Conlin nods. She nods *gravely*, trying to sell it to me just like I'm selling to her. "Yes. They're your friends. I want you to stay calm, though. This will get sorted out."

I'm stunned at how easily she lies. It's effortless, like she believes it herself. So real it's enough to leave me slightly unhinged. The only thing missing is a bit of warmth behind her gaze.

I take a deep breath. "I'm calm." Okay, so those are my friends, but wouldn't my parents be here? I let my eyes fall, then brighten, as if an idea has just popped into my head. "Where are my parents?"

Dr. Conlin sighs. "I'm afraid they passed away when you were a child. You developed your memory disorder shortly after. I'm sorry."

"It's . . . fine. It's not like I remember." I shift in my seat, feel my armor flex with me.

"No. Not yet."

I pull my T-shirt up, exposing the armor underneath. "What the hell is this?" I knock my fist on my stomach. "Is this *armor*?"

Conlin looks prepared for this too. "Not exactly. It's a suit that produces a minor electrical charge to stimulate brain function. That's how the brain works—it's like an organic computer that needs electricity. Instead of wearing some cumbersome helmet, we use the suit as a conductor. It allows us to keep the charge low. Think of it like a memory aid."

I put surprise on my face. "Wow. Pretty high-tech."

"It is," Conlin says, smiling at my buying another lie. "*We* want you to remember as much as *you* do."

I let my eyes roam over the bookshelves. At the little green plant on her desk. "So what now?" I say.

Conlin claps her hands and leans back in her chair. "Now I'll talk to your friends and explain the situation to them. We have another test we'd like to do to see if we can jump-start your memories."

"What kind of test?" I say. The dry run. What else could it be? Now I don't mind being used in their little test; if they put us near Beta team, we'll be able to stop them before anyone gets hurt. I try to keep anticipation off my face, the eagerness I feel to drop the facade and fight.

Conlin pulls a syringe from a desk drawer. It's filled with the lemonade-colored liquid. I've never been so happy to see a needle in my life—that's my first thought. Then I wonder if it just *looks* like a memory shot. It could be the first step to changing us, to making me like Grace. It's possible Conlin didn't believe my little act at all.

"It's complicated," she says. "We can discuss it more in the morning. I have to give you this shot now."

"What's it for?" For all I know, it could knock me out. Long enough to wake up with a tattoo at the top of my neck. But I have to risk that if I want to continue.

"Antirejection agent for the compound we use. It's a bit technical."

"Okay."

Conlin comes around her desk and swabs my arm, then sticks the needle in. I feel the prick and the pressure as she pushes the liquid into my vein. I wait to pass out, but don't. She pulls a cotton ball from her coat pocket and has me hold it over the injection spot. "There," she says. "Now, go down the hallway. It's the last door on your right. I'll see you in a few hours when the sun comes up."

I stand up and walk to the door. I don't feel any different. Just the usual worries pounding at the gates, threatening to show Conlin the truth.

"Miranda?" Conlin says behind me.

I turn around. "Yeah?"

She's sitting on the edge of her desk, holding the empty syringe. "Do you remember your last name?"

"North," I say.

She smiles. "Perfect. Good night, Miranda."

I walk down the long white hallway. Slowly. A little off balance and confused, maybe. A brand-new amnesiac wouldn't walk with purpose and confidence. I pass doors on both sides. The desire to see what's behind them is strong, but I keep moving. I hear Conlin leave her office and open the cell door again, retrieving whoever's next. I don't look back, fearing something in my face would give me away.

I open the last door on the right expecting to see Grace and Tobias, or maybe an alternate version of Noah and Olive. I don't even know how my Noah and Olive were captured, or how Noah managed to hide those vials in his mouth. And who knows when we'll be alone next, away from eyes and ears watching everything we do. They won't chance us faking it. They'll be on us until we're free.

Instead of Grace and Tobias, I find a room identical to the one I called home. Bunk beds on either side, a table in the middle. The table has checkers instead of chess. A fridge and some dressers line the back wall. Any cameras are hidden.

I stand in the room, feeling like a stranger. Which is perfect —if anyone is watching, they'll think I'm confused about which bed is mine. The bottom bunk on the left has a pair of boxers on it, so I count it out. The bottom bunk on the right is the one I had back home. I kick off my shoes and roll onto it.

I watch the door, expecting Grace to burst in and scream

at me for being in her bed. It occurs to me I have no idea where the other clones are right now. Maybe watching me. The thought makes my skin crawl. So I think about my team instead, listening to Conlin's little speech. Nodding at her lies and accepting her words as fact.

I lick my lips, which makes me remember kissing Peter and Noah in the cell. And what I felt when I did. The truth is I don't have time to feel, not until we're free. We haven't stopped the dry run. We're on schedule to be *used* in the dry run.

Sadly, those facts don't keep me from trying to decode the way Peter and Noah looked at me.

I pull on my hair, roll over, and grip the pillow so hard my fingers ache. Noah's kiss. Peter's kiss. I shouldn't be thinking about it when we're so far behind enemy lines.

Focus, North.

I take deep breaths, letting my mind relax. Just as I get to a comfortable point, Noah opens the door. He stands in the doorway, taking in the room like I did.

"This is great," he says. "Which bunk is mine?"

"I don't know. Maybe that one," I say, pointing at the top bunk across from me. Peter was on the bottom, and I'm going with the theory some things will be similar.

Noah walks past me to the dressers and starts going through the drawers. "Hey, check this out," he says.

189

I roll out of bed and come up behind him. He hands me a few pictures. The first one is Grace playing one-on-one basketball with Tobias, trying to shoot over his tall frame. I laugh nervously. "I like basketball, huh?"

"Guess so," Noah says.

The next picture is of Alter-Noah kissing Alter-Olive on the mouth. They look just like my Noah and Olive, except Alter-Noah's hair is a little longer, not buzzed to the scalp. "Guess you have a girlfriend," I say.

Noah snatches the picture away and stares at it. "Huh."

No way to tell if it's fake, or if the other Noah is really with the other Olive.

The next picture is all four Beta team members standing side-by-side, arms looped over one another's shoulders.

"So we're friends," Noah says. He hands me the picture.

"Looks like it."

"Good. We're smiling. That's a good thing." He chuckles and turns away, heading back to his bunk. "I was beginning to feel like a prisoner."

20

eter comes in next, followed by Olive. I'm giddy with how well everyone plays their parts, especially Olive, who sits on her bunk with a confused look I can't match. Her eyes keep darting between us.

Noah hangs an arm over the side of his bunk. "So what do we do now?"

Peter shrugs. "I don't know. What do we do every night?"

Noah points at the checkerboard on the table. "Somebody likes checkers. Anyone?"

"We could share our names?" I say. "I'm Miranda North."

Noah chuckles. "Noah East, how about that?"

Peter wrinkles his nose. "Peter West. Directions? That can't be a coincidence."

The boys look at Olive on the top bunk. "I'm . . . Olive South."

"Maybe they're codes," Peter says. "Maybe these aren't our real last names. Dr. Conlin told me this was a facility."

"Whatever," Noah says. "Too much for one day."

"Agreed. I'm going back to sleep," I say. Conlin mentioned there were a few hours left until dawn. "It's almost morning, and we have to do that experiment tomorrow." Referring to mass panic as an experiment makes my stomach sour. I take off my outer clothes so I'm just wearing my suit, or Conlin's *memory aid*. "Nice meeting you guys again, by the way."

"No one thinks there's something off about this?" Olive says. "That we just woke up in that tiny box room together?"

At first I think she's playing it up too much, but then I realize she's acting better than all of us. It's the small furrow between her eyebrows; it seems like she could burst into tears at any moment.

Noah raps his knuckles on his armor. "I would say yes, something is off. Look what I'm wearing."

Olive doesn't say anything. She just folds her legs under her on the bed and covers her face with both hands.

"You okay?" Peter says. "The doctor said we might get our memories back tomorrow."

She nods into her hands. "Yeah, I just need a minute."

"We should really sleep," I say.

She abruptly lies down and rolls away from us. For a moment, I think she's mad because I kissed Noah. But no, Olive is reasonable. She knew it was the only way to pass the vial.

"Right," Peter says. "Sleep." He takes his clothes off too, but doesn't mention the armor. I suppose we all got the same explanation.

Noah gives me a subtle look that seems to ask if Olive is okay, but I don't want to risk answering, so I pretend I don't see it. I get into my bunk and pull the covers around my neck.

Peter faces me on the lower bunk. For the next twenty minutes, I watch his open eyes in the dark. I allow a little of myself to show through when I look back at him—the real me, not the pretending-to-be-amnesic me. He does the same, but it's not enough. Noah snores on the top bunk. I can't hear Olive. The silence and waiting is killing me; I can't just lie here.

A few minutes later I pretend like I'm waking up. I set my feet down quietly, heel to toe, then pad to the bathroom. I tell myself it's to be alone, to get a drink, to stretch, but I know it's because Peter will follow me. It's a stupid risk, just to talk to him. But I need to.

Maybe he'll call me reckless. He might not comfort me at all. I shouldn't need him to, not if I'm as strong as them. I'm supposed to be.

Several toilets line the right wall. I enter the farthest stall, just before the showers. A few minutes pass. In the dim light, I can barely see the water in the toilet. It's so quiet I can hear my pulse. Until I turn around, and Peter is in the stall with me.

"What are you doing?" I whisper. "They probably saw you come in." Yet I came in here knowing he would follow me.

"I don't care," he says.

We stare at each other. I reach out through the dark and put my hand on his shoulder. "I'm scared, Peter. I'm scared we won't be able to stop them."

He doesn't offer words of encouragement. Instead, he pulls me to him. I lay my head on his chest and wrap my arms around him, and he rests his chin on top of my head. He holds me like that for a while.

"What if we fail?" I say.

"We won't." His voice vibrates in his chest. I lean away so I can look at his face, but his arms are still tight around me, pressing our lower halves together.

Tonight could be the last moment I have to talk to him. To be alone with him. Who knows how tomorrow will go, or if we'll all make it out in one piece. We don't even know who our true enemy is.

"Miranda," he says, but I kiss him before he can finish the last syllable. His mouth opens to my kiss, and what I said about him kissing soft doesn't apply now. He buries one hand in my hair to pull me closer, the other pressing against my lower back. I wrap my arms around his neck. I pull away for a second to draw breath but then his mouth is back on mine. His fingers find the seam in my suit; it cracks open along my spine. He tears his lips away and kisses along my jaw, to the soft spot under my chin. Down my throat. He peels part of the suit back, exposing my left collarbone, which he kisses to my shoulder. Every square inch of me is on fire, like I swallowed a coal and it's burning low in my stomach. Peter comes back to my lips and kisses me softly this time, lingering.

A wave of guilt crashes through me, almost physical, and I take a step back. Guilt because of Noah. Which is absurd. We kissed in the river out of necessity. That doesn't mean I'm beholden to him.

Peter holds my gaze. "You still love him."

"No," I whisper.

"Yes, you do. I can see it."

"No, Peter. How could I? I can't even forgive him."

"Yes, you can. I see it happening right now."

I put my hands on his shoulders, let them trail up to cup both sides of his neck. "Peter, I don't remember. Whatever we had is gone." Saying the words doesn't make it true, as I'd hoped. Not gone, but different. Is it different enough for Peter . . . or will it always be something that hangs between us?

He lets that sink in. "We'll see. Tycast said it was unlikely you could forget everything, no matter how long you went without a shot. Given enough time, the pieces of you that still love him might come back."

I want to deny it again, but I can't. Despite the anger I have for Noah, there is something inside me that clicks when I see him. Like looking at an old photograph and remembering the smells and sounds of it, even if the exact moment is fuzzy.

Maybe that's why Peter said no when I first asked him about my memories returning. Because he doesn't want me to remember how I felt about Noah. He said he didn't want to get my hopes up, but there could be more to it. Or most likely I'm overthinking again.

His pulse races under my palms. "Was there ever... between us, was there ever something?" I say.

He shakes his head. "Just for me. But you were always Noah's."

"I don't want to be."

He doesn't say anything.

I lean back into Peter and he puts his lips against my forehead. "Don't let this distract you," he says. "I need you ready tomorrow."

"I will be," I say.

"I shouldn't have come in here."

"No, Peter..."

"What?"

But I can't think of anything to say.

"We should sleep," he says.

"I know."

Then he's gone. The empty space around me still smells like him. I still feel his lips on my throat.

I sit down on the toilet and try to imagine the girl I was a few days ago.

Dr. Conlin wakes us a few hours later. I drifted in and out of sleep, lucid dreaming of Noah's lips under the water. Peter's hands roaming over my bare skin. Of a city on fire, burning, panicked, crumbling. Dying. Part of me feels ashamed that I'm allowing myself to be distracted. Memory loss or not, I know I was trained better than that.

Conlin has us sit at the table while we blink sleep from our eyes. The others look awful, like they spent the night boxing rather than sleeping. Olive doesn't appear any different than Peter and Noah, maybe a little sadder.

I don't know how much longer I can act; it makes me itch, like worms under my skin. But we can't make a move until we're free of this building, and know the location of Beta team.

Conlin slips her glasses over her eyes. "Now, I want to do a little test before we get on with the experiment. It's likely this will bring back your memories, and I know you're excited about that, but we still need to focus."

I want to glare at her when she refers to the dry run as an

experiment, but I keep my face placid. Images of my night-mares resurface, a backdrop to Conlin's reserved posture and face. People run and scream and die behind her. The pieces of her test are moving into place as we speak, but we're stuck here, helpless. Waiting. I blink the images away.

"Some coffee would be nice," Noah says.

Conlin smiles politely at him. "Breakfast is on the way. But first, I want you to focus on the space behind your eyes, just behind them. Can you do that?"

I keep the alarm off my face, just barely; Conlin isn't wearing a headband or a helmet. Which means she's built up a tolerance to our fear, like Tycast seemed to have. Peter and Noah are carefully blank-faced. Olive wrinkles her brow in confusion.

"Focus on that area," Conlin says, "and imagine relaxing it. Then imagine it heating up, and expanding. Can you do that? Then let it expand further, into this room. You might get a headache but that's completely normal, I assure you."

I do it. The waves build. The familiar pain returns, then narrows, until it passes through my skull, expanding. The scent of roses is immediate. Conlin smiles tightly—it's clear she's uncomfortable. But apparently they have to be sure we can create fear before sending us into the open.

Olive presses her fingers to her temples. "What *is* that? It hurts."

"That's enough," Conlin says. "I'm sorry, you can stop now." She blinks a few times, licks her lips. "Very good. Okay. Feel free to wash up and eat, then we'll get on with the experiment."

"Uh, Doctor?" Noah says.

"Yes, Noah?"

"What the hell just happened? Why does it smell like... flowers?"

Conlin looks at a clipboard. "You have all been very patient. I understand this has been a troubling time for you. So please, just a bit more patience. Can you be patient for me?"

Conlin only has to keep us in line for today. After she demonstrates us to the buyers, she can lock us up until our tattoos are ready, at which point we'll be just like Beta team. Ready for delivery. Used for some other nefarious purpose.

Controlled.

"Sure thing, Doc," Noah says.

A big smile from her. "Good. The experiment will be just like that, but bigger. Think *big*. The more you push, the more you let flow, the better chance your memories have of returning. So when the time comes, let loose."

Think big, she says. *Let loose.*

Conlin leaves. We take turns using the two showers. After I towel off, I wait in the shower until Olive comes in.

"Oh, sorry," she says.

"It's okay." Then I mouth, *Are you okay?*

She freezes. Her mouth opens, but I put a finger to my lips. Olive shrugs.

And walks past me, into the showers.

I stand there for a full minute in my towel, wondering why she didn't give me a wink or a nod. Anything. Then I dress in a fresh black suit that does nothing to warm the chill on my skin. I'm not sure what I did to make her act so strangely, but there's nothing I can do about it right now.

I eat breakfast mostly in silence, not wanting to risk saying the wrong thing while under surveillance. As Olive showers, I try to let Peter know something is off about her, but I can't communicate it with just my eyes. And writing a note would be a red flag to anyone watching us on video. The tension in the air grows. I want to scream and drop the act. I still can't believe I went into the bathroom specifically to draw Peter in. We could be back in the cell, truly denied our memory shots this time.

And we still have no real plan to stop the "experiment" from happening. Because there's no way to be sure what we're walking into. They're using all of us, so our first goal should be to meet up. It's impossible to know how far they'll space us apart, because I don't know the true range of our fear.

So regrouping will be the tricky part. Once together, we'll find a way to track down Beta team.

Unless it's too late by then. The fear waves from Beta could overtake the city by the time we reassemble. The madness I remember Tycast mentioning, how the energy ultimately drives people insane . . . how long would it take?

I bite the inside of my already-raw cheek and taste blood on the side of my tongue. I grab a pencil and quickly scribble *Find a way to meet up* on a piece of paper. I tap it with my finger, and Noah sees it. Peter comes around and glances at it. Noah picks up the pencil and—

Conlin comes back. Her white coat is gone, replaced with more casual clothes. She smiles at us, making it as genuine as possible. "How do you feel?" she says, as I palm the paper off the table and crumple it into a ball.

How do we feel, she asks. Outside we're alabaster, but inside . . .

Peter says, "Fine."

"Great. Ready to get started?"

"I am," Noah says. The sadness in his eyes cuts through me.

We stand as one, and Conlin leads us from the room.

21

Conlin leads us down the hallway to an elevator. We pass the cell, but none of us looks inside. The elevator doors open into the parking garage. Two vans wait under fluorescent lights, rear doors open.

Conlin points to the left van. "Miranda and Noah in that one." She points to the right. "Peter and Olive in that one. Okay?"

I step into the van, waving good-bye to Peter and Olive, making myself a silent promise I will see them before the day is over.

Conlin shuts the doors and Noah smiles at me in the dim cargo area. "Hey, Mir."

"Hello, Noah."

That's all we say. The van starts and a driver we can't see pulls out of the building. Noah shuts his eyes, and after a while I do too, falling into a quiet place. It might be the last calm moment of my life.

Time passes. The van stops and I come back to reality, feeling like an armed bomb. I have no weapons, but I don't need them. Noah looks like he wants to say something, but he's in the same place I am.

"Whatever happens..." he says.

"Save it. Tell me later."

He frowns, but it turns into a grin, as I knew it would. The rear doors open and bright sunlight stings my eyes. We're somewhere in the city—buildings and people everywhere. Two men wearing casual clothes wave Noah out of the van. They shut the doors, leaving me in darkness. A second later we're heading toward wherever I'm supposed to go.

It isn't far. I try to imagine how they'll place us, but there's nothing to base it on. I fall into a light meditation once more, dissolving the heavy chains of worry and doubt.

The van stops again; same drill. Two men stand at the rear.

"C'mon out," one says. The men look friendly enough, nondescript. I step onto the roof of a parking garage in the middle of downtown Cleveland, a few feet from the railing. Buildings rise up around me, echoing traffic noise from the streets below.

Key Tower stands tall in the east. It's still morning, maybe nine o'clock.

"What are we doing here?" I say.

One sticks his hand out for me to shake. "Hey, I'm Bill. This is where Dr. Conlin wants you to perform the experiment. We're supposed to record the results, then take you home."

The man who is not Bill has a gun under his jacket; he does nothing to hide the bulge.

Bill says, "We're supposed to get back in the van so you have privacy." He checks his watch. "Are you ready?" he asks me.

"Yeah, are you?" I say, as I give off the smallest wave of fear I can. This one actually feels good.

The effect is immediate. Bill and the other guy stiffen, eyes widening. I kick Bill in the chest and he staggers back, arms flailing, hands grabbing at air. The railing catches him mid-thigh and he flips over. He hits the ground two seconds later, the same sound the bodies made in the mall. This time it isn't so awful; it's hard to feel anything but freedom. Finally, after hours of pretending to be helpless, I can act. It's like growing wings.

The other guy has been going for his gun, but the fear has slowed him too much for me to care. I grab the barrel as he raises it, then swing my right hand under his gun arm to uppercut his wrist. The small bones bend, then break, and he shrieks. I pull the gun away and toss it over my shoulder.

The man tries to punch me with his other hand but I deflect it and kick the inside of his knee. He topples over with a moan, clutching his leg with both hands.

I stand over him. "Where are the others?"

He spits on my boot. I kick him in the stomach, mostly to wipe the saliva off. "Where are they? I won't ask again."

I crouch next to him and rifle through his jacket. I find a folded-up piece of paper. It's a map of downtown, scribbled in various places—Peter, Noah, Grace, Tobias, Miranda, Olive, Joshua, Nicole. I'm guessing Joshua would be Noah's double, and Nicole would be Olive's. The names have arrows pointing to specific spots on the map. I look where I am, then see *Grace* written three blocks south and one block east. I shove the paper into my pocket.

The man cowers on his back. "Please don't kill me."

I'm about to reply when I catch the scent—roses. The nearest Rose is blocks away and yet the energy is strong enough to affect my sense of smell. The dry run has already begun. I leave the man on the roof and get behind the wheel of the van. I start it and peel down the ramp, rear doors banging together because I forgot to shut them. Doesn't matter; Grace is close. I burst onto the street and hang a left, tires squealing and horns honking in my wake. People stand still on the sidewalks, confused. I'm hoping they'll be spared the brunt of the fear, since I've created a gap in the little octagon of fear waves.

Faces rush by, just people, all these people trying to live their lives. Not knowing what's coming for their minds. I grip the steering wheel tighter.

A cop car blasts through the intersection ahead of me, followed by another. I slow, even though the light is green, then pass through it as the rose scent strengthens. I make a left, following the cops east. On the right corner is an empty, weedy lot with cracked pavement, and a peeling brick building much like the one near the pier, this one only three stories tall. It's full of broken windows, with a faded sign I can't even read. I pull into the lot's north side, shocks rocking on the uneven pavement.

Grace leans against the dirty brick. The intersection in front of her is empty except for two abandoned cars, the doors still open. The drivers must have fled on foot. Across the street a homeless man claws at the wall, his collection of aluminum cans spread around his feet from a burst bag. He can't figure out how to get around the building.

Grace waves at me. I mash the gas to the floor, knowing it's a stupid idea, but feeling the need to channel my rage into something physical. The van rockets forward, aimed right for Grace; she laughs and steps away from the wall. She grows in my windshield, dropping into a crouch. At the last possible instant, she jumps straight up, disappearing above the van as I ram the building's northeast corner and gouge out a chunk of half-crumbled brick. The van rocks sideways and I bang my head on the driver's-side window. The dislodged bricks shoot into the empty street, tumbling over the pavement. I hear a soft thump as Grace touches down on the van's roof.

I open the door and there she is. She grabs the front of my shirt and pulls me out—I'm too dizzy to stop her. The pull turns into a throw. I try to orient myself midair but land on my side and skid into the intersection.

It's possible I approached this the wrong way.

Pain lancing through my limbs, my attempt at standing ends with me hunched over, hands on my knees. Blood pounds in my head; if I have a concussion because of my own stupidity . . .

Farther east, dozens of cars are smashed together, a crowd of people surging down the street, screaming. So many people terrified of something they can't see. I'll never know what it's like to be in that grip, to feel what they're feeling. But I can't help them yet, because my fight is *here*, with Grace. I can only hope they get free safely, before the fear drives them mad.

Grace stands easy, hands loose, waiting for me. Even with the city screaming for attention, it chills me to look into her face, *my* face. "I told Dr. Conlin you were probably faking. I said we couldn't be sure when you last had shots. How did you do it?"

I ignore her, pulling my shirt over my head, revealing my black scaled armor. I don't need to hide under my clothes any longer, and I don't want to give her something she can grab on to. The little scales glimmer in the sun. I unbutton my pants and let them fall to the ground. Down the street, north of me, two ambulances scream past. One of them clips a telephone pole and goes up on two wheels. A helicopter chops by overhead and leaves us in relative silence again.

"Not gonna tell me?" Grace says.

"Noah," I say, kicking aside my boots and pants. "He had vials in his mouth. He must've gotten into the cache before you guys caught him."

The stretchy armor covers my feet, thin enough to feel the pavement rumble as something explodes in the distance. Behind me, a fireball rises into the sky and dissolves into black smoke.

"He's adorable," Grace says. "So much better than Joshua. I can see why you like him."

I wish I had a weapon. Anything. Just because she looks like me doesn't mean she isn't better, faster, stronger. She could be all those things. Fighting her could be suicide. Forgetting the gun on top of the parking garage is something I want to be able to laugh about one day.

Grace steps back, putting her shoulders against the van.

"I have to fight you now," I say.

She looks a little sad, like she doesn't have a choice. Which I guess she doesn't. "I know," she says.

I run toward her as she falls into a simple stance, feet spaced properly and hands up. Right before we collide, she reaches up and grabs the lip of the van's roof, curling her legs up and over, flipping into a crouch. I plant my foot on the van's side—running at full speed now—and leap vertically. I kick out while I'm still rising; she blocks my leg with both arms crossed in an X. My feet touch down on the roof, leg tingling from her block; the metal flexes, snaps, and pops under our feet.

On the street next to us, an empty police cruiser rolls by with the doors open. The lights flash but there is no siren.

I kick Grace again while the cruiser stops against a telephone pole. Grace catches my kick this time and holds on to my leg, then *lifts* me, swinging me off the van toward the building's second floor.

Not good. The second time she's thrown me in a minute, this time at a brick wall. I brace, eyes squeezed shut against the impending impact—

I hit one of the broken windows, crash through jagged pieces of glass. The suit protects my body, but the glass slices my face and neck. My shoulder hits the wood first and I skid across the dusty floor. I've been skidding a lot lately. I roll to my feet in time to get punched in the chest.

Which makes me stutter-step backward until my heels hit the bottom of a staircase. The whole place is dusty and dark, the few remaining windows too grimy to let in much light.

209

The broken windows sketch dim yellow patches on the floor, illuminating great clouds of dust motes, which swirl as we pass through them. Grace screams, tries to drop an elbow on my face, but I plant my foot on her chest to keep her away. I shove her back and flip onto my stomach, scrambling up the stairs.

The next floor is darker. Old desks line the wall with filing cabinets piled on top of them. I run. The cuts on my face are bleeding now, but it's a good pain, hot. Not crippling like blunt force trauma.

"You can't win!" she yells after me. "The city is already lost. Let us tattoo you and you won't even care!"

Oh, okay.

Up the final flight of stairs. Grace grabs my leg halfway and tries to pull me down. I kick free and crawl the rest of the way. The door at the top is padlocked, but the lock rusted last century.

I kick it. The lock and door snap at the same time. Bright sunlight floods the stairway, blinding me for an instant. Grace uses some part of her to hit me squarely on the spine. I go down on one knee, lunge upright, desperate to put space between us. I run for the eastern edge but she trips me. On my knees again, a few feet from the empty space above the street. Another kick; I go down. My hand claws for the edge, but even if I reach it I don't know what to do. Too high to jump without breaking something.

I roll over in time for her to land on me. Our faces are inches away and she's crushing the breath out of me. I try to bring my knee up, but she has me pinned.

My head is free, so I smash my forehead into her nose. It breaks. Blood flecks my face. She punches me in the mouth and my lips crush. Blood flows between my teeth and onto my tongue. But she's disoriented. I brace my foot against her, lift her above me, over me, behind me, with every ounce of strength I can muster. Her armored legs pass in front of the sun. I roll onto my stomach, see her flail in open space three stories up. She arcs over the street in a smooth descent. Comes down hard on her side. Her head bounces. She doesn't move, doesn't twitch.

Slowly, I get my feet under me.

I stand on the lip, hands on my hips, heaving, a little shocked I've thrown two people off roofs in the last ten minutes. In the distance, two fighter jets scream low over Lake Erie and pull up into the clouds. Closer, south of my position, a fire truck lies on its side in the street, half on fire. The irony would make me laugh if I could.

The streets near me are empty; the citizens have fled. If I look east, deeper into downtown, I see people running. Nearby sirens cloak most of the screams. The people seem to be massing, funneling into one giant, insane snake that slithers through the streets.

I picture the map in my head—Peter is east. But Noah and Joshua are so close, just to the south.

Grace hasn't moved, and I've wasted enough time. I spit out a mouthful of blood and drag my hand over my throbbing lips. As the adrenaline ebbs, my body decides now is a good time to turn into a giant bruise. To stay loose, I run down the stairs to the van, which I allow myself to lean against while I decide which direction to head. It's a question of who needs my help the most. Some of my hair sticks to my bloodied face, so I gather it up and tie it into a quick ponytail. South, I'll go south.

"Miranda."

I turn around. Noah stands there, grinning. His outer clothes are gone too, just his black scaled armor shining in the sun. Relief floods through my veins, cooling my blood. Since our reintroduction, I've never been so happy to see him.

"Noah," I say, moving to him. He wraps his arms around me and squeezes. I squeeze back, letting him take some of my weight. "It's awful, Noah. How do we stop it?"

"Where's Grace? I saw her on the map."

"She's dead." I kept my vow to kill her before this was over. If only it made me feel better. I'll never know how much of Grace was the tattoo, and how much was her. During the fight I didn't even think to try to damage the circuitry in her neck. Maybe I could've freed her, turned her to our side. Even as I think it, I know second-guessing my actions will only hurt me right now. She came at me so hard, so fast, there was no opening to destroy the tattoo anyway. Not to mention I'm weaponless.

I smell something that hasn't gone away since this began, but the scent of roses is stronger around Noah.

And growing.

Noah doesn't say anything. One of his arms is moving. I try to pull back but he has me tight. "Noah," I say. He's fast. I try to jerk out of his arms but he already has the knife in his hand. I see a flash of silver as it goes around my side—

The knife plunges into my back.

White pain shoots to the top of my skull, worse than anything I've felt so far, and I cry out. He releases me and I stagger back a few steps. I reach around and feel the knife handle. It didn't go in all the way; the armor only parted so much. My fingers come back with blood.

"Joshua," I hiss, remembering the map, his name scribbled on it.

He smiles at me, a wolf with bared teeth. "Is she really dead? *You stupid bitch. Is she really dead?*"

My weak knees threaten to fold. My legs are shaking, liquid. I feel the knife inside me, my blood beating around the blade. But it's not deep. It's not too deep.

"Threw her off the roof," I say. "Around the corner. Go check." My voice is weak. The others need me. I have to keep

213

it together. The armor should act as a bandage, like when Peter cut the tracker from my ankle. Unless the knife wedged the material too far apart.

"You shouldn't have done that." Joshua's eyes blur with tears. "Grace knew you guys were faking. We didn't believe her."

I still have blood in my mouth from Grace's punch, so I spit it at his feet. A helicopter screams by overhead. While I stand here wondering if I'll see Peter and Noah and Olive one more time, Joshua continues to pour his energy into the city. I can feel the waves as they pass over me.

If stopping him is the last thing I do, well, there are worse ways to die.

Joshua pulls another knife from behind his back. "I'm sorry. I don't have a choice."

22

A figure stands behind Joshua.

Joshua raises the knife. "It was nice meeting you, Miranda."

The figure moves closer. I don't look directly at him, for fear of giving him away. But in the unfocused part of my vision, I see Noah, *my* Noah, press a finger to his lips.

I try to grab the knife out of my back, deciding to risk the increase in blood loss, but another bolt of pain freezes me in place. My hand drops to my side. Blood trickles down my leg, inside my armor.

Without warning, Joshua spins 180 degrees in place, pivoting on the balls of his feet, dropping as his legs twist like a double helix, stabbing out with the knife. But Noah is ready.

He sidesteps the thrust and slips past before Joshua can reset. He grabs both sides of Joshua's head and twists. I don't look away.

The crack is muted by the blood pounding in my ears. Joshua falls in a heap, utterly limp, no attempt to catch himself. Dead before he hits the ground. I only feel pain.

Noah turns, panting. "Are you okay?"

I open my mouth and take a step forward. The ground rushes up at me, or I rush toward it. Probably the second one. Noah catches me and eases me down.

He gasps, and I can guess why. "Oh shit," he says. "Okay, wait."

"Not bad, right?"

"No. Not bad at all. I'm going to pull it out, okay?"

He doesn't wait for me to answer. He eases the knife out and I scream, cutting it off by burying my face against the smooth scales on his shoulder. The scream turns to a keen in the back of my throat. Pure black narrows my vision, until all I can see is Noah's face as he studies my wound. Gradually, the darkness recedes. I don't pass out.

"I got you," he says. "Look, see? The armor holds the wound together." Now that the knife's out, I feel the armor tighten up.

I sit with my back against a telephone pole, next to the van. Joshua is dead a few feet away. Two members of Beta team are left, plus Conlin and whoever her buyers are, assuming they're in the city to observe. It feels like an hour has passed since my fight with Grace, but it's only been a few minutes. Still, I'm wasting time with a flesh wound—Peter and Olive are out there, probably alone.

I need to get up. As long as I don't bleed to death, we can find them.

"Miranda?" Noah snaps his fingers in front of my face.

"Yeah, I'm fine." And I think I am. The pain is . . . receding?

He crouches next to me and cups the sides of my face. "The armor was breached, but it sealed again. It'll hold until I can stitch you up. Can you stand?"

"We have to move," I say.

"I know, I know. Try to stand."

I brace myself on his shoulder as he helps me up. Dizziness hits me, then fades. I feel strangely good.

Noah smiles. "There you go. The suit has painkillers lining the interior. If you're injured, it numbs the spot. Pretty cool, right?"

"Very," I say. My back is numb and tingly. While the pain is muted, I have to remember there's still a gash that will need attention. Noah stands close to me. I touch his cheek, and he reaches up to hold my hand against his face. "Thank you. You saved me."

"Nah, you totally had him." He stares at me an extra moment, cocks his head a little.

"What is it?" I say.

"Nothing, just. Your eyes look different. You feel okay?"

"I feel fine." I know what he means, but I don't have time to worry about it. Maybe they're just bloodshot, and he's not talking about the reddish tint to the irises. I can think about it when I know Peter and Olive are safe. And when the entire city isn't unraveling around us. Random screams carry on the wind, a vile reminder.

He leaves my grasp with reluctance and walks into the intersection. The jets are back, flying low over the lake. Their passage thrums the windows in the buildings.

He waves me forward, and I find the painkiller numbs me enough to walk without a limp. I join him and look down each street—abandoned vehicles are scattered everywhere. Some with their doors open, empty. Others with smashed front ends, people slumped over the wheels. Blood smeared on the inside of one windshield. A dog trapped in the backseat of another, sniffing at a crack in the window. A van on its side, flames licking at the undercarriage. A downed telephone pole diagonal across the road, live wires sparking and dancing over the street.

Noah points to the east. "Peter is that way, closer than Olive. Time to reunite and escape before they bring in the National Guard."

"But what about all these people?"

"I don't know, Mir."

Stragglers still gather down the street, between us and Peter. They push and smash together, rebounding off the edges of the main group, limbs flailing, only to run back into the shoving match. A man sits outside the river of people, holding his broken arm, shaking. Someone fires a gun three times and the screams rise up, drowning out the echoes of the gunshots.

"What if Peter is already somewhere else?" I say, my voice trailing off. It's hard to believe what I see.

"We'll take that chance. Come on." He runs down the street. I tear my eyes from the growing mass to make sure Grace and Joshua are still dead. They are. Then I run after him. I'd take the van, but I'm afraid to sit down again.

I stop after a few feet. "Noah!"

He stops and throws up his hands. "What?"

I run back to the van and grab the map with our locations on it. I didn't give it a very good look the first time. The crumpled paper is in the foot well, near the gas pedal. I open it to check our names again, then see something else, right in the middle of the map. A star with a circle around it, unlabeled. Noah is next to me, breathing hard.

"Show me your map," I say.

"I, uh." He's blushing.

"You uh what?"

"I forgot it. I only looked at it long enough to find you."

Stupid. But it means he came for me first. If he hadn't, I'd be dead.

I point at the star, memorizing the map while I do. "I think Conlin and her buyers are in the city to witness this firsthand. Right here. Closer than Peter."

Noah snatches the paper out of my hands. "That's Public Square." He folds the map and tucks it under the armor on his neck.

We take off again, and I pause just long enough to snatch up the two knives Joshua carried. I toss one at Noah and it sticks to the armor covering his right shoulder blade.

He reaches back, feels it, then smiles.

Together, we race through the nightmare.

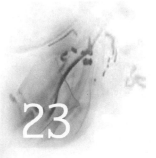

23

Public Square is pandemonium.

People run blindly, some in packs. The fear has taken them completely, and it's even worse up close. Howls surge up from low in their throats. Animal sounds. Animal faces. This is the madness Tycast talked about.

One man's face is a sheet of blood. A woman has retained enough motor function to spray mace into the crowd. People moan and claw at their faces, splitting away at random angles, tripping over bodies crushed in the street. The wind has died, and the day is hot and thick. Many of the refugees have fled south, either by car or on foot, taking the highways out of the city.

Noah and I walk against the tide. Pinned-open eyes stare back at me. I try to focus on the source of the wave, but sense nothing. The rose scent is in the air, but it's subtle and doesn't seem to be coming from anywhere in particular. It's possible these people were hit by waves elsewhere in the city, and are only escaping in this direction.

A man shivers on a park bench. His Windbreaker is open and he hugs himself inside the jacket. "Sir!" I say. He looks at me. "You can't stay here! Follow the others!"

He swallows and nods, then stands up and walks stiffly alongside everyone else. It's strange how the fear affects people differently. Some freeze, some run. Some scream. Some shake.

I see more bodies, first three, then six. Then ten more trampled in the street, limbs twisted and broken, clothing shredded, blood-streaked.

A little boy with his ankle twisted, crying on a manhole cover. I lose him in the tide, and when a gap appears, he's gone.

Before I can think about it, I drop to my knees next to an old man sprawled in front of a bus. He's barely moving, but his eyes are open. "Sir! We're going to get you help, just stay calm. Just—" Noah grabs me from behind and pulls me up. "Stop! What are you doing?" I struggle until my knife wound flares with a fresh burst of heat.

"We can't help him, Mir! The only thing we can do is stop this."

He's right, and I hate him for it. I let him pull me along, too weak to look at the old man again.

All this power, all my skills, and I can't stop the city from tearing itself apart. Another ambulance is wrecked farther up the road. All four tires are on fire. In the Terminal Tower people press their faces against the glass, watching the madness below. They seem unaffected, as if the waves don't reach higher than the first floor, or the building shields them in some way. It must seem like the world is ending. The glass doors at the bottom are barricaded with furniture from inside the mall. No one is bothering to break in.

Noah grabs my arm and I almost lash out on reflex. "What is it?" I say. He yanks me down behind a pickup truck parked halfway into the street. Someone runs past at a light jog, breathing heavily. "What did you see?"

"Look over the truck. If north is noon, they're at ten o'clock."

I shift around to get my feet under me, then slowly rise until my eyes are just above the truck's hood. Three people stand in a small parking lot across the street, maybe two hundred feet away. Calm postures, unafraid. Two men wear the familiar metal helmets, while the black-haired woman wears a headband. Dr. Conlin. The two soldiers hold video cameras, filming the action, like they're creating some kind of twisted infomercial. Their body language says they haven't seen us.

"What do you want to do?" Noah says.

"Fight them."

"Yes, I guessed that much. I was wondering *how* you wanted to do that."

"Fists or knives, pick one." I duck behind the truck's grille, locking Conlin's location in my mind. My feet itch with the urge to keep moving. My hands itch with the urge to fight back.

Another mass of people staggers down the road. We sprint across the street before they pass us, using them as cover. I leap over two bloodied bodies. Then we're against the Tower and there's only a short distance, a line of shrubs, and a fence between us and our enemies. Our feet are silent as we run. No one in the crowd bothers to look at us. At the last possible second, I plant my left foot against the wall and spring off. My toes skim over the bushes and fence. I touch down in the parking lot and roll, silent except for the muted *ting* my knife makes on the blacktop.

I feel Noah behind me. The soldiers are right in front of us, Dr. Conlin just ahead of them, watching the mania wind down as the city empties itself. An explosion rumbles very far away. I veer left and grab the nearest soldier's helmet, then flip it off his face. In the span of a second, pressure builds and releases behind my eyes. He sucks in a breath and makes a gurgling, terror-choked sound in his throat, dropping the camera and his weapon. Noah does the same thing with soldier two. I pick up the fallen gun, a stripped-down G36C—a compact assault rifle that feels familiar in my hands. I've trained with one, although I'm not sure when. This is when I would normally glare at Noah since he's the reason I can't remember, but he did just save my life.

Dr. Conlin turns around. We point our rifles at her chest. Behind her, a man wearing only a necktie runs past, limping.

"Making a sales video, Dr. Conlin?" I say.

"Precisely that, Miranda." She looks down at her panicking men. I expected robots behind the smoked visors, but they're just men, same as the ones who drove me downtown. "Although I see you've taken out my camera crew."

"Where are the buyers?" Noah says.

She sneers at him, which I give her credit for considering the firepower she faces. "Not here, you idiot. They can see your function just fine." She gestures at the nearly empty street behind her. "The whole world can."

A quiet has descended over the city, pierced only by an occasional shout, the background noise of multiple helicopters, and the dull roar of jet engines from miles away.

"You all performed as expected," Conlin says.

"Grace and Joshua are dead," I say, more to hurt her than anything. If she was anything to them like Tycast was to us, it'll break her.

And it does. Her brow scrunches for an instant before smoothing again. Her mouth becomes very tight. "I see."

"You don't," Noah says. "Not yet."

"Why are you doing this?" I say. I shift to my left, opening my field of vision behind Conlin. One of the soldiers stands up. I ram my rifle butt into his face and he falls down again.

Conlin says, "If you don't know, you have much bigger problems."

"Yeah," I say. "To sell us. I get it. But why? Why go to the trouble? There are easier ways to make money."

"Only a cynical person would think all of this was for money. Your ultimate purpose was unimportant to me. Creating you, the perfect weapon, was the real draw. There is no higher calling for a scientist than to see the limits of potential, then break them completely."

"Holy shit," Noah says. "A real mad scientist."

I take a step closer. A slow smile spreads across Conlin's face. The street behind her is completely empty now. "I don't buy it," I say. "We aren't just experiments."

"No, you aren't."

"Then what are we?" *Only a cynical person would think all of this was for money.* There's more to us, I know it. "Tell me!" I shout.

"No one is going to buy you, Miranda."

"But Tycast . . ." Tycast thought that was the plan all along; it's what he fought against, why he died.

"If Tycast knew your true purpose, he would've run screaming into the night."

Our true purpose.

Dr. Conlin reaches into her coat pocket.

"Take your hand out of your pocket!" My finger is on the trigger.

"Good luck, to both of you." Conlin pulls her hand free, but I don't shoot because at first I think it's empty.

It isn't.

She puts something in her mouth and bites down.

"No!" Noah screams.

Conlin falls, white foam bubbling from her lips. I kneel next to her while Noah covers me. I open her mouth but the poison is already working, sending her into convulsions. They don't last long. Her eyes are open, staring.

I look up at Noah with no clue how to proceed. Her last words were too vague, offering just enough of a hint to drive me completely insane. If there's something worse than being forced to terrify and kill on command, I don't know what it is.

Peter and Olive—plus the remaining two Betas—could be anywhere by now. We're losing. Or we've already lost. The damage is done, and irreversible.

I blink Noah into focus, tears of frustration clouding my vision.

Two figures stand behind him, silhouettes in the sun.

"Noah!" I shout.

Noah spins, but the first one grabs his rifle and removes it with a simple twist. Noah lunges for it. The man elbows Noah in the chest so hard his feet leave the ground. He crashes onto his back next to me, breath exploding from him. He rolls to the side, clutching his chest, gasping.

I'm coiled on the ground, ready to leap, but staring down a gun barrel keeps me still. The man holding it is really just a boy. He has white-blond hair somewhere in between Noah's shaved look and Peter's long-and-scruffy. On his belt are a sword and a silver revolver.

His suit is unmistakable—black scales, skintight. The unfamiliar Rose grins at me. "You gonna come at me or not?"

I give a small shake of my head. Noah sits up, holding his chest.

"Good," the boy says. He tosses the rifle back to Noah.

Noah contemplates the rifle in his lap, then looks up at the stranger.

Only now do I take in the figure behind the blond stranger. Black suit, black hair—it's Olive! Seeing her sends a flood of warmth spreading out to my toes and fingertips.

"Olive, are you okay?" Noah says.

She nods. "As well as I can be, I guess." Her face is stone.

The stranger claps his hands and rubs them together, tearing my attention from Olive. "Now then. There is a pressing issue."

Noah scratches his head. His cheeks are red, like he's embarrassed this guy just put him on his ass. "I'm sorry, who are you again?"

The stranger grins. "Right, sorry. I'm Rhys." He hooks a thumb over his shoulder. "You know her, I'm sure."

Rhys. The rogue. Here in front of us.

And we're not dead, even though he had the drop on us. He returned Noah's rifle. I watch Noah to see how he reacts, but he seems to draw the same conclusion.

Which means my attention can return to Olive, who appears lost, like she doesn't know where to stand, or what to say. "Hey, Olive, are you sure you're okay?" I say. For some reason I can't bring myself to say, *Do you remember me?* I finally stand up and give Noah a hand. I check behind me to make sure no fear-crazed citizen is about to jump us, then step over Conlin. A step closer to the rogue.

"I'm fine," Olive says. "I'd be better if I knew what the hell was going on." She doesn't say it like a comment on the situation's insanity. She says it like she truly doesn't understand. A cold spike twists in my gut.

"Noah," I say, reaching out to grab his arm.

"I got it," he says. He raises his voice. "Olive, why did we leave home without telling Peter?"

Olive stares at Noah for a moment, brow wrinkled. Rhys nods at her, as if granting permission to answer. The wind cuts over the small parking lot, whipping her hair around her face.

"I don't know what you're talking about," she says.

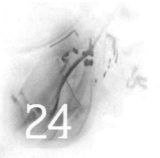

24

Her words hang in the air. I know what it feels like to say them.

Noah gave her the vial. It should've been enough. Maybe too much time elapsed, since she was the last to see Conlin; maybe her metabolism burns hotter; maybe using her fear to guide us in the forest was too taxing.

"She was the last one Conlin saw," Noah says softly, barely shaking his head. "She was the last one to get a real shot."

"But how long were we asleep for?" I say. "How long did she go between shots?"

"I don't know. I don't know. It was close. Sometimes..."

"Sometimes *what*?"

His lower lip trembles, and for a second I think he might

cry. But he just presses his lips together. "Sometimes Tycast gave her a little extra. Her body temp was higher, he said."

My stomach flips and I think I'm going to throw up. When I thought she was doing a superb acting job . . . she wasn't. She truly had no clue. And I knew it, too, deep down, but I told myself it was the stress that made her different.

I remember the look in her eyes when she confessed her love for Noah. . . .

All of that gone now. She doesn't know us. She's in the same place I was. Or worse, because I had Peter to guide me.

It's not fair. That's all I feel—this pervading sense of injustice. For her, for all of us.

Then again, what if it's another trick?

It could be Nicole, Beta team's version of Olive. Instantly I harden. It's so much easier than actually feeling something.

I keep my finger tight on the trigger, and the rifle tight against my side, not quite raised, but not lowered either.

"You gave her the vial, right?" I ask Noah.

"I watched her take it," he says. His gun points at the ground. Sloppy.

In a blur, Rhys pulls the long revolver off his waist. I prepare to fire, to squeeze just another fraction, but his gun points between me and Noah. He fires a single shot. Behind me, a helmeted soldier falls on his face in the street.

My trigger finger relaxes a millimeter.

"A little warning next time?" I say. I don't mention how I almost shot him.

"Sorry, go on," Rhys says.

"Who *are* you?" I say. Part of me wants to kill him, just for being the reason Noah wanted to "protect" me in the first place. But if he hasn't killed us yet, maybe he can help.

"That's a bit complicated. For now, trust that I'm a friend. Otherwise, you'd be dead already, right?"

It's true. But I can't rule out some larger game just yet. No way to tell if this is the rogue, or some other version. The speed with which he drew his gun leaves no doubt he's faster than me *and* Noah.

"Where did you find her?" I say, picturing the map in my head.

"In the care of two of those guard types on the south side. She was using her fear waves until I stopped her." Rhys slips the gun back into his belt. His left hand rests on the hilt of his sword.

Of course. Olive wouldn't know what she was doing. She would just follow instructions, thinking it was a real experiment.

Noah's eyes are wet with tears—now both of us don't remember him. Unless enough phantoms of Olive's love remain inside her, like they do for me. The thought makes me dizzy and sick all over again.

And yet, Rhys could still be lying. He could've known where Olive was, where the other version of her was too. There's no way to be sure, except to let my guard down....

I lower my weapon all the way. Rhys and Olive don't make a move, which isn't conclusive, but it'll do for now.

"Listen," Rhys says. "While I'd love to introduce myself properly, I'm afraid one of your friends is in danger. Peter."

"Where is he?" I say. The dizziness evaporates.

Rhys tilts his head to the right, south. "He's being chased by Nicole and Tobias as we speak. Saw them enter the baseball stadium. I came here to gather you, seeing as you were on the—"

I don't hear the rest because I'm already running. South of Public Square is the arena and stadium, then the highway. I sprint down the empty street, dodging bodies in the road. Some of them are clumped, as if they fell together. Wait—by the freeway ramp a quarter mile ahead, I see a few survivors standing together calmly enough. With Tobias and Nicole pursuing Peter, I guess the waves have finally abated. Now I just have to keep it that way.

To my right, Noah keeps pace. We move onto the sidewalk and round a corner that brings the stadium into view. We're at the fence a few seconds later. I leap onto it and pull myself up, then jump off the top and land on my feet. We're at the left field entrance of the stands. A quick jog to the railing reveals the entire field, and the timing couldn't be worse. All I can think about is how if Rhys had told me about Peter a minute earlier, I might've been able to help.

Peter stands alone on the pitcher's mound, holding a staff in both hands. In front of him, closer to second base, is Tobias. Behind Peter is Nicole, the girl Olive fought in the forest. They move in like closing jaws, as Peter raises the staff. He spins and twirls and whips the staff back and forth, but he's outnumbered. They have four striking points total, while he works with two. Nicole snaps her staff behind Peter's knee, buckling it to the dirt. Peter barely blocks a downward strike aimed for his head.

"*Peter!*" I scream. All three look. Peter uses the distraction to shove his staff point into Tobias's neck. Nicole strikes him between the shoulder blades.

The staff slips from Peter's grasp.

I run down the aisle, preparing to leap from the stands to the field. Noah is right beside me. Then the familiar background buzz of a helicopter grows louder as one crests the stadium wall behind right field. The black helicopter swoops low over the grass and rotates, showing us its side. In the open door a soldier sits behind a minigun. I see the orange flash and throw myself against the barricade at the bottom of the stands. Behind me, chairs splinter and snap into shards, filling the air with hot powdered plastic. Noah lands hard next to me, hands covering his face.

"Are you okay?" I shout. The minigun is deafening, filling up the stadium with its terrible whine.

"I'm fine! Can you see Peter?" Noah shouts back.

The stream of bullets sweeps across the stands, away from me, and I'm safe to peek for a moment. The helicopter touches down on first base. Peter slumps between Tobias and Nicole, who hold him upright and carry him toward the waiting helo. His feet drag on the dirt. My ears ring. I stand up and scream with all the air in my lungs. Tobias turns around like he can hear me, but it's impossible over the roar of the helicopter. I see the white of his smile. Then everyone is inside, and the helicopter takes off, rising across the stadium and out of sight.

Now the stadium is eerily quiet, just the muted drone of sirens far away. I stare at the pitcher's mound, the grooves Peter's feet made in the dirt.

Noah's hand on my shoulder startles me. "We'll get him back," he says.

"Now, *that* is unfortunate," a voice says behind me.

I turn and stalk toward Rhys, who looks somber even though his tone is all snark. I try to punch him but he deflects with the edge of his forearm, puts his other hand on my throat and shoves me backward. Noah catches me before I can fall on my butt. He helps me upright.

"That was rude," Rhys says. Olive hops the fence behind him and walks toward us.

Noah moves like he's going to attack, but I grab his arm, if only to save him the embarrassment. It's sweet he wants to protect my honor, but Rhys has us outmatched. And besides, he's not our enemy.

I keep my voice steady. "Why didn't you tell us right away? We could've made it before the helicopter."

"Or got caught on the field, mowed down by the large machine gun. Either way, I'm glad they took him."

"Why?" Noah says.

Rhys smiles, and I want to punch it right off his face. "Because I know where he's going. And now we share a goal."

25

"What goal?" I say.

Rhys begins climbing the fence. "The end of the creators and their work. If you want your Peter back, you'll help me destroy them. I'll tell you more when we're less exposed."

I remind myself he's the rogue. Not to be trusted. He had no way of knowing they would capture Peter, not kill him. It makes sense for them to keep Peter alive, but Rhys couldn't be *sure*. "Why should we trust you?" I say.

Rhys heaves himself over the side and lands in a crouch, where he stays, scanning the empty street. "Because you need me, and I need you."

"That's not good enough. Where did you come from?"

He turns around, putting his back to the street. "I'm from the original Alpha team. I said hold the questions, all right?"

The original Alpha team. I turn the phrase over in my head. So he's a Rose, but not a copy of anyone from the Alpha and Beta I know. Not sure what that makes him, besides a rogue.

"Excuse me," Olive says, hands on her hips. "I'm done following you guys until someone tells me what the hell is going on."

No one speaks.

"Really? That's great. Because first I wake up in a plastic cube with three people I don't know, and then this guy"—she points at Rhys—"is telling me we're all super soldiers with the ability to inflict psychic fear on others."

"That's pretty much it, yeah," Noah says.

Olive raises her eyebrows. "So, what, you're a fellow psychic soldier?"

Noah shrugs, but his face doesn't match the gesture. "You could say that. And now the people who raised us want to enslave us, and . . . we're not sure what they want to do."

Two gunshots echo off buildings in the distance. Rhys shakes his head and begins to walk away. "Fine, stay in the street, wait till they come scoop you up with a helicopter too."

"We follow him?" Noah asks me. To Olive he says, "Will you stay with us? I can explain more, but please don't go."

Olive swallows, nods. "I'll hold you to that."

We take off at a light jog through the empty streets, passing a few stragglers too disoriented to get into much trouble. We check nearly every body for a pulse, but there are fewer and fewer the farther we move away, and some are so trampled it's obvious they're dead.

We pass burning cars and empty storefronts. Glass scattered over the street. The scent of roses is gone, but who knows how long it will be until people return. I wonder what they felt, what they saw. What terrors their mind showed them.

We run the entire distance, but not fast enough to blur the death and ruin.

Rhys has a luxury apartment on the Cuyahoga River, which curls around the west side of Cleveland. The building is tall and made of blue glass. I'm breathing hard by the time we get there.

"How can you afford to live here?" I say as we approach the massive glass doors. The bulk of downtown is to my right, empty and silent. Two black helicopters circle the city, the same kind that picked up Peter. I think it's a good idea to seek cover.

"It's amazing what you can rent with a down payment," Rhys says. His carefree attitude grates on me. He's obviously not blind to the destruction around us, and if this is his way of dealing with it, well, that says something about him. I'm too tired to figure out what, exactly.

He opens the door and holds it for us. I know none of us feels comfortable going inside, but there isn't much of a choice. We ride an elevator that looks over the flat, gray river. Rhys's condo is on the top floor. He ushers us into one big room with a vaulted ceiling. The far wall is made entirely of glass, providing a huge, wide view of the river and the city.

"Don't think I indulged," Rhys says. "I chose this apartment because it's the last place the creators would look."

He's probably right. My instincts would be to go to ground, not settle down in the open.

"Where's your medical kit?" Noah says to Rhys.

Rhys lifts one blond eyebrow. "You hurt?"

"Where is the kit?"

"Bathroom, below the sink. Just down the hall."

Noah takes my arm. I'm too weak to fight when he guides me into the bathroom and shuts the door. Everything is made of creamy marble. The lights are a little too bright.

"What are you doing?"

"Crack your suit, please," Noah says, bending down to pull out the kit.

Then I remember. The knife wound in my back. I turn away from him and pull at the suit, near the nape of my neck.

It splits open, and Noah is all business. His gently pushes the suit off my shoulders, and I cross my arms over my chest. I look at his face in the mirror as he studies my back.

"It's not too deep. Stitches will work, but you'll need a tetanus shot and some antibiotics to be safe."

"Whatever," I say. It's not his fault I'm hurt; I just want him to get it over with.

"Excuse me?"

I don't want to get into another argument. I don't want to see his hurt puppy dog eyes and hear his apologies. It should be Peter here stitching me up. It should be Peter scolding me, telling me I should've been more careful.

Yet, if Noah never changed my shots, this would make sense.

If, that night on the train, I had told Noah I didn't trust him. Told him to purge any crazy thoughts he had. Or made him tell me the truth before giving him vague authorization to alter my identity.

That's when I realize I never loved Noah at all. And he never loved me. He loved some other Miranda, whoever I was before. I'm sure that Miranda loved him, but I'm not her now. I'm someone else.

These echoes of my love for him, they don't truly belong to this new person I've become. Claiming them would be selfish, because Noah obviously still thinks of me as the Girl Before. Who knows how he'll feel when he realizes she's long gone.

I tell myself these things to make it easier, but it would help if I could completely believe them. Again I wonder if Olive shares this with me, if she's destined to fight with shadows of love. I have to keep her secret, assuming Noah has no clue. What good would it do if I told him, *Oh, by the way, Olive? She was in love with you. That's why she left with you in the first place. Thought you should know.*

"Miranda," he says.

"I didn't mean it like that. Please just stitch it."

He kneels down and I feel his fingertips on the small of my back. The sound of his rummaging in the case. The sharp prick of a needle. Again. And again. I bite my already-cracked, already-swollen lower lip. The rhythm of the needle scatters my thoughts, and I feel myself slipping into the past again. You'd think I would be used to this by now. . . .

I'm running in an autumn forest. The sky is cornflower blue, the trees aflame. Feet stir the leaves behind me—I'm being chased. A wide tree ahead has branches ten feet off the ground, bloodred leaves. I run straight for it, then push off the tree and leap, fingers grasping for a branch. Swing myself up. Set my feet. Leap to the next branch. Mechanical, yet graceful, that's how I have to think of it. See the next action in my mind, then make it a reality.

I kick my heel on the wood to shake free a cloud of leaves. Climb.

The wind buffets the tree, clacking the smaller branches together. Leaves catch in my hair, crackle in my ear. My pursuer is close. I hear his breath, the scrape of his boots on bark.

Then I see it.

The neighboring tree is orange and just as big. Its branches mingle with those of my tree. I run down the limb, feet gripping the rough bark easily, then jump to the orange tree. My left foot slips off the smoother bark, making a zipper sound. Without thinking, I hook my right arm over the branch to catch myself. Too slow. My fingernails drag on the bark, then on nothing.

I'm falling. Branches bite into me like teeth; they snag and tear my clothes. The red and orange leaves rush upward like a film reel. I hit the ground hard, touching down with my right heel first. A bone bends, then snaps. Pain lances from my ankle to the top of my head, then down my right arm. I lie in the scattered leaves, groaning, curled up on my left side. My ankle weighs a thousand pounds.

Behind me, I hear two boots land on the forest floor. A combination *thump* and *crackle* in the leaves. My pursuer, come to finish me off.

Peter kneels at my spine, places his wide hands on my right arm. He gently eases me onto my back. Leaves tickle the skin beneath my hairline. I look up into his ice-blue eyes, notice they're the same shade as the sky behind him. Wide with worry.

"Where does it hurt?" he says.

"Everywhere."

"Come on, Miranda."

"My ankle."

The dull pain is now fire, brighter than the trees around me. Peter fishes something from the pocket of his vest.

"Open up," he says.

I part my lips and he slips a pill between them. I swallow it. His hands roam down my leg tenderly, easing their pressure as he nears my ankle. He touches it with his fingertip. I moan. Squeeze my eyes shut. Hear a knife snap open. Fabric tears. Cool air on my exposed ankle. His warm fingers on the swollen skin. The pill is working now, dulling the pain.

"I have to carry you," he says.

I suck in a breath. "We're miles from home."

"It was my idea to come this far. Tycast is going to kill me for leaving the perimeter."

The pill works harder. I wiggle my back up the tree until I'm sitting. "I'm not letting you carry me. This was my fault."

Peter smiles at me while I talk.

"What?" I say.

"I don't think that pill is going to give you an option."

My mouth falls open. "What was it?"

But I know. I feel the tug on my eyes. My muscles relax. "Why are you so good to me, Peter?"

My head tilts back against the tree. My eyes are too heavy to keep open. I feel the vague sensation of his hands sliding under me, weightlessness as he lifts me up and settles me against his broad chest.

On the edge of sleep, I hear him whisper, "That's for me to know, and you to never find out."

I open my eyes, feel the prick of the needle. My ankle tingles.

The memory fades slowly, leaving me with an aching emptiness. It couldn't have come at a worse time—I don't want to think about how Peter is gone, I want to think about getting him back.

If Noah took notice of me checking out of reality, he doesn't say so.

"How were you able to get those vials," I say, the first question that pops into my head, "if they were waiting for you?"

I feel the skin tug as he pulls the stitches. "I found the crate easily enough. Opened it. Got a handful of vials. Then two hands grabbed my shoulders and pulled me back. Guys in scuba gear. I managed to elbow one, and there were bubbles everywhere, so I crammed the vials into my mouth. It just happened to be four."

Four. But it didn't matter for Olive, who was unlucky enough to go last in her one-on-one with Dr. Conlin. Makes me wonder how close the rest of us cut it.

He puts his hand on my shoulder and uses me to boost himself up. "All done."

"Thank you." I slide my arms through the suit, and Noah pushes the self-sealing seam together.

"It was a little different last time I had your shirt off."

"You had to say something, didn't you?" My cheeks and ears burn.

He grins. That same grin. I refuse to smile with Peter still out there, with the city shattered the way it is. "I guess so," he says.

I pat him on the chest once and leave the bathroom, feeling the stitches tug in my back. But they don't hinder my movement, and that's the important thing. The view hasn't changed at the floor-to-ceiling window. The sky is hazy with smoke from dozens of fires.

I turn away. The whole room is wide open—on the left side are leather couches and a TV, on the right a massive dinner table. Between those and farther back is an open kitchen with a marble island. You have to step down to get to the couches. I put my hand on a couch, not willing to sit down. Rhys is at the island, preparing some kind of meal. Noah sits Olive down on a couch and talks to her in quiet tones, probably telling her more about who we are, like Peter did for me.

I stare at Rhys until he looks up. "We're here now, safe. I think we deserve an explanation."

He sucks a bit of red sauce from his finger and wrings his hands together in a rag. "Right. What's your first question?" He leaves the island and walks over to me. His irises are reddish-brown, and I'm struck with the memory of looking in the mirror at Elena's house. How my eye color had brightened since the mall.

"Who are you?" I say.

"Already answered that. Said I was from Alpha team." He cocks his head to the side, looking directly into my eyes. "C'mere, let me see you." He grasps both sides of my face, gently, and I fight the urge to pull away.

His eyes narrow; one of his fingers twitches against my cheek.

"When did you use the machine?" he says, not kindly.

"What machine?"

"Don't play with me." He's still holding my face. All that easygoing nature has evaporated. "Your eyes have changed from green to red, or didn't you notice?"

"Let go of her," Noah says from the couch, injecting false calm into his voice.

"It's fine," I say.

Rhys turns me toward the big window, examining me in the better light. "Tell me," he says.

I speak slowly since he didn't understand the first time. "I have no idea what you're talking about."

Noah stands up. "You have five seconds."

Rhys looks at him, still holding my face. "Oh, does this bother you?"

"It does."

Me too, but I won't pull away. Something has him spooked and I want to know what.

Rhys faces me again, close enough to feel his breath on my cheek. He rubs his rough thumb over my chin. "Say *ah*." I open my mouth, and he says, "Interesting."

"What?" I say.

"You have exceptionally beautiful teeth." As Noah takes a step closer, Rhys says, "I could snap her neck, you know. One twist and she'd be gone."

"Enough," I say, refusing to let him scare me. Standing still as a statue in his grasp. "You know where Peter is. Tell me now."

"I believe you don't know why your eyes have changed. I can usually tell when someone is lying."

"That's progress," I say.

"You'll have an easier time with this, I think, because you've done it before."

"Done what?" I say.

"Had somebody else's memories transferred to your brain."

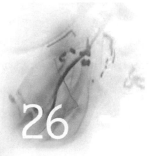

26

His words don't make sense right away. I sound it out in my head.

Sombody else's. Memories.

Transferred to. Your brain. Your *brain*.

"No," I say. I could say *I don't understand* or *What are you talking about?* but I can only manage No.

Noah is at my side. "Explain," he says.

Rhys holds up his hand, palm out, warding us off. "Hey, don't kill the messenger. I only said she's gone through the process before. I didn't say what it meant." The suspicion and malice I saw when he held my face is gone, for now.

"So say what it means," I demand.

"I don't *know*," Rhys says. He turns away and goes back to the island in his kitchen. "Who's hungry?"

"I'm talking to you."

He spins around and throws up his hands. "What should I say? Would you like me to make something up?"

"A theory would be nice."

His face is...careful. Like he's preparing to hold something back. "A theory. All right. I don't think you are who you think you are. How's that?"

"Then who am I?"

He raises his eyebrows, turns back to the kitchen. "Now that's a question."

I stand there for a moment with my eyes on the floor, thinking. Memories transplanted, memories lost.

What if I'm not the Miranda they grew up with?

She could be in a cage somewhere, hidden. Or dead in the ground. I could be a mole, planted in the group to sabotage them. Controlled by means other than the tattoo. But no, that doesn't make sense—if they wanted to use me against my Alpha team, they would have by now.

I grab on to that logic like a lifeline.

Olive and Noah wait in front of me, grim. Their faces blur as tears well in my eyes.

"You're you," Noah says. "I know you. I promise."

I nod. The sympathetic look on Olive's face makes me want

to cry more. She doesn't remember anything, but she feels bad for me. I don't deserve her pity.

I wipe my tears away as we walk toward the kitchen, forcing my voice to harden. "Is it possible I'm not Miranda North?"

Rhys licks his lips. "Anything is possible."

"Bullshit," Noah says. "She's Miranda."

"Noah, please," I say. "Let me talk to him."

Noah clenches his jaw and faces the big window.

Rhys raises an eyebrow at Noah. "As I was saying. Is it likely you're someone else? Who knows. I think the answers are coming, and I think you need to focus on what's in front of us for right now." He tries a tentative smile. "The mission of rescuing your friend and destroying the creators. And the food I'm preparing."

I'm speechless for a second, then the words come out low and cold, like ice. "I don't care about food. I need you to stop playing games. Peter is out there. The city is wrecked. And you're saying it's possible I'm not Miranda North, then making like it's no big deal."

Rhys lets five whole seconds pass. "Think logically. Maybe we can restore our strength, and then figure out the best way to recover your friend and bring the evildoers to justice. That should be acceptable."

Acceptable? No. But if he has the answers, we have to play by his rules.

He gives Noah a look and gesture like, *Is this girl for real?*

Noah gives him nothing in return, not even a glare. Rhys shrugs and returns to the kitchen.

We stand around the island while Rhys finishes the meal. He adds basil and crushed pepper to a pot of red sauce on the stove. A pot of pasta boils next to it. My body is hungry, but the sight of food makes me ill; I need to move, not eat.

Rhys says, "Sorry, I was in the middle of making lunch when I looked outside—and what did I see?—the whole city going to hell. And the faint scent of roses. Which is better than psychic energy that smells like a skunk, I suppose."

No one laughs.

"I've been hiding," he says. He dices mushrooms on a cutting board. "In plain sight you could say. When I first escaped the original Alpha base two years ago, I hid in vacant buildings. Would've stayed if they didn't look there first."

I glance at Noah, who *was* searching for Rhys. He nods once.

"Right, see? I've been keeping tabs on Alpha and Beta teams since I escaped. I've skills, no doubt, but I'll need help if I want to strike that fatal blow."

"Against *who*?" I say. "With Dr. Conlin dead, who is our enemy?"

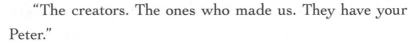

"The creators. The ones who made us. They have your Peter."

The ones we were cloned from. When I was falling off that building, I had a phantom memory of my creator, the woman handing me over to Phil. Not my mother, just an older version of me.

I notice Rhys is still armed with his revolver and sword, like he doesn't trust us enough to take them off. I don't blame him. But I don't trust his story either, not until all the holes are filled. For starters, shouldn't there be other versions of him running around? Why did the original Alpha have a Rhys, but my Alpha—and Beta—do not?

"Where is Peter?" I say again, leaning on the marble island. Noah rummages around in the fridge. It might be the last time I ask before I just leave to go find Peter myself.

Rhys lifts his chin to the window behind me. "You won't like it."

Outside the window is downtown. "What?"

"He's in the tallest building," Rhys says.

Key Tower is the tallest. It's a normal stone-colored sky-scraper until the top, where the point becomes silver-white.

"My old home, where I lived and trained . . . everything was in the silver cap." His voice is flat with old memories. I know the feeling.

The cap of the tower looks white in the sun, lots of sharp angles. It reminds me of some fantasy ice palace plopped down on top of a skyscraper. I can't tear my eyes away, wondering if Peter is behind its walls right now. Wondering if it holds the answer to the question that burns in my mind like a furnace.

Who am I?

We've barely had a moment to rest, but now, behind the safety of this glass, with the city emptied before me, I know what drives me. I want to know who I am. Not just who I was or what I've done, who I might become.

Who I am.

Is it so much to ask?

"It doesn't make sense," I say. "Why draw attention to themselves? Why not test us in a city they don't *work* in?"

"Attention?" Rhys says. "How will the government ever in a million years link what happens above the fifty-seventh floor to what happened here today? Eventually life will return to normal. There is no evidence." He pops a mushroom into his mouth. "Hiding in plain sight. Test complete. The Roses are a success."

He dishes up pasta for each of us, and we sit at his dark wood table next to the kitchen. I drink a glass of water, not realizing how thirsty I am until it touches my lips. Sitting down like this, eating a meal, it feels wrong. Peter is somewhere, alone, maybe hurt, and we're eating?

"You're impatient, I know," Rhys says. "But we move at

dark. I have a plan that will destroy the cap and rescue your friend."

"But will it stop them," Olive says. "Will it stop the people who . . . our creators."

Rhys frowns. "Maybe, if they're there. But it will cripple them, or at least reveal them to the world. And maybe that'll be enough for us to live out the rest of our lives without looking over our shoulders."

Through it all, through every moment, a phrase keeps looping in my mind—

Transplanted memories. Transplanted memories. Transplanted memories.

Rhys cleans his plate before any of us. "You wanted to know who I am," he says. He pulls his revolver from his belt and sets it on the table with a thunk.

"I do," I say. "But I'd like to know more about why our eyes are changing color. What you said about memories."

Rhys smiles. "Luckily, I can do both at the same time. But you might not like what you see. In fact, I guarantee it."

"I can handle it." At least I think I can. I try to remember the last time I slept. That short nap in the cell, then another nap in the Beta's room before coming downtown. My eyelids feel caked in cement. I check the clock on the stove—12:04. A few hours ago, nothing bad had happened yet. We were still together. The dead were still alive.

"All right, then," Rhys says, pushing away from the table. Noah visibly tenses at the movement, but I put my hand on his forearm and he relaxes. Rhys goes to a closet near the door and opens it. And pulls out a headband. Almost like the one Tycast and Conlin wore to negate our waves, but thicker, and stiff—it holds its circular form.

Rhys points at the nearest couch. "Lie down, please."

I'm confused, but I figure the answers are coming. I step lightly to the couch, wishing I could feel the plush carpet on my toes. I've had this suit on for so long, I'd give anything for cool air on my skin. I remain standing for some reason. Maybe instinct.

Rhys steps down into the couch area, holding the headband. The thick material is charcoal in color, but catches the light weirdly, shimmering at the edges. "Before, I said you've had memories implanted."

"Yes," I say.

He holds up the band. "This is how it happened, with one of these machines. The creators had a plan from day one to make more of us. The trick would be to take our experiences—those of Alpha and Beta team—and use them as a template to imprint on new versions of us. Ready-made experiences for the clones they could continue to grow. Copies of the same person, with the same memories. Basically an endless supply of . . . us."

"Exactly us," Olive says softly, standing up from the table.

The reality of that weighs on us for a moment. I try to imagine other copies of me running around, not just identical in body but in mind.

"I stole this from the Tower when I left, from the office of Mrs. North herself."

All traces of humor are gone from Rhys's eyes. Noah and Olive sit down on the other couch.

"What does that mean?" I say. "For me."

Rhys shrugs. "It could mean anything. It could mean they've already taken your memories to give to the next Miranda, or whatever they call you nowadays. I once knew a Peter, a Noah." He looks at Noah and Olive on the couch. "I knew Olive."

Back to me. "And you, Miranda. When I escaped, I copied my memories in the hopes I would meet people from the other teams. I would have to . . . explain myself, show them the truth. And seeing is believing. I could talk to you all day long, but you won't truly believe until you see it."

"See what?" I say.

"Why we have to stop them. Why we can't fail."

Olive says, "If the original Alpha team had our names, why does Beta team have different ones?"

Rhys shrugs again. "I suppose it got confusing to keep tabs on several beings with the same name. If we fail and they grow another team, say, Gamma team, I bet they'll have different names too." To me, he says, "You'll want to lie down for this. Really."

I settle onto the couch, waiting.

He hesitates.

"What?" I say.

"It won't feel good."

"I can take it." I hope I can take it.

He gently lifts my head, so unlike the last time he touched me, and eases the headband over my eyes, blocking Noah and Olive from sight. The metal band is icy at first, but then warms against my skin.

"Relax," Rhys's soothing voice says. "Relax, Miranda," he says, as a thousand knives pierce my skull.

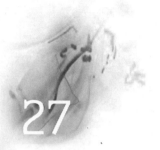

27

I open my eyes.

I'm sitting at a computer. The monitor displays a 3-D model of Cleveland. I tap a few keys and a pinkish-red cloud spreads within the city. At the bottom, it says ROSES NEEDED: 1. The number goes up as the cloud widens, until it envelopes the entire downtown area at 7.

Terror cuts through me like a sword. I cover my face with my hands, and only then do I see that the hands belong to Rhys.

I am Rhys.

I close my eyes. When I open them, I'm in a room just like the one back home, just like the Beta room, too. Bunks on either side, but an extra one on the left. Peter is there, and so is Noah on the bunk above him. And there's Miranda, across from Peter, fighting with a knot in her shoelace. It's *me*, only it's not. This is the original Alpha team....

But where are they now?

"You don't understand," I say. Rhys's voice sounds different coming out of my mouth.

Peter shakes his head. "What don't we understand, Rhys?"

"They're going to *use* us on the city. I saw a computer simulation. They want to test us on Cleveland."

Miranda laughs at him. "That's ridiculous. You know how insane that sounds, right?"

I nod. "Yes, yes I'm aware."

Olive jumps down from the top bunk. "They can't make us do anything we don't want to. Look at how strong we are already."

Noah jumps off his bunk too, then begins a stretching sequence for tonight's training mission. "I think you might be overreacting a bit," he says. "How do you know what you saw?"

Peter holds up his hands. "Guys, stop. If Rhys says he saw something, he saw something."

I throw up my hands. "Listen to me. Why do you think we're here? I mean, what is our *purpose*?"

Miranda stands up. "Rhys, indoor voice please."

"Don't tell me what to do," I say.

Miranda shrugs. "Fine. I'll get my mom, and she can tell you how crazy you are."

I stop her with a hand on her shoulder. She looks down at it, then up at me. Why is she acting like this? Good plan—let's tell her mom I've found something bad, when I'm saying her mom is the one behind it. Her bright green eyes hold mine steadily.

"Sit down, Miranda," I say.

Noah laughs from the floor, stretching over his extended leg. "Giving orders now?"

Peter is the only one taking me seriously. And maybe Olive, who is uncertain and quiet, as always. They're too trusting. They always have been. We've been living here for years, training, learning how to use this power we don't fully understand. I shouldn't have been in the server room, but it doesn't change what I saw. I still remember the headline—

PROJECT ROSE/
PROJECTED WAVE RELEASE PATTERN FOR CITY
Min: Four (4) Roses

Then, at the bottom—

Two roses can be used effectively in smaller cities. Recommend pairing with partner. Roses One and Three can be paired. Do not recommend pairing Three and Five. Do not recommend pairing two of the same clone. Roses Two and Four can be used in any configuration.

I make a final plea to my friends. "They gave us numbers. The program talked about what configuration we could be used in. It said 'projected wave release pattern for city.' You tell me what that means. It said we were *clones*."

Olive almost laughs. "Clones, huh? You lost me there."

Noah finally stands up, pulling his arm across his chest. "You swear to God you're not kidding?"

"Rhys's jokes are usually believable," Peter says.

I take a deep breath. "I swear. I saw it."

"Then let's look into it," Noah says. "You probably misunderstood, but let's look into it. Then when it turns out you're an idiot, you can clean the bathroom for the next six months."

"Deal," I say.

Noah glances over my shoulder, and I turn. Miranda's mom stands in the doorway, one sculpted eyebrow raised. She is beautiful like her daughter, not yet forty and only a few lines on her face to show for it. She's wearing a crisp gray business suit.

"Everyone out," Mrs. North says. "I'd like to speak with Rhys alone."

"I don't know, Mrs. North," Noah says.

Mrs. North rolls her eyes. "Really, Noah? Get your ass moving." They file out at once. I'm in trouble and they know it. I want to scream at them to stay. No one is grasping the severity of the situation, and it's my fault for not explaining it right.

We are going to be used to hurt innocent people. How's that for an explanation?

But I let them go. I will let Mrs. North explain herself, and then I will take my next course of action. We've lived in comfort for so long I don't blame them for being blind to the truth. If I hadn't seen it, I might not believe it either.

"Rhys," Mrs. North says. She points at the table. It has a half-played game of Monopoly spread over it. "Have a seat."

I sit down across from her, closer to the door and the weapon hidden in my bunk. Mrs. North is our martial arts instructor. She taught us how to use a staff, a sword, our fingers and feet. She folds her powerful, delicate hands on the table. Hands I've felt so many times, but never in kindness. Always on the mat, always when I was too slow and a strike slipped through, cuffing me on the head or neck.

Mrs. North sighs and moves one of the hotels on the board with her thumb. "I feel any explanation I give you will not be good enough."

I lick my lips.

She nods. "Yes, I see that. What were you looking for, Rhys?"

"Something has been off for as long as I can remember. Even my earliest memories are from this tower, all of us living together. And you never explained *why*. None of the parents did. The others . . . they know something isn't right, but they're afraid to see it. They don't want to see it."

"What were you looking for, Rhys?"

"The truth," I say.

She nods. "Did you find it?"

"Yes. You're raising us to be weapons. We can create fear from nothing, and I bet some people are willing to pay you for that power. You're . . . you've made copies of us." Saying the word makes me feel silly, but I say it anyway. *"Clones."*

My own father died years back, but the other parents stuck around to help raise us. Because we're special, they said. A family.

"You're wrong," Mrs. North says.

"No, I'm not."

"You are," she says. "We aren't cloning you. You are the clone."

"What? No."

"Yes. All of you. Miranda? Who do you think that is? Look at me." Mrs. North's green eyes are flecked with brown and gold. "Look at my face, Rhys. Who am I?"

"No . . ." I say.

"Yes. We made you. And we can do what we want with you." She lets that sit for a moment.

"What happens now?"

There is new tension in Mrs. North's shoulders. I've never been able to beat her one-on-one. Only recently have I been able to hold my own.

Mrs. North unbuttons the front of her business suit. "I'm going to put you in holding and keep your memory shots away. After a while you will forget this, and then I can place you back with the others. I'll have to do the same for them, too. Which is your fault, Rhys. *Your* fault. You go poking your nose where it doesn't belong, and stuff like this happens."

I think about going back to the way things were. Clueless. With the same outcome—our use as the ultimate weapon. I can't have it. I can't let them make me forget.

Mrs. North takes off her slender wristwatch. "Now. Will you come with me, or do I have to force you?"

Neither of us moves for a long beat. Mrs. North blinks. I spring out of my seat and lunge for my bunk. My revolver is there, under the pillow. We aren't supposed to keep the weapons in our room, but I do. I hear Mrs. North step onto the table and spring off; she'll be on me in the next second. I slide my hand under my pillow, feeling cool steel. My fingers close around it as Mrs. North hits me so hard in the back of the head my vision fuzzes black for a second. She wraps her arms around me and twists, throws me across the room. I land on my back, sliding, but she doesn't see I had already closed my hand on the gun. I aim it at her heart and pull the trigger. The gun bucks and a red hole opens in her chest. Another step before she falls to one knee. She covers the hole on her blouse with one hand, then falls.

I don't waste time. I roll off the floor and gather what items I have and throw them into a pack. I kneel over Mrs. North and check her pulse. Still beating. I missed her heart. I put the gun against her forehead and hold it there. But I can't do it. I don't know why. Because she was a mother to me all those years, alongside the others? Even if she was as brutal a mother as I can imagine, she still helped raise me. It was a lie, I know, but I can't. I can't pull the trigger. The gun leaves a pinkish ring of burned skin on her brow.

A guard kicks in the door with his rifle up and ready. I fire a shot between his eyes. He falls in the doorway, wedging it open.

I stand up, sparing Mrs. North a final glance.

Then I run.

More guards fall before me, faceless men who've been there my whole life but have never spoken a word. They die. In Mrs. North's office I find more ammunition and a strange metal headband. They go in my pack. I find a parachute stashed

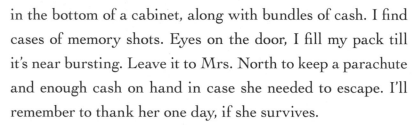

in the bottom of a cabinet, along with bundles of cash. I find cases of memory shots. Eyes on the door, I fill my pack till it's near bursting. Leave it to Mrs. North to keep a parachute and enough cash on hand in case she needed to escape. I'll remember to thank her one day, if she survives.

I close my eyes and open them.

Now I stand in front of a window overlooking the city and the lake. Gunfire erupts behind me. The window shatters and I jump through the falling shards, out into open air. The wind rushes through my hair...the violent tug as the parachute opens. The scent of roses.

I close my eyes.

You're Miranda. Not Rhys. Miranda. I am Miranda.

Miranda North.

But at the same time, I'm Rhys.

As my eyes open once more, I lose myself completely.

I'm in a forest. The Beta team base is nearby—I've seen the other versions of us training in the woods. They're almost as far along as us, maybe a year behind.

Dr. Tycast seems like a good enough guy. I wonder if I can warn Beta team without getting myself killed. But my Alpha team is a lost cause. They're in the woods, chasing me, blind to the truth. They think I've gone mad. My friends, turned against me because of a lie. They'll be used. Sold to kill. And there's not a thing I can say or do to convince them it's true.

"Rhyyyyyys!" Someone calls to me. They're closing in. I jump onto a low branch of the nearest tree and start climbing. It doesn't matter if they kill me. All that matters is what will happen to them after they do.

There is only one thing I can do to save them.

I wait in the branches for an hour. Maybe more. My breath stays shallow through force of will, muscles relaxed but ready. Then I see Peter crouched under the tree, unaware I'm directly above him. He scans some bushes across the path, calm as still water. Now is my chance. I slip off a branch as silently as I can and free-fall, pulling my revolver. I land behind him in a crouch, then rise up. Peter, who might have believed me. Peter, who was fair to everyone.

"Rhys," he says, without turning around. He raises his hands slowly.

I shoot him in the back of the head. The tall grass around me rustles as small animals flee the explosion. I'm running again. The forest thickens around me, branches snagging my suit. My passing sounds like an elephant trampling through the brush. I leap over a large bush into a clearing. The sky is purple, speckled with stars. Noah stands in the clearing with his sword out.

"Who did you shoot?" he says. He's breathing heavy.

"Peter."

"Why, Rhys? Why?"

"Because I won't let us be monsters. Mrs. North will make us forget everything."

"She won't. You have to trust her." Noah unslings a rifle from his back and holds it vertically, barrel down.

I point the revolver. "Don't."

"Are you crazy, Rhys? She told us you were crazy. That your body was rejecting the memory shots."

"Listen to yourself. *Memory shots*. Who are we, Noah? Why are we here?"

"You killed Peter." He lifts his rifle, but too slowly. Like he was giving me time, or afraid to shoot. I pull the trigger and a bright red hole opens on his forehead and he disappears into the tall grass.

Olive bursts from the tree line where she was hidden, sword raised. I spin, lose the gun when she chops it from my hand. She kicks, slim heel connecting with my Adam's apple. I fall into the grass, struggling for breath through my aching throat. She jumps on me, screaming, and raises the sword above her head. My own sword is jammed on my belt under her thigh, so I slam my knee into her butt, and she wobbles forward and rolls off me. Her sword point sticks in the dirt next to my head. I grab her leg and twist her over, pulling her close. One hand grips her throat and the other pins her sword arm to the ground. A quick pinch of her delicate wrist bones and the sword falls from her fingers.

"I'm sorry," I whisper, squeezing until the little capillaries in her eyes burst and she stops struggling. I squeeze some more. Until she's dead. I start crying. Big fat tears falling onto Olive's black suit. But my friends can't be used to hurt anyone now. No one will make them forget.

I slide off her, still crying, and find my gun in the tall grass by luck. I stand up and drag my forearm across my eyes. My breath hitches. When I open my eyes, Miranda stands at the edge of the tall grass. Her face is resigned, sad. I wish I could say something to make it okay.

"I love you," she says.

I start crying again, face pinched, cheeks aching. But I keep my gun on her, shaky though it is.

"Don't do this," she says. "I love you, Rhys. You're my brother."

Is she just saying that? Is this her cunning? Does it even matter? I can't trust her. She came with the others.

"Show me your hands, Miranda."

She holds them up, palm out, and steps into the clearing. I hear a helicopter in the distance, the faint rhythmic buzz of its blades.

"Don't come any closer," I say.

Because it's Miranda, she ignores me and moves closer. Soon she's right in front of me. My resolve crumbles as she pushes my gun away and wraps her arms around me. Her body trembles against mine.

She's afraid.

"Come back with me," she says. "Come home."

"I can't."

"I'm sorry, Rhys." She pulls the knife off her back and pushes away, slashing sideways at my throat. I block it with my forearm; the blade pierces my suit and flesh, clicks off the bone. Pure, hot pain. I put the gun against her breastbone and pull the trigger. She gasps. I pull the knife from my arm and catch her as she falls against me. I hold her upright and she stares into my eyes.

"I hope you're right," she whispers. "I don't believe you are, but I hope. I hope you . . ."

"I am," I say.

"Then kill them all." She rests her forehead against my chest and dies.

Now I'm truly alone, but it doesn't make me sad. There are no tears because they've been boiled away by rage. With shaking hands I lay her in the grass, next to the only family I've ever known.

They created us to be weapons, and I'm going to show them what happens when you don't use one responsibly.

I'm going to kill them all, like Miranda said to.

Slowly, I make my way out of the woods.

28

I open my eyes and burst into tears. Sobs rack my body. The sight of Rhys stirs something within me. I reach for him and he reaches for me. I bury my face in his shoulder and cry and cry and cry. And not because of the residual pain in my head, the throbbing needlepoints where the band touched my skin. It's because the horror he felt is now my own. I still feel the weight of the trigger, the spike in his heart with each one he killed. The loss dwarfs anything I've felt so far. That pain is the only reason I haven't run screaming from the apartment, why I haven't pushed him away in disgust. As impossible as it seems, I understand what he did, and why.

"Now you see," he says.

"You killed them," I say.

"Yes. I did."

"You would've killed us—"

"If you hadn't found out the truth on your own, or I couldn't show you in time..."

His memories stay with me, but the vividness fades until I can breathe normally again. Rhys holds me the whole time. I want to ask where Noah is, but I know he's not here. Otherwise he'd be beside me. Outside, noon has become afternoon. I check the stove—3:47. I spent hours in Rhys's memories, though it felt like minutes.

"Why are we different?" I say.

His breath tickles my ear when he talks. "Your team was the first one raised outside of our 'parents' influence. You came a year behind us, and the current Beta team a year behind you. Maybe it was the creators' influence that kept my team from seeing the truth, something you never had growing up." He pulls back. I want to hide my puffy wet face, but he puts a firm hand along my cheek.

"Your team never knew me," he says. "If there were other versions of me, I've never found them. Maybe I'm special. Or maybe they removed my clone from your memories."

He pauses, blond brows furrowing. "But that doesn't explain why you've used the memory band and the others haven't...." He shakes his head and sighs through his nose. "I just don't know. What I do know is the tattoo for the Betas came shortly after I left. It was only a matter of time before they controlled you, too."

I wipe my nose on my armored forearm, which works as well as you'd expect. "And then we wouldn't be here to fight."

"Exactly." He waits while I take a moment to pull myself together, sniffling and rubbing the tears off my cheeks. "Do you hate me?" he says.

The question startles me. "No." I swing my legs over the side of the couch. He stands up. "Where's Noah and Olive?" I say.

"I sent them to recover my cache of H9 and memory shots. I stole enough to last."

"H9," I say.

"The stuff we'll use to destroy their labs. You're already familiar with it."

The fires that consumed my home. Yes, I'm familiar.

He doesn't try to hide the pain in his eyes. Maybe he doesn't care if I see. I can't imagine what it's like to meet us, an almost exact copy of his team. The team he murdered, to save them from the fate of monsters. I can't wrap my head around it; there had to be another way. It only makes sense he would kill us, too, before letting us be captured.

"Where did you get the memory band?" I say, pushing the horrible thoughts aside.

"I stole it. You saw, in Mrs. North's office. Along with a

good supply of the memory serum. And some weapons and H9 from the Beta team armory. I've been watching you ever since, both teams, waiting to make my move, seeing who I could trust."

Trust. The concept sounds funny when it's reversed. The whole time my instincts have been screaming not to trust him, simply because I don't know him. I didn't stop to consider that maybe we have to earn his trust too. I want to fight this strange bond I feel toward him now. But I don't think I can do that any more than I can fight being me. I have a piece of him inside me. There is no going back, no way to erase the shared memory.

"Don't be alarmed," he says, "but the redness of your eyes has deepened. The machine works by..."

"How?"

"It pierces your skull with microscopic needles, I think, much too fine to see. Once it's jacked into your entire brain, it can recreate the memory as if it's actually happening. I'm guessing this includes the eyes."

The thought of needles in my eyes doesn't do much for my stomach. "And they built it to create more versions of us? To store our identities?"

"I don't know what else it would be used for."

Oh, I'm sure there's all manner of nefarious uses for it, ones we can't even think of. "Will you show this to the others?"

He shakes his head and sits down on the couch again. "No. I won't tell them, either. Not until this is finished."

"Just show them. You showed me."

"It's too painful the first time. Physically. Or it was for me. If we're going after Peter tonight, they need to be ready. And I don't want to distract them. They may not take it as well as you have."

"I'm taking it well?"

He shrugs. "You're still here."

I nod. It's suddenly awkward here on the couch, alone. Rhys's emotions for the other Miranda flood through me as I remember them. How much he cared for her, like a sister.

He must see this. "Don't worry," he says. "I know you're not the Miranda I knew. I know that."

"Okay," I say. Something occurs to me. "What's your name?"

"Rhys..."

"Your last name," I say.

His mouth grows tight. "My father's last name was Noble. The silly compass thing was from a training mission when we were kids. I guess your team did the same mission, the one where you each start in a different place on the map? I never got a direction. I'm just Rhys."

I don't remember the mission. "And Mrs. North?"

He almost smiles. "That's what the creators had us call them. Mrs. North, Mr. West. Guess they didn't trust us with real names. I only found out my dad's real name because he told me the night before he disappeared."

"What happened?"

"He was gone in the morning. Just gone. They told us he died. No other explanation."

The apartment door opens; Rhys has the revolver in his hand a half second later. Seeing the gun again makes me sick. I've never touched it, but I know exactly what it feels like.

It's only Noah and Olive, carrying enormous black duffel bags. Noah sees me and drops the bag on his way over.

"Are you okay?" he says, stopping at a distance. "I didn't want to leave you."

"It's fine," I say. "I'm fine." But I'm not.

"What did you see?" Noah asks.

I shake my head. "Later. We have to focus."

"Miranda—"

"I need you to trust me, Noah. Please."

He's about to say more when Rhys claps his hands and says, "That's more like it." He stands up and walks back to the kitchen table, where Olive is counting out bricks of H9. "I hope you're all comfortable with climbing."

We each take another memory shot and discuss what we hope to accomplish.

Rhys wants to burn the building to the ground, hoping that will get the creators off his back for good.

Olive pretty much wants the same, so nothing like this can ever happen to her again.

Noah wants Peter free, and more answers about where we came from and what we're designed for, since Dr. Conlin made it seem like we have uses that aren't yet apparent.

I want it all. I want to be free. But most of all I want Peter back where he belongs, with us. If I have to level a skyscraper and kill the creators to make that happen, so be it. Peter should be good through the night, but we agree they'll deprive him of shots to wipe him clean, reuse him. I pull Olive aside while Rhys and Noah argue over entry plans.

"How are you holding up?" I say. I grab a bottle of water from the refrigerator and take a sip.

She shrugs. "Fine, I guess. I remember snippets. I remember you. Noah seems familiar. What can I do but go with it, you know?"

I smile. "I know. That's how it was for me in the beginning."

"I guess it's not hard because I have nothing to compare it to. This seems . . . normal. But more is coming back. Maybe because I didn't go without a shot for too long, you know? I remember Dr. Tycast and I remember riding a black motorcycle with you on a winding road. Do you remember?"

"I do. That was a fun day." In truth, I don't remember, and I want to so bad it hurts.

She doesn't seem to believe me. "We'll do it again when this is over, yeah?"

"Deal."

I walk back to the table, where Noah is shaking his head.

"We'll be exhausted after the climb. There's no way we can break in, plant the charges, and get out undetected."

"You have another idea?" Rhys says, sitting back in his chair and folding his arms across his chest.

"Yeah. We go up from the inside, blast our way in. Use the stairs like sane individuals would."

Rhys shakes his head. "You don't know the security like I do. We climb up the side of the building or we don't go at all. We don't have to climb the *whole* way, Noah, just high enough. They'll obviously be watching the lobby."

Noah says, "Well I don't like being exposed on the side of a building like that, darkness or not."

Rhys shrugs. "There are other entrances, sure. All of them watched by cameras."

I sit down at the table. "And how do we get out?" I say.

"Parachutes," Rhys says. He might as well have added *Duh*.

Noah says, "How do you know they do the cloning there? They could have a separate facility."

"I *don't* know," Rhys says. "But the mothers and fathers are there. It's where they conduct research. And they might have more labs in the basement. I remember them going down there when I was a child."

He doesn't have to explain it—*mothers and fathers.*

Our "parents."

Olive says, "I like the idea of destroying what we can while searching for Peter, but maybe we don't stick around afterward and tempt fate. What does a wolf do? Cripple the prey then wait for it to weaken before moving in for the kill."

"Wolves do that?" Noah says.

"Actually, I may have made that up. The point is, blowing off the top of the building will get noticed. Being greedy might hurt us in the end."

"Noted," Rhys says, picking up a marker. His tone says we won't be going anywhere until the job is done, which is fine with me. He walks to the big window overlooking the city. I see emergency lights flashing in the distance, a few camouflaged Humvees rolling down the road. On the glass, Rhys draws a horizontal line where the tower ends and the cap begins. "The base is from here up. The first level was our living area. The second was a laboratory. The third was where we trained." He draws a vertical line from the cap to below the building. "And here is the basement. I don't know what happens here, but I know they have an elevator running to it. One the rest of the building can't use."

"Will using H9 destroy the entire building?" I say.

Rhys caps the marker, taps it against his lips. "It shouldn't. But their real estate front owns it anyway, so who gives a shit. If we do this right, it should only melt the cap. They'll have a hell of a cleanup job, but the building will remain structurally intact."

He smears the marker on the window with his hand, turning away.

The tower looms in the distance, hazed by smoke from fires still burning. Waiting for us.

29

From Rhys's armory, which is really just a closet, I choose a straight sword and extra magazines for the G36C assault rifle. Noah takes his assault rifle too, along with a collection of black throwing knives he wears across his chest in a bandolier. Rhys sticks with his revolver-sword combo. Noah hands me a tiny radio for my ear.

Olive stares into the armory. I hold my sword out to her, hilt first.

"Do you want to try this?"

She looks at the sword, then at me. She shrugs. "What am I good with?"

I smile. "I think you're good with a little bit of everything."

She reaches into the closet and pulls out a metal staff, then holds it in both hands, testing its weight. She gives it a quick twirl.

"I think I'll take this," she says.

"It's worked out for you so far." I rap my knuckles against her back. "Stick it here."

She slides the staff onto her magnet, then pulls out two handguns and a belt holster. I start to back away. It feels like a private moment. She's rediscovering the weapons she trained with her whole life. She holds a Colt up to the light, racks the slide back, and peers inside the chamber.

She lowers the gun. "Thank you. For helping."

"I know what it's like."

After arming ourselves, we stretch on the living room floor. It's hard to stop moving; it feels like the sun will never set. Rhys passes some food around for us to nibble on, and water. Noah turns the news on, but Rhys turns it off after a few minutes. The world thinks there was some kind of airborne chemical or biological attack. The city is quarantined, only military and the CDC allowed in until it's deemed safe again. They show footage from helicopters of abandoned cars in the streets, of ragged people standing a hundred feet from a block-ade lined with armed soldiers. People are trapped in the city. I'm glad when Rhys yanks the cord out of the wall.

Soon the blue sky turns purple. Key Tower appears empty and dark, an office lit every few floors. Ambulances and yellow

CDC trucks patrol the streets, flickers of red light moving between buildings. Our psychic energy has disappeared, but the core of the city remains empty.

The plan is less than ideal. Climb up the side of the tower, high enough to be invisible. Then break in and plant H9, rescue Peter, and make it out with the three parachutes we have. Which means two of us will have to go down the long way, or climb down, or something. There just isn't enough time to find more chutes. And we're okay with that. We are Roses and we are set on a course, and we will follow it. For now, I wear a thin chute on my back, and so do Rhys and Olive.

Once it's completely black outside, we leave the condo and walk the empty streets. Helicopters fly above, shining their spotlights on the ground, but we avoid them easily. They aren't looking for us anyway, I don't think. Down one street I spot men in white hazmat suits, testing the air with handheld instruments. We have to duck into an alley when a Humvee roars around the corner, the big diesel engine like a thousand falling hammers. The soldiers wear full-face gas masks and green plastic ponchos.

Soon we reach the base of the tower. I tilt my head back and look to the top. Rhys aims skyward with his grapnel gun and fires—a sharp *ping!* The hook and line fly high into the night. I don't hear it catch on the ledge, or see it, but Rhys gives a couple of tugs.

"See?" he says. "Perfectly safe." Without another word, he plants his feet on the side of the building and climbs, hand over hand. I lose him in the gloom.

A few minutes go by, then my earpiece crackles. "All right, North, you're up."

I take a deep breath and grab the line. I'm not afraid of heights, but there's a difference between leaping over rooftops you know you can clear, and climbing up the side of a sky-scraper on a line secured to something you can't see. I plant my right foot on the wall.

"Miranda," Noah says.

"What?"

He opens his mouth. Closes it. "Be careful."

"Always." Which seems a funny thing to say considering the last couple days. I focus on my hands, putting one over the other. My black-scaled feet grip the windows firmly. My fore-arms and fingers burn, but I ignore them. I don't look down. A hand reaches out and grabs my wrist. I almost scream, but it's just Rhys. I'm already at the first ledge. He swings me up and over the side. I plant my feet on solid ground, then move to the opposite edge, gazing over the dark city. It's only a hundred feet up, maybe less.

My earpiece clicks. "Olive, you're next," Rhys says.

Truly no going back now, not that I would. Still, the climb has left my nerves frayed. While Noah and Olive climb, I

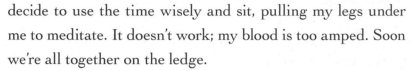

decide to use the time wisely and sit, pulling my legs under me to meditate. It doesn't work; my blood is too amped. Soon we're all together on the ledge.

Rhys draws his sword and slashes at the nearest window. It shatters, creating a jagged hole big enough for us to slip through.

We enter the dark office, find the stairs, and begin the ascent.

Moving slowly, in shifts, listening for the smallest sounds, it takes us nearly two hours to reach the fifty-seventh floor. Rhys and I watch for surveillance equipment the whole time, while Olive and Noah cover our rear.

The door to the fifty-seventh floor is locked with a keypad. Rhys slices off a thin piece of H9 and slaps it over the pad, then pushes one of the tiny bullet-shaped detonators into the semisoft material. It burns through in a flash. The door sighs open and we're inside the office.

Rhys points to the ceiling. "Above us is the first floor. This corner of the building was our bunks. It should be empty."

"*Should?*" Noah says.

"Well, yes. I don't have X-ray vision, do I?"

"I suppose not," Noah says.

"Guys," I say.

Rhys shakes his head and jumps onto someone's desk,

kicking aside a pile of papers. He removes the ceiling panel, then takes a bigger slice of H9 from his satchel and sticks it into place. Hands still in the ceiling, he looks down at us. "You'll want to move to the other side of the office."

We do. He hurries after us. For a second I think it failed, but then sparks spit down from the ceiling, followed by chunks of molten steel that plop on the desk, which promptly bursts into flame. The headquarters of Project Rose is officially breached.

"Sorry," Rhys says, as if the desk's owner can hear. Noah grabs a fire extinguisher off the wall and sprays the desk with white foam.

We assemble under the hole and look up into darkness. The opening changes the acoustics of the office; I can *hear* the empty room above.

"Right, then," Rhys says. "Who's first?"

"Wait. This isn't right," Noah says.

Rhys throws up his hands. "Oh, good. Now he gets doubts."

Noah says, "Actually, I had doubts before. But all I wanted to say was we should split up."

Olive hooks her thumbs into her gun belt. "Um, why?"

Noah faces her in the dim light. Behind him, out the window, I see the vast expanse of Lake Erie gleaming with moonlight. "Think about it. All four of us in tight corridors? We can't be very effective. They could take us all at once. If we split up, plant charges on opposite sides, then meet somewhere, it'll be better. Faster."

"No. We stick together," I say. While his point is valid, there's too much risk, too many unknowns. I will not have one of us pinned down or captured, forcing the others to either look for that person or leave them behind. We all win, or we all die.

Olive nods. "What she said."

"She's right," Rhys says. "Only I know my way around this place. You guys would get lost."

Noah has no response. I take the lead by jumping up through the hole. I'm careful not to touch the still-glowing ring with my hands, instead using my foot to piston off the hole and into the room. Touching it for a second leaves the bottom of my foot roasting. The air feels baked.

The room is too dark to make out details, just the rough outline of the bunks. Then suddenly it's not too dark, because red lights flash from every corner. A terrible alarm pushes on my ears.

They know we're here.

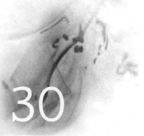

30

Rhys jumps through next, pulling his sword and revolver while he's still in the air. Then Noah, who lands in a crouch and unslings his rifle. We look ethereal in the strobing red lights.

"Noah, cover the door!" Rhys shouts as he pulls a brick of H9 from his satchel, still holding his gun. Noah aims his rifle at the door, and so do I.

From the corner of my eye, I watch Rhys cut another slice off the brick, then stick it on the ceiling. Two soldiers burst through the doorway and crash to the floor as we open fire. I only shoot a quick burst to conserve ammo. The number of targets up here is unknown—there could be a dozen soldiers or more, plus the creators, plus Tobias and Nicole.

Over the alarm I hear the hiss and sputter of melting metal as the H9 goes to work on the ceiling. A tiny grenade flips into the room from the open doorway, spiraling. I identify the flashbang for what it is—a grenade that disorients with sound and light instead of shrapnel. It bounces once on the floor and disappears down the hole we made in the fifty-seventh floor ceiling. The white flash of light and the bang don't affect us. We affect the guard who comes in thinking we're blind and deaf.

The new hole Rhys created is directly over the first one, so the molten metal drops all the way down to the fifty-seventh floor rather than piling up on this level. After a few seconds the hole above us stops glowing. Noah covers us as we jump straight up through the opening and roll clear—to fall back through would mean a two-story drop onto a pile of half-cooled jagged metal.

I pop up, leveling my rifle at the next threat.

There is none.

No flashing red lights in this room, no alarm except the muffled blare from beneath us. We're in an operating room, complete with gurneys and banks of monitors and fluorescent lights. The relative quiet is almost startling. Red light from the hole paints the ceiling bloody.

Only one bed is occupied. I recognize the memory band right away, circled around a girl's head like a thick blindfold. I recognize the auburn hair pinned tight to her ears.

It's me, another Miranda.

Another clone.

I go to her, slinging my rifle onto my back. Noah stops next to me, keeping an eye and gun on the door. I lift the band off the girl's head slowly. Under the sheet she's naked.

"Miranda," Noah says to me.

"They have my template," I say. To my right, Rhys plants a whole brick on the wall. He sets a timer on it. The numbers flash red, then disappear, an invisible countdown. I look back at the other me.

Her eyes open.

She sits up, inhaling sharply. I step away and lift my rifle automatically.

She clutches her chest, which is bare because the sheet has fallen away. But she isn't covering herself; it's like she's in pain.

"I was shot. There was blood," she says. She looks at me as if I have two heads. Then she sees everyone else. "Noah? Olive?"

Noah looks at her, then at me. "Oh my God," he says.

"What do you remember?" Rhys says. He finds a balled-up gown on the next bed and unfurls it. He slides it over her head and forces her arms through.

She still clutches her chest. "I was shot. Noah, why did you leave me?" She doesn't cry, but tears fill her eyes. Rhys helps her off the bed. Noah stares at her with his mouth open, remembering something I can't. He left me. But how would she know that? Is this some kind of awful trick to distract us?

"Noah!" I scream.

Two more soldiers burst into the room, helmeted, assault rifles out and blazing. A bullet ricochets off Noah's suit. I fire and crumple the left soldier's helmet while it's still on his head. Olive's handguns crack a few times, lighting up on my right.

Noah checks his suit. "Dammit, that. That really hurt." He's staring at my clone again.

The other Miranda is off the bed, shivering, dressed in the flimsy gown. Olive takes her hand and pulls her to the rear. She tells Rhys, "I'll watch her. Keep moving."

The alarm shuts off. The lights stop flashing on the floor below.

Rhys nods and readies the next brick, keeping his revolver out. We leave the operating room behind, heavy one Rose.

We move to the next room, and the next. Rhys doesn't say how much time we have left. Some of the rooms resemble offices, some are laboratories. Each one gets a brick of H9, not a sliver. All the timers are synced.

Rhys holds the final two bricks. He lifts one to me—*Want it?* I nod and he tosses it. I stuff it into the satchel strapped to my lower back, below my chute.

One thing is becoming very clear to me.

Peter is not here.

"We have a few minutes," Rhys says. My skin itches because it shouldn't be this easy.

And it isn't.

We round a corner, coming out of a hallway. Tobias and Nicole stand in front of the elevator. They have us cold. We freeze in the hallway entrance, not bothering to raise our weapons because we know they won't give us the chance. Tobias and Nicole have their rifles pointed at us, center mass. In my peripheral vision, I see Noah back into the hallway slowly; since we stopped at the corner, the angle hid him from sight.

"Drop your weapons," Tobias says.

I kneel slowly, lifting the strap of my rifle over my head and placing it on the floor. Wondering if they know we have just minutes left before this building does its best impression of a volcano. I pull my sword and toss it on the floor too.

Nicole grins. She has malice in her eyes that I've never seen in Olive. I wonder what they did to make Beta team different; it can't all be the tattoo. Or maybe the malice is just a twisted form of joy—they won, after all.

"Where is Peter?" I say as steadily as I can.

"In the basement," Tobias says, grinning behind his rifle. "We knew you were coming, so Mrs. North decided to keep him down below." His eyes narrow. "Where's Noah?"

He's creeping up behind you. Noah puts a finger to his lips. He must've run up some parallel hallway to get behind them.

"Just kill them," Nicole says. "They're too dangerous."

"You're right about that," I say. Noah slips into the space next to Tobias, knocking his rifle toward the ceiling. I dive into a shoulder roll and scoop up my own rifle. Rhys is faster than all of us, kicking his revolver off the floor so it pops straight up. He snatches it out of the air as Noah breaks Tobias's neck with a wet snap, just like Joshua's. Nicole opens fire. The flash from her gun blinds me. Rhys fires too, once. Nicole falls to the floor. I run over and kick her weapon away, even though she's already dead.

"How much time?" I say.

Rhys checks his watch. "Six minutes."

The other Miranda cries out behind me.

I whirl.

Olive is sprawled on her back, arms out.

There's enough blood for me to know right away some of Nicole's bullets found their mark. Still I go to Olive, falling to my knees, lifting her up and holding her to me while the others stand around, helpless.

There is nothing they can do.

Olive is dead.

I don't know how much time passes before Rhys grips my shoulder. "We need to go. The clock is ticking."

My tears have dried and the only thing inside me is fire. I thought I knew what rage was, but I was wrong. I feel rage for our creators. For the other versions of us. For the mutated brains that give us these strange powers. Rage for our purpose as weapons. For the people who want to use us. For all of it. It surges through me and gives me strength.

I lay Olive down and stand up, shrugging out of my parachute.

"What do you think you're doing?" Noah says.

Rhys fashions his final brick of H9 to the wall. Our escape.

Their escape. Not mine.

"I'm going to the basement," I say.

Noah's eyes flare, and he thinks he can stop me. I hold my hand up to silence him, then spread my arms for a hug. He can't resist. He moves forward as the H9 burns a hole to the outside. The air pressure changes and a gust of wind blows my hair around. I grab Noah's arm and jerk him off balance, stepping behind him and wrapping an arm around his neck. He struggles at first, but is unwilling to hurt me. Rhys watches me choke him into unconsciousness, a dead look on his face. I set him down gently, next to Olive. Then I push the button on the elevator.

Rhys watches me, framed by a jagged black hole.

"Get the chute on him, get him awake. Get out of here. I'll meet you outside."

He wants to argue, but there's no time. He nods once. I step into the elevator.

"North," he says.

I look up from the buttons. There are only two—one labeled B and one R.

He tosses me his revolver. I pluck it from the air. His sword comes next—it's the most beautiful thing I've ever held. Solid, light, and straight, with just enough give in the blade.

"I call it Beacon," Rhys says, nodding at the sword.

I feel like I should say something more to him, some kind of good-bye. There's a bond between us I can't explain, his memories ever-present in my mind. But I don't need to say good-bye, because I'll see them again. I'm getting Peter out.

"Keep them safe," I say. I press the B button.

I hold his gaze while the doors close between us. The car descends.

31

I check the load on the revolver—six shots. He must have reloaded between shooting Nicole and pulling me away from Olive. The rifle I left behind might be high-tech, but it was cumbersome. I see why Rhys chose this combination of weapons; it feels elegant just holding them. Maybe if I live long enough, I'll use them too.

The elevator drops faster than normal. I feel the lightness in my stomach and watch the floors wind down on a tiny readout above the two buttons. I thumb back the hammer on the revolver and point it at the door.

The car stops hard enough to bend my knees. The doors open.

A near pitch-black tunnel leads to a strange blue-green

glow. I step out, gun leveled straight, Beacon in a reverse grip, tucked flat against my arm. The doors hiss shut behind me, and cables twang as the car ascends.

I walk the whole way like that. One step, then another, the only sounds my shallow breath and the light crunching of grit beneath my feet. The gun grows heavy, but I can handle it.

A hundred feet later I enter a room with a black ceiling that could be a thousand feet high. A steady hum fills the air, a soothing hum, peaceful. It comes from the four rows of tanks lined up in the room, each three feet taller than I am. Nothing else is here. Four rows, ten deep. All of them glow blue-green. All of them illuminate the person suspended inside them. Each row has a name branded on top of the tanks—

PETER

NOAH

MIRANDA

OLIVE

Rhys is absent.

The Miranda row is the third from the left. Two of the tanks are empty and dark. Each tank seems to hold a different-aged version of us. Some are children, and some appear to be our age.

I came from here. This is where I was born. There are no thoughts beyond that. Just a general lack of understanding. A question, maybe—How is this real?

Staring at the field of tanks, I let my gun drop toward my side. It snaps back up when I see two figures at the other end of the field, in between the second row—Noah—and the third row—Miranda.

It's Mrs. North, the origin of me. Whatever you want to call her. Peter is on his knees next to her, arms bound behind him, mouth gagged with a white cloth. He has a black eye, blood crusted around the gag.

I don't waste time. I simply squeeze the trigger and the revolver crashes in my hand, scraping the skin on my palm. The endless ceiling swallows the noise. Smoke curls from the barrel, but Mrs. North is gone. Peter is still there, on his knees, screaming something behind his gag. I take a few steps into the field, hating how the tanks illuminate my suit with eerie light.

To my right, a flash of black scales amid seafoam. I fire again and hit one of the tanks. There's the snap of plastic followed by a stream of blue-green goo that arcs out and splatters on the floor. She's baiting me. She wants to draw my fire until I click empty. Movement again, closer. I look up—Mrs. North stands on one of my tanks. I raise Beacon just as her blade crashes down. She wanted me to see her; she could've just dropped down behind me.

My creator is toying with me.

She leaps over my head to the row of Noahs. I raise the revolver and she slashes it out of my hand before I can aim. It fires, a flash of orange light between us. The gun tumbles away, barrel to grip, and stops in the spreading pool. Mrs. North jumps down, and I move forward with a flurry of slashes. She doesn't bother to parry them, instead walks backward into the goo, ducking her torso when needed. Her feet splash in the liquid and I stop. She looks exactly like me, just aged, fine lines around her eyes. Same reddish-brown hair. Same red eyes from the memory band.

Her breathing is smooth. "You're better than the last Miranda. I'm impressed."

The revolver is half submerged in the liquid between us. "The Miranda from the original Alpha team," I say. "The one Rhys killed . . ."

Mrs. North laughs. She's standing near the two empty tanks in my row. One for the Miranda we found in the operating room upstairs.

And one for . . .

"No," Mrs. North says. "The one your Noah stole and left in Columbus." She raps her knuckles on the empty tank. "Go on, you remember. I left some of the memories intact. Buried, but intact."

"No." I shake my head, fighting to stay in the room. I can't let a memory take me, not now.

"Yes. Remember." She lowers her voice and speaks a string of numbers. Too fast to decipher individually, but hearing them tugs at my brain. The code dredges up another memory, buried deep.

Then I can't help it anymore.

I remember.

I don't know where I am. It's a city. Tall, unfamiliar buildings. I'm in a small park, one of those dingy ones they set down on an empty lot and then forget about. A boy stands in front of me. The pain in his eyes almost rips me in two.

"You won't understand this for a while," he says. "I don't know how long."

"Why can't I remember anything?" I say.

He takes my hands and I let him, even though he's a stranger to me. He rubs his thumbs over my knuckles. "I hope you can forgive me one day. I'm trying to keep you safe. It's the most selfish thing I've ever done." He gives a short, helpless laugh. "I would take it back if I could, but I can't."

Behind me, a girl with black hair stands in the street. She's watching us. "Noah, hurry," she says.

Noah holds up a finger. "I'm doing this because I love you. When I figure out how to keep us safe, I will come back. I will find you. Just stay here. You're resourceful. Don't get in trouble, Miranda, okay? Just lie low."

"Why can't I come?" I say.

"Because I don't think we can win." He hands me a

folded-up piece of paper. "This has instructions. If you're still alone on the date I wrote down, call this number. Ask for Peter. It tells you what to say."

I take it from him, not really understanding.

"But it won't come to that," he says. "I swear I'll find you."

He leans in and we kiss. It's automatic. Do I normally kiss strangers? What did he say about loving me? It feels like I'm dreaming.

I sit down on the park bench and watch the boy leave with the girl. They don't look back.

I'm running. I don't know where I am. I'm in a city with tall buildings I don't recognize. It's raining and my clothes are soaked. Night has fallen, and I don't know where I'm running to or what I'm running from.

Wait. Yes I do. People are trying to shoot nets at me. Something is wrong with my head; it's too hot. I think I have a fever. Pressure builds behind my eyes.

I turn down the next alley and slip on a piece of wet cardboard. My shoulder hits the slimy brick wall and I stumble forward. It's a dead end. I turn around to see a woman standing a few feet away. She has pretty red hair and bright eyes. I feel like I know her.

"Mom?" I say.

"Hey, honey. What are you doing?"

"I don't know. I think people are chasing me."

Mom waves me over. "C'mere sweetheart."

I can't remember how I got here. I was running and people were chasing me. A man steps out from behind her. His short brown hair sparkles with rainwater. He looks familiar, like a boy I saw earlier. Like that boy but grown up. Like I went to sleep for a very long time and woke up to find he is much older now.

This isn't right. Someone told me to run, to stay free. That isn't my mom. Names flicker and fade in my head—*Peter Noah Olive*—and I bend down to pick up a rusted piece of pipe. It feels gritty and solid in my palm.

"Let me through," I say.

The woman says, "Miranda, let us take you home."

"You're not my mother. *Get out of my way.*"

"No, Miranda. Put down the pipe."

I charge them, raising the pipe above my head. I jump. They're frozen with surprise, and I'm going to hit them. Something yellow flashes on one of the rooftops lining the alley, and something punches me in the chest. I hit the ground and skid on my knees before toppling over. The pipe rolls into a puddle.

"*NO!*" The woman shrieks. "Who fired? Who fired?"

"Jesus," the man says next to her. A radio crackles and he says, "That was unnecessary."

On my belly it feels like the water under me is growing hotter, and spreading out. I can't breathe. I can't take a single breath.

Mom kneels and rolls me onto my back. Blood bubbles out of my chest, mixing with the rain. She smoothes the hair off my face. I look into her eyes, thinking, *Please give me comfort. Please tell me what all this means.*

"I'm hurt," I say. Or at least I think I say. I might just mouth the words.

"I know. I'm sorry, baby. It was an accident."

My mind catches up. That flash on the rooftop was a gunshot. Of course it was. They shot me and now I'm bleeding.

"You won't die for good," my mom says. "I promise."

I try to say something but my mouth doesn't work. She looks up at the man. "Do we have another body ready?"

"Two, actually. They're already prepping one."

"We need to hurry," Mom says.

She bends over to plant a kiss on my wet forehead, but my eyes close before she reaches me.

I open my eyes. Bright white light above me. Something beeps steadily in the background. I lift my head and see I'm naked. I remember the alleyway, the water and blood and pressure in my chest. But there are no wounds. A nightmare, then. I sit upright, pulling on the sensors and needles plugged all over my body. I have to get out of here. I don't know why, but I know it's true.

"Relax," a voice says. "Easy, Miranda. Easy."

On the operating table to my left is a girl with reddish-brown hair. She's naked like me, with a gaping red hole between her breasts. On a table between us is a thick black hoop of metal with wires running off it, and an empty syringe with a wide-gauged needle.

"How do you feel?" the voice says. Mom steps out of the darkness.

"I'm dead," I say, not knowing what it means, but knowing it's true.

Mom stops between the two tables. She puts a hand on my leg, and a hand on the leg of the dead girl. She looks at the dead girl's toes, sees they're painted a dusky red, almost identical to the girl's hair. "Dammit, I have to paint your toes," she says to herself.

I point at the corpse. "That's what happened to me. Something hit my chest. I'm dead."

Mom shakes her head. "You were just born, sweetie." She sees I don't understand, and sighs. "Do you remember anything from home?"

I don't even know where home is.

She hands me a pair of jeans and a black tank top. "Put these on. You won't remember this, but you'll get to go home."

From the rolling table in the middle, she picks up the syringe. It's not empty. There's a little pill-shaped object inside. She holds my foot still and sticks the needle into the soft skin behind my ankle. I hear a blast of compressed air, and the little pill thing disappears. I don't even feel it.

"I hope this isn't for nothing," she murmurs, rubbing my ankle. Her voice drops to barely a whisper. "I hope you can go home, and we won't have to intervene." She gives my ankle a final squeeze.

Tears run down my cheeks, but my breathing is normal. I point to the dead girl on the table.

"That's me," I say.

Mom stares at the dead girl. "It was," she says.

I open my eyes back in the present, between the rows of Peters and Olives and Noahs and Mirandas. Unsure of how much time passed while I relived the memories. Mrs. North hasn't moved. She's just watching me.

She lays her palm flat on the empty tank. "This was yours."

My blood has been swapped with lead. I am not the Miranda North everyone grew up with.

I'm just a shell with a few scraps of her memories. . . .

I'm nothing.

But that's not true. Peter still kneels at the end of the row, and the look in his eyes heats the lead in my veins until I can move again. My team cares about me, and I won't fail them. I remember what Peter said to me in the bathroom. Words spoken in the past, giving me strength right now.

We'll make new memories, he said.

Mrs. North twirls her sword once. "You were our first template, that night you died. Then, when you murdered Grace, I came down here and made our first copy. You. Using the fragmented identity your idiot boyfriend created when he tampered with your shots."

She pauses to let that sink in.

"What should we call the girl upstairs?" she says.

"It doesn't matter," I say. "She's already gone. And so is everything above the fifty-seventh floor."

If this fazes her, she doesn't show it. "Look at the room you're in. There are plenty more of you to make."

The past isn't mine. It died with Miranda in that alley.

But the future can be.

Mrs. North crouches to pick up Rhys's revolver, but I slide forward in the pool and kick it down the aisle to Peter. I slash across with Beacon but Mrs. North dives forward, past my right side, and slips over the floor. She rolls to her feet as I turn, and we engage again. It's hard to keep track of who attacks and who defends. She seems to know every move I make before I make it. The sound of steel scraping steel rings out continuously.

She ducks under a horizontal slash, a backhand, and Beacon bites into one of Noah's tanks. A wide, flat stream of blue-green liquid spews out, soaking us both. It has no smell. I pull my sword free, but it takes a second, which is long enough for Mrs. North to open a foot-long gash in my suit, just above my navel. I cry out, backpedaling through the puddle. I stab forward for her throat, but Mrs. North throws her head back, and the sword passes above her neck and face harmlessly. She keeps going into a full-on backflip, her foot coming up and kicking the bottom of my sword hand. The little finger breaks, and I cry out again. I step forward, off balance from the thrust, and she completes the backflip perfectly, slashing across and opening another line on my cheek. Blood runs off my chin. A hank of my hair floats to the floor.

She moves in again, a thrust. I do exactly what she doesn't expect, what I don't expect. I drop Beacon and use both hands to catch her wrist, bowing my torso out of the sword's path. I rotate in until we stand shoulder to shoulder, all four arms outstretched and fighting for grip on her sword. She turns her face to mine, and I bash my forehead into her nose. I feel it crunch between my eyes and hear a low moan burble in her throat. I push her to arm's length. She blinks rapidly, fighting to see. I hook my foot behind her heel and sweep her leg out. She goes down, practically swimming, and her sword skims down the aisle. By the time I snatch up Beacon and prepare to bring it down like a hammer, she's already pushed off a tank after her weapon, leaving a wake in the fluid. I could give chase, but I have to free Peter in case she strikes me down. Leaving him at her mercy is not an option.

I sprint for him. He's had no luck with his bindings. I hook a hand under his armpit and hoist him up, then reach down to pick up Rhys's gun. I point it at Mrs. North and fire three more times as she struggles to stand. The bullets knock her right leg out from under her, and she falls hard on her back.

"C'mon," I say, dragging Peter down a parallel aisle.

Peter moans something behind his gag, looking down at my waist with wide eyes. Blood oozes between the scales and down my legs, mixed with the fluid. I barely feel it. My cheek, however, is on fire.

"Mirandaaaaa!" Mrs. North screams. We're at the archway. Mrs. North stands just inside the aisle, wavering on a bloody leg, holding her sword with both hands. Tank sludge plasters her hair to her face. She glows in the aqua light, ghastly.

"There is no escaping true earth," she says. She takes one limping step. Her right leg is useless. I have no idea what she's talking about; she seems delirious. "You can't run."

I shove the gun into my belt and pull out the brick of H9. I press the red button and thumb the timer down to ten seconds.

I look at all the tanks behind her, all the blank slates that could be us but never will.

"Good-bye, Mrs. North." I leap up and stick the H9 against the top of the arch.

"NO!" she screams.

00:08

I run, half carrying Peter to the elevator, counting down in my head. Over my shoulder, Mrs. North has made it a few steps by the time the arch begins to sizzle and spark. Chunks of molten rock drip down, then the whole support goes, rocks cracking and shattering and falling to the floor. The rocks grow into boulders. A few fist-sized chunks skitter to the elevator, passing us.

A wall of smoking rock blocks us from the tank room. Behind it, I hear the muffled screams of Mrs. North. Her frustrated cries.

I sit down against the useless elevator, groaning against all the fire in my body. The revolver digs into my ribs, so I pull it out; it's soaked, probably ruined. "Rhys is going to be mad about his gun."

Peter sits next to me. I start pulling at the rope around his wrists. He moans something, and I pry the wet gag out of his mouth and toss it away.

"Rhys?" he says.

"The rogue. Never mind."

"I feel like I missed a lot."

"You did."

"Why aren't we in the elevator?"

"It doesn't go to any floor but the top, and the top is on fire."

"Ah."

Rock dust hangs in the air. It's probably bad for us to breathe, but neither one of us cares at this point. I lean my head against the elevator and close my eyes.

"I won't tell anyone," Peter says.

I open my eyes.

"I won't tell anyone. Who you really are. That's what Mrs. North was saying right? That our Miranda was dead."

Hearing *our Miranda* stings my heart, I can't deny. "Yeah," I say. "She's dead."

"You're our Miranda," Peter says. "This changes nothing."

"It changes everything." I can't look at him, not yet.

He covers my hand with his, and we listen to the rocks tick and pop as they cool. We sit with the steady pressure of his hand squeezing mine. I could sit like this for a while.

"Not for me," he says softly, after what feels like an hour.

I don't say anything. I do lean forward and kiss him lightly on the lips. Then the pain in my stomach is too much and I lean back against the elevator.

"I knew you'd come," he says.

"You would've done the same for me, for any of us."

Minutes pass, and the rocks finish settling.

Then Peter notices the manhole cover in the floor. "I guess we live to fight another day," he says.

"I guess."

But he smiles, and so do I. Living another day doesn't sound so bad. Not if it's with him.

I bleed against the elevator while he pries the manhole cover up with Rhys's empty revolver.

A foul smell fills the tiny, choked space. Call it the smell of freedom.

Peter looks down in the dark, then up at me. "Ladies first?"

32

The sewer is another nightmare, but a welcome one. We trudge through calf-high sewage running under the city. After a few hundred feet, we find a ladder that leads to the surface. I shoulder through, then reach down and pull Peter out, grimacing against my wounds.

We're next to the tower. It's a massive birthday candle. A torch in the night that says it's safe to go home. We're alone on the street, but not for long.

Rhys walks over with Noah and the other Miranda in tow. Noah glares at me, and I can't blame him, considering I choked him out less than twenty minutes ago. But he's also happy to see I'm alive. Rhys ignores us, watching the surrounding area instead.

"Nice to see you, Peter," Noah says dryly.

Peter laughs and nods his thanks, then wraps Noah in a hug.

"Ew!" Noah says, pushing him away. "You smell like shit." He drops a hand on the other Miranda's shoulder. "Um, there's someone I'd like to introduce."

Peter stares at the other Miranda.

"Hello, Peter," she says. A little scared. I would be.

Peter says, "Where's Olive?"

I look at the ground. I've got that itch again, the urge to move, to seek the darkness.

"Was it bad?" he says, and wipes at his eyes.

"No," Other Miranda says. "It was fast."

Rhys holds out his hand to me. "My weapons?" I can tell he doesn't like standing in the open, either. But we earned a minute.

I drop the goo-covered gun in his hand.

"This is awful," he says, so tonelessly I laugh. He quirks one blond eyebrow. "The sword?"

"I'm keeping it, I think."

He sighs, wraps his arm around my shoulder, then faces the burning tower. The fires are dimming, fizzling out before they reach the floors below. Soon Peter comes over and wraps his arm around my other shoulder.

"I'm Peter," he says to Rhys.

"Nice to meet you," Rhys says.

Noah walks in front of us, and stops. "You guys ready to take off?"

The streets are quiet around us, but they won't be for long.

While the fire still burns, we disperse into the shadows, then run through the streets, avoiding the Humvees rolling in force. They're all going the same direction. Halfway home, I make us stop near an intersection. The view is perfect here, on a dark street that runs straight to the tower. It's so quiet I can hear the bulbs click in the stoplight as they change.

Together we watch the fire go out.

It takes weeks for the city to sort itself out. No one is sure what happened. Most puzzling of all is the strange fire on top of Key Tower. Stern faces on the news ask, *Are the events connected? What did the top floors hold?* There's an elevator shaft that runs to the basement, but it's blocked by too much rock, and no machine can fit down there to extract it. In all, six hundred and twelve people died, most of them in fires. Many of them trampled. Some from heart attacks. They show the bodies on the news. Emergency vehicles, volunteers, people in yellow jackets flooding through the city, combing first the streets, then the alleys and buildings for bodies. Always flanked by National Guardsmen, rifles at the ready. Twenty-nine people drowned in Lake Erie. They cart the bodies away on stretchers. Everyone in the city wears a blue mask over their nose and mouth, for fear that whatever caused the mania was in the air.

It could've been so much worse, had we been forced to participate. Had we not stopped the dry run when we did.

Strange, then, it doesn't feel like a victory.

The five of us stay at Rhys's, our new home. I have my own room. Peter and Noah share one. The other Miranda—Rhys calls her Sequel—sleeps wherever. We fight over who can use the shower first. It's the good kind of fighting. It's nice to worry about stupid, pointless stuff for once. The boys have backed off each other, but not completely. We try to adjust to the other Miranda, and she tries to find her place in our group.

But it's hard. She's *me*. And I don't know how much of us is the same. We're living different lives. We have different opinions about things. Is it enough I like onions and she doesn't? Is it enough I'll get in an argument with Rhys or Noah, and she'll act as mediator? As time passes, the hope is we'll grow in different directions. I'll be able to walk around without feeling like I could be killed and no one would know it. That Sequel, or some other Miranda, could step into my shoes and take over the tenuous identity I build on each day. At least the red scar on my cheek makes it easy to tell us apart.

She remembers some of the same fragments I do, like the blip of Noah leaving her on the bench. Thankfully, the memory of the original Miranda dying is muddled, a nightmare. Like me, the rest of her is coming back in pieces. Pieces that don't really belong to either of us. The official explanation is the creators obviously had possession of me at some point, and made my identity into a template. Then they released me, knowing I would lead them to the rest of Alpha team. Of course, the truth is a little more complicated.

We don't talk much, because we can't look at each other for more than a few seconds. It was different with Grace; Grace was not me, even if she looked the same. Seeing Sequel, on the other hand, reminds me of where I came from. A pod. Born this very summer.

One day she comes to me when I'm in the bathroom. "Do you still see it?" she says.

I freeze. "See what?"

"I wake up every night in an alley, feeling the blood pumping out of me. I swear it's real." She tilts her head down, auburn hair hiding her eyes.

I have the same nightmares. Slowly, I lift my hand and rest it on her shoulder. "It's just a nightmare. Sometimes . . . it's hard to tell the difference." I don't want to lie, but I can't tell the others who I really am. Not yet. It would destroy Noah if he found out his attempt to protect the original Miranda ended with her death.

Peter knows. He can keep my secret.

"We aren't that girl," I say to her.

"Then who are we?"

I smile at her, and it feels good. A real smile. "That's the beauty of it ... we're just finding out now."

After a moment, she smiles too. But it fades. "The others are ..."

"Treating you different, I know." I pause, searching for the words. "I went through all this—I still am. You feel it in your chest, right? The gap ... it'll fill. I promise you. It just takes time." It hasn't filled for me, not completely, but that won't help her. The promise is as much for me as it is for her.

"Will it ever be normal between us?"

Normal. I wish. Sequel doesn't make understanding my own existence any easier. But every day is better. Every day we are more our own person.

"It will be normal," I say. "I promise."

Sequel nods once and leaves abruptly. I hear the door shut, and I guess she's crying because it feels like I'm about to.

We gaze out the big window from time to time, watching the city stitch itself back together. The streets are wary. Helicopters are always overhead. National Guardsmen patrol in gas masks. Scientists spout theories on cable TV. A few religions claim the end is nigh.

There is still fear on the streets, even if we aren't the cause.

We watch. We wait. We train and spar and stay in shape. We take our memory shots. Sequel has flashbacks about Noah in the middle of the night, and she'll say his name. He'll come into the room, not knowing who called for him. He'll stand there with his mouth hanging open, until Sequel says it was just a nightmare. I can never tell Noah that without his actions I'd still be growing in a pod. I can never tell him that, because of his actions, the Miranda he loved died in an alley, bleeding in the rain.

Peter and I take out the trash one night. I recognize the tension in his shoulders. A Humvee rolls down the street. The gunner in the back watches us, then nods. We nod back.

"What's wrong?" I say.

Peter throws a black garbage bag onto the pile. He looks up at the cloudy sky. The first few raindrops plunk down around us.

"Nothing," he says.

"Peter..."

He laughs. "You're right. There is something."

I smile, fighting the inevitable just for the fun of it. "You know, I think Sequel likes you."

"She likes Rhys," Peter says matter-of-factly. "And Sequel didn't rescue me from Mrs. North."

I wait. He stares at me, and I stare back. The wind ruffles his hair, but otherwise he is still. There's nothing else to say. I go to him, closing the distance until I'm looking up into his eyes. I rise on my toes, and he kisses me gently. I rock back down to my heels, but his mouth doesn't leave mine. He kisses me like he did before, softly at first. Then harder. And once again I'm glad we made it out of the tower. Because I'm starting to realize my life doesn't have to be about an identity, or a lack of one. If I can focus on the little moments, however fleeting, they become my own. No one experiences them the way I do but me.

I find the hem of his shirt and pull it over his head, our lips breaking just long enough for the fabric to pass between them. He tosses it aside, onto the trash pile, as his watch begins to beep.

He looks at it, frowning, like it's a tick trying to burrow into his skin.

"Time for shots?" I say, my voice hoarse.

"Yeah," he says, the frown turning into a smile. "I wouldn't want to forget this."

He grabs his shirt, shakes it out, and puts it back on.

"Maybe I'll be out here tonight around midnight, to look at the stars," I say.

"I like stars." He loops his arm around my shoulder, and together we walk inside to take our shots.

One day at the end of summer, when the others are out on a run, I take the memory band into the bathroom and shut the door. Call me paranoid, but there are some moments from this summer I don't want to miss. Just last night we "borrowed" someone's boat and went fishing on the moonlit lake. It was so nice that, for brief seconds here and there, I was able to forget the people who would have us captured or killed. And so that memory goes into the machine, in case I ever forget again.

I put the lid down and sit on the toilet, easing the band over my eyes. My finger skims down the side until it finds the small button that enables the copy function. The pain is brief now, almost negligible, as the microscopic tendrils snake through my brain.

Thinking back on that moment, the way the water resembled dark glass, I prepare to hand the memory over to the machine.

Instead, the machine decides to hand one over to me.

A memory Mrs. North left behind.

The elevator ride is the longest of my life.

She's never summoned me before, not like this, not without notice. I can't help thinking that after decades of waiting, this is it. We will finally be called to serve. I make a mental note to record this memory later, so the others can hear the words as they come from her mouth, not from mine.

I clasp my shaking hands behind my back. The elevator doors open, and I step into her office. The glass walls form a pyramid, but she's left them tinted. The sun is just a small glowing marble on the left pane.

She sits behind her desk. It's the only piece of furniture in the room.

Without looking up from her papers, she beckons me forward with a hand. I cross the plush carpet and kneel at her desk, even if it makes me feel silly. Things are done differently here.

"Rise," she says.

I do.

Her armor is scaled, but golden instead of the black I wear. The scales shine like mirrors. Her hair hasn't lost its red-gold luster yet, as mine has. Her face is still seventeen, like the Miranda I'm raising as my daughter. I must appear old to her, so very old.

She studies me with youthful eyes that have seen more than I can imagine. Perhaps, if I please her, I will be able to see as much one day.

"I summoned you because I would like to hear of your progress, from your own mouth. Is everything on schedule?"

"Yes," I say at once. "There may be a minor snag, but your test will go on as planned."

"What kind of snag?"

"Nothing to be worried about. I think Rhys is suspicious of the Roses' true nature, and I believe he will try to investigate further if left unchecked. I recommend we remove him from Alpha team."

"That's very sad. Do what you think is necessary."

Her attention goes back to her papers. I can't tell if I'm dismissed or not, but I don't want to risk turning my back without permission. This woman is my true mother, the source of all Miranda clones, my own *blood*, and yet she makes me feel like a cockroach. Insignificant, a pest to be crushed underfoot.

My mind goes to dark places as the seconds tick by, and the urge to see her new weapons is too much. I've put my time in. I deserve to see them.

I work up some nerve, and ask, "May I see them?"

"Them?" she says, seemingly surprised I'm still here.

"Your . . . the ones you will have working alongside the Roses. The ones who will conquer our world."

She smiles. "Afraid to say their name? Afraid they'll hear you?"

Since she'd know if I was lying, I don't. The monsters have a name, but if you think it, they can hear you. I don't want them to hear me.

"Yes. A little."

This seems to amuse her, not disappoint.

"I wouldn't want to plague your sweet sleep with nightmares."

326

"Thank you."

She dismisses me then, but must sense my disappointment, because she calls after me. "Be patient. You will see *them* soon, along with everyone else in the world."

I take off the memory band and set it in my lap. The door to the apartment opens and I hear four people come inside and kick off shoes and open cupboards and laugh at someone's joke.

Two years. That's how old the memory is. So much time has passed.

Mrs. North has a creator of her own. And there are monsters that will conquer the world. Monsters with a name Mrs. North is afraid to say.

"Miranda?" someone calls for me. It sounds like Peter or Noah.

I look down at my hands holding the band, and wonder what my team will have to fight next. I wonder what could strike fear in a heart as black as Mrs. North's.

Then I realize it doesn't matter.

Whatever it is, we'll face it together.

ACKNOWLEDGMENTS

Thank you:

To Adam Lastoria, for reading my early novels and not crying about it. And for handing me that book not so long ago, which sparked my love for reading again.

To Suzie Townsend, for everything. Maybe that's a silly thing to say, but we both know it's true. Thank you for everything. This book is here because you wouldn't give up on it, or me.

To Janet Reid. With you in my corner, I feel like I can do anything. Thanks for the snacks, and the glasses of water. Thanks for QueryShark.

To Catherine Onder, for showing me the book's true

potential. And being an all-around champion. And to Hayley Wagreich, her tireless assistant.

To Pouya Shahbazian, for movie and TV stuff. Especially for being my screenplay resource.

To my parents, all four of them, for raising me to believe I can do whatever I put my mind to. And, you know, for keeping me alive.

To Adam Grisak, for the medical stuff.

To Lastoria's BP, for 9.5 years. It's there I dreamed up my stories. And got paid to read a few hundred books. Sorry, Don.

To the crew of EB Games at Randall: Mike, Rashad, and Aaron. For the talks. And the EB Stow crew, specifically Will Lyle, for dreaming with me. To Mike Mockbee, for whatever.

To Joanna Volpe, Meredith Barnes, Sara Kendall, for reading early, and for helping me find my inner teenage girl. And to Brooks Sherman, who did not help me find my inner teenage girl, but did other things.

To Sean Ferrell and Jeff Somers, for being my mentors. No, really.

To Josh Bazell, for inspiring me. To Suzanne Collins, for the same.

To everyone at Disney-Hyperion Books, for helping to create a book I'm proud of.

FORGET WHAT YOU KNOW

FALSE
SIGHT

A FALSE MEMORY NOVEL

DAN KROKOS

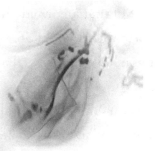

Thomas David asks me about my eyes.

Over and over again.

"Are they seriously red? Let me see and I'll stop asking. Kristin, let me see."

Kristin isn't my real name. It's Miranda. Kristin is pretty generic, but that's the point. And at least I don't have two first names, like Thomas David, the boy who keeps asking about my eyes.

"They're not bloodshot," Thomas says to me. "Gina says the irises are red like a vampire. Hey." He pokes my arm. His fingernail is a little too long, so it bites into me.

Keep it together. Do not react.

"Don't react," I say aloud by accident.

"What?" Thomas leans over his desk so he can see my face better. "Say again?"

If he were a Rose, making him stop wouldn't be an issue. But Thomas David is not like me; he's fragile. We can't sort it out with fists. Not that a normal girl would use fists. I don't know what a normal girl would do.

"Kristin, if you have red eyes, that's okay. It's kind of hot. I love vampires."

The teacher is rambling about the global economy and how the markets interact. She hasn't looked back in five minutes. Noah is slumped on the other side of the room, dozing. Doom impends for the entire world, yet economics can bore him into relaxation. Then his face turns toward me a millimeter, and his eyelashes flutter. The boredom is an act; he's watching us.

"Gina said you're crazy. She said you hit her. Are you going to hit me? Hey, Kristin."

Gina Daly first saw my eyes in the girls' bathroom. She caught me cleaning my contacts. I wear them to cover my red irises, because red eyes freak people out. The colored contacts turn them a muddy brown color no one looks at twice.

Gina didn't notice them at first. She started with, "How'd you get that scar?" Her nose wrinkled like she smelled something bad. The horizontal slash on my cheek is just a thin white line now, but it's still obvious. Rumors have already spread about it—that my dad gave it to me as a kid, that I did it to myself, that I let a boy do it. They say I have more scars hidden by my clothing, probably self-inflicted. To me, it's just a mark on my face that reminds me I don't belong here. I am not a normal student with normal problems, no matter how badly I want to be.

So when Gina asked about the scar and how I got it, I told her, "A sword," because it's true. I kept my eyes down and scrubbed the contact in my palm.

"Whoa, let me see your eyes." She put her hand on my shoulder and tried to *turn* me.

I've killed people and had people try to kill me. So when Gina Daly, just a regular girl with regular problems, moved me against my will, it got to me. She was not dangerous or scary—I know, because I am familiar with those things.

I put my hand on her throat and shoved her away, maybe too hard. She stumbled until her back slammed against the hair dryer.

"What is your *problem*?" she spat.

"You touched me."

She looked directly into my eyes. My right one was muddy brown, and my left, bright red. My eyes are blood-colored because they're colored with blood. I'll get to that later.

Her anger melted into disgust. "What is *up* with your eye?"

I turned back to the mirror, pulled my lower lid down, and popped the lens into place. "Nothing. What's wrong with your face?"

Gina curled her lip. "Okay, Snake Eyes."

She clacked out of the bathroom in her heels, and I became Snake Eyes. Snakes don't even have red eyes. I looked in the mirror at my scar. At my lank auburn hair and the bluish veins around my eyes. I thought about makeup and nail polish and other things girls use. I didn't know where to start, and a part of me was confused about why I didn't care to.

My new name spread through school in a day, and people started asking to see my eyes sans contacts. They asked Sequel, my "twin," what the story was. She was slightly more abrasive with her responses, especially when someone noticed she wore contacts too.

Peter stopped me outside my locker a few days later. He kissed me lightly, took my books, and leaned against the dark green lockers. "We need to talk."

I shut my locker and spun the dial. "What's up?" I knew what was up.

"You punched a girl and she told the entire school about your eyes."

I started walking to economics, wondering again why we were pretending to be real students. "I didn't punch her. I shoved. And I acknowledge it was a stupid thing to do."

"It wasn't stupid. You reacted, that's all. If you had thought about it first, then it'd be stupid." He smiled, almost.

I nodded, unsure of what to say.

He grabbed my arm and gently pulled me to a stop. People streamed past us on both sides. A rogue book bag hit me in the kidneys, but I didn't budge. "It wasn't your fault, *but* . . . Noah and Rhys think we need to move on. People are starting to talk." His blue eyes dropped to my scar. "With your scar, and now your eyes . . ."

"Yeah?"

His eyes went right back to mine, which I was grateful for. "I'm just saying we should think about it. You're not attached to this place, are you?"

I wasn't, but I didn't like the idea that we *had* to move. This was our grand attempt to put the past behind us. Moving somewhere else wouldn't fix the problem.

Peter leaned in to kiss my forehead. When he pulled away, he was smiling, which made me smile on reflex. "Just think about it. We can start over a hundred times."

I wanted to ask him to just make a decision, but in the last few months our roles have become less defined. Peter was always our leader, but without something actively trying to kill us, it's been hard to tell who's in charge, if anyone.

"You're smart," I said. "And cute."

"I know. Just think about it," he said, squeezing my hand. Then he entered the stream of moving bodies and disappeared.

Now I'm in economics and Thomas David won't stop asking about my eyes.

"If you don't answer me," Thomas says, "I'm seriously gonna touch your eye."

Keep it together. Do not react.

I need Noah to do something. If Thomas sees Noah perk

up, he'll stop, because Noah is scary. He can put this dead look on his face that needs no words. The best I can do is glare, which only seems to egg Thomas on. I'd have to make a scene to shut him up, and I already discovered that's a bad idea. My frustration is manifesting as prickly neck sweat.

I shear the eraser off my pencil and roll it between my fingers.

"Why are you being weird about it?" Thomas David says.

I toss the eraser at Noah. It hits him in the ear. His lip twitches, but the rest of him stays still. Maybe he wants to see if I can handle the situation in a nonviolent manner, which I can't blame him for. If I had shoved Gina just a little harder, she might've ended up in a wheelchair.

"He can't save you," Thomas says, after making sure Noah didn't notice.

I finally look at Thomas's face. He's sneering, the way people do when they're trying hard to show they're amused or having fun. His lips are like pale worms, glistening with spit.

"Hi," he says. "Now just move your contact. A quick peek."

He reaches out like he's going to touch my eye.

I don't know if he actually would have; he never gets that far. I reach out too, grab his index finger, and bend the whole thing back a few degrees. I stop before it breaks, because I'm in control. It probably still hurts.

For some reason, Thomas David opens his mouth and screams. Everyone jumps in their seats.

"She broke my finger!"

"I did not," I say calmly.

The teacher turns around and lowers her glasses. On the blackboard behind her it says CHINA VS INDIA VS US???

"He tried to touch me," I say, as if that will explain every-thing. Thomas David is clutching his finger, so nobody can see it's not really broken.

Noah rolls his eyes at me. Thomas David gets sent to the nurse, and I get sent to the principal.

I sit in a stiff chair until Principal Wilch calls me into his office. He tells me to sit in another stiff chair across from his desk.

"What's the problem?" he says.

I tell him a version of the truth. I say I have a rare corneal disease that discolors my irises and Thomas David would just not stop making fun of me and he even tried to touch my eye, and I just—I snapped, and I'm so sorry, I didn't mean to grab his finger.

"What should I do about this?" Wilch asks. He folds his hands over his substantial belly and leans back in his chair. "I can't have students assaulting each other. Even if Thomas David is a punk."

I don't point out that the finger in question is, in fact, unbroken.

"Give me a warning?" Get me out of here.

"Will it happen again?"

"Not unless he tries to touch my eye...." Wilch's brow furrows. Wrong answer. "I mean, no. It won't happen again."

"That's good. I want you in this office on your off-periods. We need aides."

I have a strange feeling I won't be around to comply. So I just nod and say thanks and leave his office.

Noah is waiting for me in the hallway. "You're lucky they didn't call the cops," he says.

I pick at my jeans. "Why? His finger's fine."

"What was the guy saying?"

It sounds kind of silly now.

"He wanted to see my eyes. He wouldn't shut up about it." A girl carrying a hall pass walks by and gives me a funny look. I ignore it. *Don't react.*

Noah doesn't say anything. I can't tell if he's not amused or just pretending to be not amused.

"He was going to touch my eye."

"Uh-huh. Well, Rhys wants to meet us in the gym."

"Did you tell him what happened?" I think I know what the meeting will be about, if he did.

"I texted that you were going to the principal's office."

"Thanks for telling on me."

"Hey. I told him you didn't do anything wrong."

We start walking toward the gym. My shoes pinch my feet, and my jeans and shirt make me feel naked. Give me my armor any day.

"Just relax," Noah says. His hand briefly massages the knots in my neck. Thomas David is probably already telling everyone what a psycho I am. Noah takes his hand away before I have to tell him to remove it.

In the gym, Peter and Rhys are playing one-on-one under the hoop while Sequel stands off to the side, disinterested. Rhys jumps three feet off the ground and sinks a jump shot over Peter's head. Peter gets the rebound and stops dribbling when he sees us.

"What's wrong?" I ask, hoping I don't sound defensive from the start.

"Nothing," Peter says. "I just thought it was time for a chat."

"We're leaving," Rhys says.

Peter sighs. "Thank you, Rhys."

"But don't feel bad," Rhys adds quickly. "If you hadn't pushed that girl, one of us would've gotten in trouble eventually."

"That probably doesn't make her feel better," Sequel says. We're biologically identical, but Sequel's hair is dyed black and styled in a pixie cut. Changing her hair was one of the first things she did—we had found her in the lab with shoulder-length auburn hair, exactly like mine.

Noah says, "Look, we knew we'd stick out here. So we learn from the experience. We don't make the same mistakes at the next school." He's making eye contact with Sequel while he says it, even though he's talking to all of us. It's cute he thinks we don't notice the way they look at each other. Cute in a lead-ball-in-my-stomach kind of way. I swallow and pretend I don't care, mainly because I don't know *why* I care. I should be glad —if Noah and Sequel really do have some kind of romance going on, then I don't have to worry about what he thinks of me and Peter being together.

Rhys holds his hands up and Peter passes the ball. Rhys sinks another jump shot. "Screw going to another school. I don't see the point. We're smarter than these imbeciles. I should be *teaching* calculus." The ball rolls back to his feet, and he picks it up and shoots again, nothing but net. "What good is school when the creators plan to conquer the world?"

He's got a point. Once we figure out what the creators are up to—creators, as in the people who cloned themselves to create us, and who gave us the ability to create mass panic with only the power of our minds—we'll have to stop pretending to be real people and start trying to save the world. Or something along those lines.

Going to school is just a distraction until that time comes. It started with the question *How do a bunch of kids raised as super-soldiers live normal lives?* The answer is they don't. But the decision to try came one night after a brutal training session on the roof of our apartment building. We'd been talking about it for the last hour. Bruised and achy, we pulled ourselves into a loose huddle that was almost like a group hug. It was corny, but we did it every time after training. We just stood like that as our breathing returned to normal. It reminded us that we were the only family we had, and that we couldn't afford to let things come between us. Not anything. And so far we'd done a pretty good job of that.

"The creators will show up again," Peter said. "Count on it. But until then, we should try to live. Otherwise what are we doing?"

Rhys smiled. "I could take a dose of real life."

I was in. I wanted homework, and a locker. I wanted to try it all. One day we might need social security numbers and diplomas. After that was the possibility of real jobs, with paychecks and health benefits. I could work in an office, have my own desk with pictures of people I love on it. I could go home to a family and think about what to do for dinner instead of how to avoid becoming a slave.

What good is school when the creators plan to conquer the world? Rhys says now.

Peter gets the rebound again and tucks the ball against his hip. "You have a point," he says to Rhys. "Noah?"

Noah bites his lower lip and looks at each of us in turn. "I don't know. Is school really hurting us in the meantime? I mean until we have to fight again."

If school makes us softer in the long run, then yes, it's hurting us. We should train more. There's a reason none of us have been able to relax here. The creators haunt every shadow. They are every stranger on the street. They're our unfinished business. And living each day with eyes in the back of your head is no life at all.

In unison, our watches begin to beep. Time for our memory shots. Without speaking, we each pull syringes from our bags. My thumb pushes the lemonade-colored liquid into my arm, and a fist unclenches in my stomach; for a little while longer, my memories are safe. I imagine how this looks to someone else—five kids sticking needles in their arms under a basketball hoop.

"Can we just decide tomorrow?" Sequel says, capping and pocketing her syringe. "After homecoming. I already bought my dress. Let's do normal one more day, okay? Then we can go to Prague for all I care."

Rhys tosses the ball up, but it bangs off the front of the rim. "Fine, we stay another day." He's only agreeing because he already picked out nice clothes for the dance. The girls like him, and he likes that they like him.

"Fine," Peter says.

I don't care what we can do, we're still teenagers. While I'm not sure hanging around is the best idea, it isn't selfish to grasp at a few extra days of normalcy.

Not selfish—just an error.

I had my run-in with Thomas David just a little too late. Because staying that extra day turns out to be the biggest mistake we've ever made.